FOUR DOGS IN SEARCH OF WISDOM

Robert Stewart

ISBN: 978-1-8381272-4-4 (paperback)
ISBN: 978-1-8381272-7-5 (ebook)

The stray

Cloud was having an argument with a wood pigeon.

'What do you know about it?' said Cloud.

'What do I know about it? What do *you* know about it?' cackled the pigeon.

Cloud was a Border Collie. He was a junior but respected dog in a den of dogginess called Easthill. Easthill was a small hamlet. It was in the East. And on a hill.

The pigeon was not a respected member of the community. Most animals found him annoying. He was a moaning trash-talker who was always complaining about the dogs and ridiculing them. And when he wasn't doing that, he would poo on them.

The dogs called the pigeon Mr Whinger.

'I know more about it than you!' said Cloud defiantly.

'Then you know slightly more than nothing – which isn't much of an achievement! Then again, there's nothing to know, so it hardly matters!'

Mr Whinger was enjoying himself.

But what was *it*? What were the Border Collie and the wood pigeon having an argument about?

They were arguing about the Thumbald.

'You could at least show a little respect.'

'Respect! When have you lot ever shown me any respect? Pah! I poo on you and your bum-bald from a great height!'

And, with these words, Mr Whinger about-turned. Cloud just managed to sidestep the bombardment.

'Now then,' called out Cloud, 'you know how important today is for us – and I don't want anything to get in the way. We haven't always seen eye to eye, I know, but I hope we can be reasonable. You're a pigeon. I'm a dog. But we live in the same place. We can at least try to get along.'

'You were the one who lost your temper with me! I was only trying to be helpful!'

'All right, all right, I'm sorry,' said Cloud, trying to stay calm.

'I don't really see how you can get wound up by a bum-bald, anyway.'

'Thum…' Cloud began, then checked himself, 'I came to you for a simple reason. It's no secret that you don't share our belief in the Thumbald. It's also no secret that you have spread rumours about it, and pushed dogs into other things, like competitive ear-grooming, and potato management.'

The pigeon sniggered.

'But the Thumbald is special to us. It's a symbol of where we belong. It gives us an identity.'

The pigeon didn't look impressed. In fact, he couldn't have looked any *less* impressed.

'The point is,' continued Cloud, 'that I have heard a rumour. Today is our special day. And we have heard a rumour that you have seen something.'

The pigeon cooed.

'A rumour? Who told you that?'

'If you have seen something that will affect our festival, then please, I would be grateful if you told us.'

'What do I care about your stupid festival?!'

Cloud turned in a full circle (he wasn't sure why).

'Your festival is a gut-full of gooseberries! You do exactly as you please – I have seen nothing!'

Cloud wasn't convinced and didn't want to let the matter rest. He knew Mr Whinger wasn't to be trusted (generally speaking, pigeons were untrustworthy). Other dogs had claimed they had seen Mr Whinger whispering with birds from far-off lands. Or worse, some predicted he would gradually convert the dogs to birds.

'What's going on?'

The question came from behind Cloud, in a gritted growl.

Cloud turned.

It was Francis, the Greyhound. He raised his eyebrows at Cloud.

Cloud was flustered.

'I… this bird… I just… I heard a rumour.'

'You heard a rumour?'

'That's right.'

'From this bird?'

'Yes.'

Francis looked into the tree. Mr Whinger was shuffling about indignantly on his branch.

Francis hadn't lived that long with the dogs in Easthill. He had come to them less than a year ago. He claimed that he was descended from one of the original twelve packs that founded the community – his grandfather had gone in search of new uses for potatoes, but he had come to an unfortunate end. His parents had been imprisoned in a far-off settlement. Francis had managed to escape and found his way to the land of his ancestors.

When they heard Francis's story, some dogs were sympathetic. The more traditional dogs believed his heritage gave him a high-ranking status. For other dogs it was obvious that Francis *knew* a lot – he had learned many things on his wanderings, which helped them all to manage Easthill in a better way. Francis certainly had a lot to say about who should run the hamlet and how. The top dogs – the elders – needed to have a lot of power, he said. If they didn't, the dogs would just end up barking at each other and biting each other's tails off.

Cloud could also see that Francis didn't much care for him. From the first time they had met, Francis had criticised him publicly, and for just one reason: that Cloud did not have a proper pedigree.

Cloud didn't know where he had been born. He couldn't remember his parents. He had only the faintest memory of how he had come to live in Easthill. He had been found as a puppy. This was why, deep down, he had always felt alone. Unlike the other dogs on the farm, he had no connection to the community. Did he really belong with these dogs? Or somewhere else? Did he not belong anywhere?

Francis never said so directly, but he clearly thought that Cloud had no rightful place on the farm.

'What was the rumour?' asked Francis.

'There was... one of our beagles told me that Mr Whing... that this bird had seen a stray dog.'

Francis looked at Cloud suspiciously.

'*Which* beagle?' he asked, narrowing his eyes.

It was a curious thing: whenever Francis looked at him in this way, Cloud thought that he looked like a bird of prey. The resemblance was uncanny.

'He's called Bartholomew.'

'Bartholomew the beagle!' laughed Francis. 'He's a joke! I wouldn't trust him to trim his own tail!'

'Nevertheless...'

Francis interrupted.

'You! Bird!' he shouted at Mr Whinger. 'What do you have to say about this?'

'Why would I go raising a rumpus about stray dogs?' replied Mr Whinger. 'You all look like stragglers to me!'

Francis, once again, raised his eyebrows at Cloud.

'Perhaps what the bird says is true. I just wanted to make sure nothing affects...'

'... *If I were you*,' interrupted Francis, 'I wouldn't trouble yourself over things that don't concern you. We all need to know our place, after all. But that's right – I forgot, you don't really have one, *do you?*'

Cloud's anger pulsed. But he didn't have enough confidence to challenge Francis.

'Perhaps I should let the matter rest, then,' he said.

'Just one more thing,' said Francis. 'I can't help but wonder. Let's say the bird is telling the truth. And let's say I don't believe a word about the ridiculous beagle

Bartholomew. I wonder if this story about a stray might have come from somewhere else. You, for example. *Pretending to be concerned. Blaming a bird.* That would be a good cover for someone who is secretly planning... well, *who knows* what.'

'But that's... that's ridiculous!' stammered Cloud. 'Why would I do that?'

Francis replied with venom.

'Because you're nobody! You came here from nowhere. You have no family or loyalty to these traditions. And because you *resent* being an outsider, you pay back all the kindness and comfort you have received by tearing it all down – or trying to!'

'Honestly, that's... I would never...'

'... I don't want to hear it. Why don't you run along and leave this innocent bird alone. But be warned, Cloud – I have my eye on you!'

Cloud did as he was told. He tried to keep his mind on the business of the festival, but he couldn't help but feel the sting in Francis's words. They were all things he felt about himself. Many – most – of the dogs had welcomed him in Easthill, even as a puppy. But no matter how much they tried to make him feel at home, he knew that something was missing. He knew that he would never belong to Easthill, like the others. It also upset him that Francis knew all these things – the Greyhound almost took delight in drawing attention to the most painful things Cloud felt about himself.

In some sense, then, Cloud had always felt lonely, but ever since Francis had been around, he had felt more alone. Like he wasn't there at all. He was still part of the community. He helped out. He discussed matters with the elders. But some part of him was always somewhere else – and he didn't really know where that was.

Once or twice, Cherry the Red Setter had urged him to stand up for himself when Francis bullied him. After all, she said, Cloud might not have been born into one of the packs from Easthill, but he had lived there much longer than Francis. For all they knew, Francis might have been making things up. And his attempt to wield more power through the farm's elders was not really at all in keeping with their customs and traditions.

Despite this advice, Cloud could never stand up for himself. He thought it would make him look more ungrateful. If he were to challenge another dog in that way, he would be sowing discord in a place that had given him the only sense of belonging he had. Cloud didn't want to cause a fuss.

Porter the Irish Water Spaniel was howling. The ceremony was about to begin. He dropped all his thoughts and concerns (they would have to wait). He scampered back to the farmhouse, but on his way, he thought he saw something out of the corner of his eye: a strange-looking, and very unkempt, black dog.

*

So what *was* the Thumbald?

It was wisdom. It was beauty. It was goodness. It was justice. It was happiness. It was love. It was the *truth*.

It was also kept in a bread bin.

The dogs held the Thumbald inside a locket on a chain, which they stowed away in the farmhouse. For a measure of extra security, they stuffed it inside an old bread bin.

They needed the locket because they had one big problem: *the Thumbald could never be seen*. Even if you tried to look at it, you would never be able to see it. Except it was worse than that. If you tried to look at it, you robbed it of all the power, goodness, wisdom and meaning it had.

This was an odd idea. How was it possible that something could be all those good things and not visible? One dog said that to understand the Thumbald, the dogs had to imagine that they were like frogs at the bottom of the well. The frogs had become familiar with their dark, wet and slimy existence, and most frogs thought only about how to survive where they were. But if they were to look upwards, they would see a light. They might not be able to see all the fields, trees, buildings, animals, and the rest of the wonderful world. They could only see the light.

The Thumbald was *like* this light. It was a *waymark to the truth*.

According to the loosely agreed story, Easthill had been founded when a single dog (the *first* dog) brought the Thumbald to the farm. The dogs could not agree when exactly this happened, except that it took place *a very long time ago*. But even agreeing that it took place *a very long time ago* was not helpful, since they didn't agree what counted as a long time. Last week seemed, for some dogs, like a long time ago. So, some thought that the Thumbald (and the entire community of dogs) were no more than a week old. They also disagreed about how to count the time, which didn't help. Some said they should use hours and minutes. Others thought it was better to use something else, like artichokes.

Once a year, the dogs brought out the Thumbald to celebrate its virtues and their origins on the farm. The ceremony wasn't too complicated. Twelve separate packs lived on the farm and its buildings. The day would begin by re-enacting the arrival of the community. All twelve packs would retreat to the perimeter of the buildings. There they formed a near complete circle around it. The Leader – currently an ageing mountain dog called Saddleback – would dress up as the first dog and lead everyone slowly, solemnly and in silence towards the buildings.

All twelve packs would advance, until Saddleback reached the entrance to the main farmhouse. At this point, they would come to a halt. A nominated dog from the elders would let out a low and lingering howl. Then Saddleback would lead the pack in a long procession through the farmhouse. The Leader would be followed by elders, juniors and members from the twelve packs. Throughout, Saddleback would, in his deep growl, repeat the words, *Oh Bald Thumbald.*

The difference between *the Thumbald* and *the Bald* was poorly understood. The dogs believed that the Thumbald was only one of many precious objects that had been brought to create communities like theirs. All these tokens came from one unifying spirit: the Bald. The Bald, itself, was difficult to define. It was too much like the air to really understand; try to grasp it and it would slip through your fingers. But, like the air, somehow you knew it was there, even though it had no obvious features. This meant that the Bald was only ever visible through the tokens that brought its power and mystery to life. The Thumbald was the light at the top of the well, and the Bald was the world from which the light came.

So, the Thumbald was the main reason the dogs

couldn't agree anything. If it was anything, it was unknown. It wasn't too surprising that some dogs weren't convinced. Recently, more and more of them had started to think that it was just a lot of nonsense.

Cloud cared about the Thumbald. He cared about it in the same way other dogs care about their ears and noses – which is a lot! Even so, he often wondered about it. How was it possible to know that the Thumbald existed? Was it, for example, a bit like smelling a piece of cheese that you couldn't see, taste or touch? If you could smell a piece of cheese, but not see, taste or touch it – did the cheese really exist? Cloud had once voiced this thought with an energetic spaniel. The spaniel came away believing that the Thumbald was a piece of Double Gloucester.

*

Saddleback walked into the farmhouse, followed closely by the elders. The other dogs lined up behind, pattering over the flagstones. Inside, they all bowed before the Thumbald, and the leaders of each pack gave an offering (which they left in a pile on the kitchen table).

Outside, as they waited for the rest of the company, some dogs performed *pinch-a-sniff* dances. These were short bursts of movement inspired by smells that came their way. Some said they were temporary responses to the near presence of the Thumbald. Others said that only dogs who were 'all bounce and no brain' behaved in such a foolish way. But this year whenever a dog tried to dance, they broke into fits of sneezing. One dog came to smell the dog standing next to Cloud but burst out coughing and spluttering.

'Some dogs don't know a bottom when they smell one,' said the offended owner of the bottom.

Silence only fell when Saddleback reappeared from the farmhouse. The company bowed as they waited for the next and final stage of the ceremony. Saddleback stopped. The dogs looked at him, awaiting his words, but many dogs gasped or dropped their jaws. Cloud, in particular, glared in horror at the locket that swung around Saddleback's heavy mane.

It was open.

There was a cry. It was almost hysterical. A Setter took two steps forward, and, with a note of pity, said:

'Look at it, Saddleback. Look at it!'

Saddleback, clearly conflicted by the very idea of *looking at it,* lowered his head; but before he could reply, several things happened. A peal – something like a cackle – rang out over the heads of the dogs. Was it Mr Whinger? Or someone else? Then the dogs broke into uproar.

Cloud winced. He saw Saddleback stumble and collapse from within. The ruckus made it difficult to hear what anyone was saying. Some dogs shouted, several looked tearful, others howled and wailed, raising such a noise that all the birds flew from the trees, and creatures of the field set off in an opposite direction.

Opinions were quick to follow.

'It's true! It's true! It doesn't exist!'

'It never did!'

'Lies! Lies! It was all lies!'

'I can't see any pies!'

'I said 'lies'!'

'Oh… yes, I see!'

Other dogs, who hadn't quite grasped what was going on, walked up and down the same spot looking indignant and barking at one of the farm's geese.

Many dogs were trying to think of offensive things to say to each other (like 'Why don't you go fart in a flannel!') but a howl brought the din to an end. The howl was unlike anything they had heard before. It was high and piercing, full of pain and melancholy. The voice, though unnatural, was unmistakably female.

The dogs turned to look for the sound. A stray black dog walked towards them.

'I've come with a message,' she said. 'I've come to tell you that, yes, as you fear, the Thumbald's no longer with you. And I've come to tell you that one of you – and one of you alone – must retrieve it.'

The assembled crowd gasped, then descended, once again, into uproar.

'Fart in your own flannel!' said one dog.

*

Francis the Greyhound was eyeing Cloud again. In fact, his eyes were so narrow that Cloud felt as if he was being crushed between them (like a pineapple in the armpit of a gorilla). For now, though, Francis kept quiet. Saddleback was doing the talking – and he was trying to understand more about the mysterious stray.

'I don't see why we should trust you,' said Saddleback to the black dog. 'You show up here unannounced, and then we find – for the first time in our history – that the Thumbald has disappeared. Surely that's no accident!'

'Here, here!' said Francis.

The black dog spoke softly.

'It's true – I did arrange to open your locket, but only so that all of you might see what you have lost.'

'Ha!' cried Francis disdainfully.

'It's a common problem – we have seen it in many places.'

'*We?*' cut in Francis.

'Food, property, shallow appearances – all these things and more have become obsessions for many dogs. I mean, look at the rampant bottom-grooming in this place – it's out of control! And a few too many of you spend too much time eating cheesy puff potatoes!

'But don't misunderstand me. All these things are excellent and good – in *moderation*. The truth is that your selfishness and self-interest has blinded you to the Thumbald. It's no wonder you can no longer see it!'

'Tsk,' said Francis.

'That's a fine-sounding speech,' said Saddleback, 'and I'm sure there's some truth in it. But it hardly answers our accusation! Why should we believe anything you say? I mean, look at you – you're a complete scruff!'

The black dog lowered her head, and then quoted something the dogs of Easthill had never heard before:

Leaves may obscure a path,
Or give grace to a branch.

The dogs looked confused.

'What does that mean?' asked Saddleback.

'This thing that you celebrate, the most you have seen of it is the locket that keeps it from prying eyes. It's unknown. Well, let me tell you, I am to you something unknown. So perhaps I also deserve your duty and respect. One way to look at it might be to say that we belong to the same category of things.'

The dogs still looked confused.

Cloud wondered – *how* had the black dog opened the

locket?

Francis's eyes flashed with calculation.

'If I might be allowed to speak, I think it's my duty to ensure my fellow elders have all the facts.'

The assembly of dogs in the farmhouse turned their attention to Francis.

'A little earlier today I took it upon myself to carry out some security checks. Like others, I wanted to make sure our ceremony went ahead without incident. I only wish I had been more vigilant! But you should all know that there were rumours about this black dog before she worked her mischief.'

The small crowd of elders murmured.

'Our junior *friend* here,' said Francis, nodding at Cloud, 'was discussing the matter with a wood pigeon not long before the ritual began.'

The dogs all turned to look at Cloud. Cloud could feel his stomach deflate like a wrinkled balloon.

'Do you deny it?' asked Francis.

'No,' replied Cloud in an inaudible croak. He cleared his throat and repeated 'No' so that everyone could hear.

'Except,' continued Francis triumphantly, 'when I spoke with the bird, he professed complete ignorance of the matter. And if that's true, it begs the question – *where did the rumour come from?* How did our Border Collie friend *know* about the stray dog?'

Cloud wanted to speak but he couldn't find his tongue. He feared whatever it was that Francis was about to say.

'If you will permit me, I have a theory,' continued Francis. 'I have observed Cloud closely ever since I first arrived here in Easthill. His behaviour has always struck me as odd. You will notice that he is often very quiet. Some might think this looks like shyness. I am not so sure. We all know that Cloud was not born into one of the packs at Easthill. He was adopted – mainly due to the kindness and compassion of Saddleback. You might hope that kindness and compassion would be repaid in kind. But experience has taught me otherwise. All too often, by a strange act of pride, dogs return such favours by harbouring a grudge against those who help them. Experience has also taught me to sniff warily around quiet dogs – shyness is not always the sign of a good nature!'

'What are you saying?' asked Cherry, her blood rising.

'It's obvious, isn't it? Cloud doesn't belong here and he knows it. So, quietly, he has been planning the destruction of everything we stand for. He arranged for this vagrant to undermine our ceremony. He is trying to sabotage us! I wouldn't even be surprised if he is secretly working for Animo!'

Cloud could see many dogs staring at him, their hackles starting to bristle. The loneliness he felt reached a new peak. He wanted to run from the farmhouse and run from Easthill. He wanted to keep running and never come back.

'I don't know,' said Saddleback hesitantly, 'that seems a bit... I have known Cloud longer than you, Francis, and I can't believe...'

'... You are too good-natured, Saddleback. I'm not sure you see what's really going on here.'

The black dog cut in. As she spoke, she fixed her eyes on Francis.

'I have been to many places. I have seen many things. And I am sure that in one way the Greyhound is right: *things are not always what they seem.*'

Francis was rattled by these words. He couldn't tell what exactly the black dog meant by them.

'In what way are things not always what they seem?' asked Saddleback.

'In many ways,' the black dog replied. 'How things *seem* and how they *are* affect so many different things. It sounds as if, to many of you, this Border Collie *seems* innocent enough. But to this Greyhound, that's not the way things *are.*'

'Quite right!' growled Francis.

'And the Greyhound's words make the Border Collie

seem quite different. Still, we haven't heard anything from the Border Collie. So how do things really stand?'

'Isn't that what we're trying to find out?' asked Saddleback.

Cloud wondered where all this was going. Should he speak? How should he defend himself?

'Indeed. The Greyhound even says that he wouldn't be surprised if the Border Collie is a spy working for Agent Animo.'

Saddleback held back a low growl in his throat.

'I don't like all this talk of Animo. These days we hear too much about it. And, thankfully, we have escaped his malevolent tricks so far.'

'Or so it *seems*,' said the black dog.

'What do you mean by that?'

'Isn't that what you're trying to find out?' asked the black dog playfully. 'Animo. Animo. That's the name he has in these parts. It's in his nature (in so far as he has one) to go by many names, but we know him by a different name. We call him Nous.'

A few tails shivered.

The black dog looked surprised.

'Why do you react like that? How much do you know about Nous?'

'All that I want to,' said Saddleback.

'Then no wonder he is darkening your home. If you

can't face up to who he really is, then you are already vulnerable to his power. He thrives on deception – in many ways, that's all he really is.

'Nous, as you say, is a trickster. He has no real character, no place, no home. He is a string of words, a spell, a charm. Do you know what he does? Do you know how he operates?'

The dogs were silent.

'He lives by stealing the bodies of living creatures. In truth he is nothing more than an airy spirit, or a malignant force. But he will rob creatures of their body, imprisoning their spirits in lonely places – the hollow of a tree, the bottom of a well, in the dark crevices of a cave. Then he will use the body he has stolen to control the lives of other creatures, gradually binding them to his will. And he won't stop. Nothing will temper his appetite for control. He wants to cast the whole world into his spell!

'He has been successful, too. He has built a city some way to the north of here. And everyone in it – everyone – is controlled by him and his apparatus of power! It's hardly surprising that you have heard more about him. And it wouldn't surprise me at all if his spies *are* operating nearby.'

Cloud thought he could detect a flicker in the black dog's eyes, but he couldn't see where she was looking.

'And it surprises me no less to find that you have lost sight of the Bald. The Bald is largely forgotten, wherever you go. It's only in the small out-of-the-way settlements like this that any memory of it lingers.'

The dogs in the farmhouse were thinking about all this very hard. Even the most seasoned elders found it a bit much. They wanted to hide under the table where no one would see them and they wouldn't have to trouble their brains about it.

'Why should we believe any of this?' asked Saddleback.

'A very good question!' said Francis.

'True enough,' replied the black dog, 'but that's my point. All these matters are related. Is this Border Collie a spy or an innocent? Am I his accomplice or am I to be trusted? Is Animo at work in your hamlet or not? How do things seem and what's the *truth*?

'That, my friends, is the beating heart of it. And that is the one thing you know that is missing – the truth, or how things truly are. *The Thumbald.* If it is anything, then the Thumbald is the truth. But even here I see that you are wavering, because I have already heard some of you ask: is the Thumbald real or just a made-up flight of fancy?

'How can you possibly know the answers to any of these questions, unless one of you seeks it out?'

The Stray

Hoo Hoo

The way opened before Cloud. As he pattered light-ly over the unfamiliar road before him, he thought about Easthill. This gave him some comfort, but it was small comfort when he thought about the dangerous world beyond. Looked at in this way, his memory of home was just a flickering candle at the end of its wick, waiting for the darkness that would follow.

A little gloomy, he tried to spur himself forward. He met very few other creatures. Sheep greeted him with a thin foot-stamp of defiance. Then they moved on, grumbling. Once he had passed them, he would often look over his shoulder to see them staring after him (and, quite often, weeing at the same time).

He glimpsed a field mouse, sporting its luck in the open air. It jumped out of the long grasses with a sort of confident and overexcited step into the unknown, only to find a large dog pawing towards it.

'Yikey mikey!' it exclaimed and dived back under cover.

Rabbits stumbled in their usual cabbage-brained habit, and then more or less trod on each other to get out of his way. And as he stopped to drink at the bank of a river, a trout floated to the surface. It considered him for a little while. Then it said:

'Are you a tuna fish?'

'I'm sorry?'

'I said are you a tuna fish?'

'A tuna fish?' asked Cloud, not sure what a tuna fish was, and so whether he was one or not.

'Only I heard there was one about.'

'I'm a dog,' said Cloud.

He was confident that this was, if not an answer to the question, at least true.

'Oh,' said the trout a little disdainfully, and then disappeared.

The track followed the gentle rise and fall of the hills, imitating the reptilian meanders of small streams, quite often under the cover of trees, which contorted their long limbs to drink from the water. He trotted through meadows of long grasses, weaving around thistles, in the glow of buttercups and the pinkish cheer of foxgloves glowing from dry-stone boundaries. Until, eventually, he climbed higher into the foothills of forbidding mountains.

Being completely alone was, at first, a challenge. Every sound, every rustle, every gust of wind, every note in the chorus of nature, was a voice coming from somewhere. Noises flew out of sweetbriars and field maples, through the cracks in the kindled dead wood on the floor of a wood, from the burrowed holes in the banks of a sunken lane, from eruptions of gorse. He wanted to respond.

Then he heard a very distinct sound: scratching, or something very like it, accompanied by a whine. It seemed to come from somewhere inside the hills. He followed the path, which had been hugging a stream. It kinked its way around a corner, where the stream disappeared into the mouth of a cave.

There, he heard a distinct voice calling out:

'He's coming! He's coming! At last, I'm free!'

Only a small stream trickled from the mouth of the cave, but its entrance was strewn with rocks and large boulders, tossed and displaced by the inconstant waters channelled down through the hillside. Cloud traced the water into the dark interior.

'Welcome! Yes, Yes! Welcome!' the voice called out, sounding so excited that it couldn't sit still. 'I'm your servant! Get me out of here and I'm your servant. Come closer! Come closer! Why do you hang back, Master? I can smell the rosemary a mile off.'

'Who are you?' asked Cloud, treading warily. 'Why don't you show yourself?'

'Listen to that,' laughed the voice. 'Show myself?! How innocent you are, Master! And of all the misfortune poor Hoo Hoo has suffered! Here I am, locked up in this cave.'

'Locked up?' asked Cloud. 'Well, who locked you up? And why?'

'Oh,' said Hoo Hoo a little hesitantly, 'it was nothing much. A trifle really.'

Cloud dared to tread a little further. He could just make out the shape of a natural chamber impressed into the rock wall. It was locked in on all sides by stone. The only way into it at all was through a small hole at its base, which had been sealed off with metal bars. This was some sort of natural cage.

'These officious types. They work themselves up over the smallest… it was nothing, really. But you try telling that to Avebalderheda. You try telling that to her!'

'Who's that?'

'Oh, you know Avebalderheda. You must have met her. Of course, she has all sorts of disguises, but I'll bet a thousand angry badgers that you met her as a black-haired vagrant. That's how she likes to parade around (between you and me I'd say she's got no self-respect).'

'The black dog?'

'Yes, yes, you see I know all about it, Master. I know all about it. You couldn't get me out of here, could you? It's very uncomfortable, and it smells of sheep.'

'How do you know the black dog? And why do you keep calling me Master?'

'Because you are my master, Master. That's how the stones stack up. And I know a lot more than that! Oh yes! Just answer me this: are you not travelling to the Lake of Gifts? And are you not going there with a tall task: to put the Bald back into your Thum?'

Cloud was suddenly a little afraid.

'How can you know that?'

Cloud noticed the sudden pitch of pride in the tone of the reply.

'Because I'm Hoo Hoo, High Lady of the Mountain-Tarn Cave for the Deliverance of Lost Creatures! Oh, but Master...'

'I'm not your master!'

'... couldn't you get me out of here? I'm sworn to guide you on your quest. And I'm assailed by malicious birds from far-off lands who call me rude names in foreign languages! I will bring all my many talents to the task!'

Cloud was flummoxed. He had scarcely come to

terms with his appointed task. It had all happened so quickly. In the chaos that had followed the opening of the locket, the black dog had made it very clear that Cloud should be the one to recover its secrets. She had only asked his name. When he replied with the answer, something cold and mysterious shimmered at the back of her eyes and she stated matter-of-factly, 'Then it must be you'.

In less than a day, he had been packed on his way and told to seek out a place somewhere in the far corners of the west called the Lake of Gifts. There he would find the answers that had confounded his community. The black dog had taken the locket and placed it around his neck. In the empty chamber, she had placed several sprigs of rosemary. Some creatures, she explained, would help him on his quest and the rosemary would help them to identify him.

He hadn't wanted to leave his home, but of all the dogs in Easthill, he believed in the Thumbald more than most – at least, unlike most other dogs, he had little else in which to believe. Something in the way the black dog had urged him to take up the challenge also made it impossible to refuse.

Cloud thought he could hear the creature scratching at the walls of their prison with a faint whimper.

'But what makes you think I can set you free?'

'First of all, you must want to set me free. And second of all, you need to stick your nose in that hole you can see just above the grating.'

'My nose?'

'That's right.'

'In the hole?'

'Yes.'

This was a leap of faith, a real question of trust. Cloud was not the sort of dog who liked to casually poke his nose into holes. After all, you never knew what might be in them! But, more than that, the nose was, of all his protuberances, the one he valued most, and he didn't want to put it in jeopardy lightly.

'Why should I trust you to put my nose in the hole?' he asked. 'How do I know that someone hasn't locked you up for some good reason, and that nosing around that hole won't leave me damaged beyond repair? Or even nose-less?'

'It's a fair question,' replied Hoo Hoo, 'but you don't need to take my word for it. Trust the words written on the wall above the hole.'

Cloud peered towards the hole. He could, squinting a little, just make out an inscription above it. It read:

Be Bald.

'I see,' said Cloud, who was beginning to understand that there was more at work here than met the eye (or even the nose).

'Besides, Master, do you know the way to the Lake of Gifts? It's a long and dangerous way.'

Cloud thought a while, and then he said:

'I will get nowhere on this journey if I trust no one and everyone. You might be tricking me, and I might be about to fall, even at the first hurdle. But something tells me – I almost smell it – that you are among those I should trust.'

Hoo Hoo didn't like to say that the smell could just be sheep poo as she thought that might delay her moment of liberation.

'Yes, yes! Excellent decision, Master! But, please, when you release me, I warn you to withdraw. I'm radiant and I've been known to blind even the most venerable eyes with my resplendence!'

Still puzzled, Cloud poked his sniffer into the hole, half expecting to have it bitten off. Something like warm moss tickled it, and a watery substance he didn't recognise overwhelmed his nostrils. He sneezed violently. Then he retrieved his nose – thankfully still intact – and stumbled out of the cave in a fit of sneezing. His eyes watered, but his nose settled down as the fresh air blew it clean.

He could hear the scraping of stone against stone, slab against slab. Then there came a yawn, thrown out by the stretching of cramped limbs, followed by the light patter of paws.

Cloud recoiled a little, and looked around, thinking that perhaps he should arm himself with a stick or stone of some kind. He narrowed his eyes, somehow expecting a streaming ray of light. He cowered in this anxious state, as a small Spaniel staggered into the daylight. It had a gunshot coat and a back leg that seemed to misbehave with unpredictable skips. Its eyes peered over a speckled white nose and blinked through a brown face. Cloud almost laughed.

'Well, where are you, Master? Oh, there you are!' said Hoo Hoo.

Her eyes were still adjusting to the light. She sat down to scratch her ear freely for the first time in a long time.

'So, you are a dog,' said Cloud, still amused.

'What did you think I was? An iguana?'

'A what?'

'Well, my name is Hoo Hoo,' she said, trotting down to the company of her new master, and sniffing at everything with interest, 'and from this moment, I am your disciple.'

'Then I hope we can also be friends.'

'Oh, I'm sure we shall. But perhaps you think we need something more. Perhaps you think I need a name that fits the worthy aims of our adventure. But you needn't worry, Master! I have already got one.'

Cloud had no idea what she was talking about.

'My name for this purpose is Bald-but-difficult.'

'Okay,' said Cloud, still confused, 'but tell me, how did you come to be locked up in these hills, and how do you know about my quest?'

*

'I don't remember from where I came,' said Hoo Hoo. 'But I do know that one of my earliest memories was a voice. I heard it as I came down out of the mountains. And the voice said:

These creatures, every last one of them, is a mixed-up mess of spirit and earth, so we should never be surprised by the peculiar things they do.

'So, you see, all I can really remember from that time is wandering about the hills until, eventually, I fell in with a pack of wild young pups.'

Cloud and Hoo Hoo had found a sheltered spot down by a small stream. Cloud lay on the ground, his back legs tucked underneath him, and his front paws spread patiently before him. Hoo Hoo paced about at the edge of the stream, giving little involuntary skips whenever she was enthralled by her story.

Straying with her pack of dogs, Hoo Hoo came to a large tarn in the shadow of some cliffs. The grasses around the tarn were scattered with wildflowers. The water, they discovered, was drinkable. As they peered across the tarn, they could see an opening in the cliff edge. It looked like the entrance to a disused mine.

'What a shame none of us can swim,' said one of the pack. 'This is a very beautiful place. If only we could get across the water to see if that mine is inhabitable.'

'I can swim,' cried out Hoo Hoo.

Except she didn't know how she knew this because she couldn't remember ever swimming before.

She stepped up to the water's edge and plunged in. She paddled all the way to the mine's entrance. And inside, she found something extraordinary. The opening had only the outward appearance of a mine. Really, it was more like a large carved-out cave. A small stream ran through it, and into the tarn. Little niches in the walls had been hollowed out to create small sleeping quarters. There were even stone bowls laid out for eating. Carved on one wall was an inscription:

This is the Mountain-Tarn Cave for the Deliverance of Lost Creatures.

Hoo Hoo helped her pack of friends to settle in the Mountain-Tarn Cave for the Deliverance of Lost Creatures. They found a routine, each with appointed duties, and they even built a small bridge from the entrance to the cave onto the nearest shore. And because she had brought them to their home, they appointed her High Lady in All Things.

'You see,' she said, 'I took the title High Lady of the Mountain-Tarn Cave for the Deliverance of Lost Creatures. Quite a title, wouldn't you agree! And, just as I discovered I could swim by swimming, I also discovered that I knew all sorts of other things. In no time at all, I knew the best way to fry a fish, and the most becoming style for ears. But I noticed I had other abilities, which, even then, I could see were not fully formed. I could affect the movement of stones and cause loudmouthed birds of prey to lose their sense of direction.'

Cloud listened openly to Hoo Hoo's stories, but his brow was beginning to furrow a little over some of the detail. And he was not totally surprised when she suddenly exclaimed:

'But I soon got bored with all that! You know making fish forget their whereabouts becomes quite tiresome after a while.'

She wanted a new challenge.

And she found something new to aim at the day a sheep fell off the mountain. It landed in an unseemly clatter at the entrance to the cave. Hoo Hoo thought the sheep might be plotting a raid on the cave. She said she would turn the sheep into a pile of vomit if it didn't leave promptly.

'Think you're one of those Proteanimators, do you? Bah!' the sheep muttered.

It limped off grumpily.

Hoo Hoo soon learned that Proteanimators had special powers, which could be developed with training. Just as naturally athletic creatures could become more athletic with practice and exercise, natural Proteanimators could transform one arrangement of things into another. But to really master this secret and highly unusual skill, Hoo Hoo would have to study under a Ponderous Proteanimator, or one who has pondered Proteanimation in depth.

Hoo Hoo was so excited that she might be able to turn cold air into fire or transform the ears of misbehaving dogs into cabbage leaves, that she could scarcely sit still in her cave.

In fact, she couldn't sit still. She set out to search the world for Ponderous Proteanimators.

*

It took Hoo Hoo years of wandering, arriving at many

dead ends, and straying into inhospitable, out-of-the-way places. Eventually she caught a rumour about a sage, who lived in a specially constructed burrow deep in a forest. After sniffing around for a while, she got a reaction. She heard rummaging, and an unusually elegant squirrel popped its head out from a felled log.

'What's all this disturbance?' the squirrel said.

'I have come to study the art of Proteanimation,' Hoo Hoo replied.

'You don't look up to much,' said the squirrel. 'Even so, my Guide and Seer, who at present is imparting the fruits of his learning, told me to attend at our front door. He foresaw, correctly it would seem, that someone would approach seeking his instruction.'

'That must be me!' Hoo Hoo replied eagerly.

'Follow me, then,' said the squirrel.

Hoo Hoo followed the squirrel into the burrow via a small hole concealed by the log. The passageways of the burrow led into a larger room, hollowed out and sparingly decorated with simple paintings of the natural world: branches, flowers, leaves, the meander of a river. A small fire glowed in the corner of the room. Near to it was the head of this little underground school.

The Ponderous Proteanimator was a Bearded Collie. He seemed to take a long time to weigh things up. Hoo Hoo said that he was old. She said that he was 'very,

very old' and that he was also 'very, very hairy'. He was curled up on a little dais before some other pupils: two Dalmatians and an Airedale.

Hoo Hoo lowered her head.

'Venerable Proteanimator, I am humbled by word of your great powers, and would dearly like to study under you. I believe that yours is a gift I share. Under your guidance, I should like to become a Proteanimator.'

'That's all very well,' said the Ponderous Proteanimator, sizing up Hoo Hoo slowly and carefully, 'but first I need to know your name and where you have come from.'

'I have wandered for many years. My name is Hoo Hoo, High Lady of the Mountain-Tarn Cave for the Deliverance of Lost Creatures.'

'Oh shoot!' said the Proteanimator. 'Scuttle off with you; that must be a lie. That's too far for one dog to come alone. Besides, I know that land is good for nothing. No one lives in that cave.'

'But please,' cried out Hoo Hoo, 'ponder this ponderously, oh Sage! I am speaking the truth. I have walked across mountains, swum oceans, and ridden clouds to get here.'

Like many other points in her story, Cloud thought that Hoo Hoo was being a little free with the facts.

'Well,' said the Proteanimator, 'let's suppose you're

in earnest. What is it you would like to learn so much? Tell me that!'

'Oh, above all things, Proteanimation, Proteanimator. That's what I want to learn!'

'But Proteanimation is not like sailing down a stream. It's a wide estuary with many tributaries. To properly understand it, you must explore them all. And it's not something to undertake lightly. It's no frivolous party trick.'

The Ponderous Proteanimator explained that to think of Proteanimation in this way was to misunderstand it.

To the eyes, everything looked fixed and solid. Most creatures, because they took this for granted, acted towards the world accordingly, which meant the world had a fixed and solid shape. But Proteanimators could see through the appearance of solid things. They could recognise their shifting and unstable elements. When the whole was seen from the point of view of these empty parts, it could quickly disappear or fall apart.

This was why they were called *Ponderous* Proteanimators. Their power came from pondering the true nature of things. In the experience of many other creatures, they also deserved this title because they rambled on at length about things that no one really understood. Some even said they talked a lot of 'duck waddle'.

But with natural aptitude, study, and a clear, concentrated mind, Ponderous Proteanimators could cultivate the rarest of skills. By seeing things through their unsettled core, they could act in such a way that disarranged the stuff of the world and reassembled it in new ways. They could channel the natural habit of change through their own powers of judgement.

Put very simply, Hoo Hoo explained to Cloud, this meant they could turn a pea into a pot plant.

'Except it isn't meant to work quite like that,' she said hastily.

The Proteanimator explained:

'Acts of the body depend on acts of will; acts of will depend on the acts of mind; acts of mind depend on knowledge of the world; and knowledge of the world depends on a body that acts upon it. You must learn to see all these parts at work. You cannot just decide to be a Proteanimator!'

Hoo Hoo was disappointed.

'Well, what must I do, oh Proteanimator?'

'You must begin somewhere. What about art? Perhaps you could begin with that.'

'What's art?'

'It is the meticulous rendering of worldly things in their true light.'

Hoo Hoo's tail drooped.

'Is that useful?' she asked.

'Well…' said the Proteanimator uncertainly, 'well… it isn't really meant to be… that's not the point! But since you don't seem very interested in it, what about Natural Philosophy – could you start with that?'

'What's Natural Philosophy?' asked Hoo Hoo.

'You will consider how creatures think. And you will ask tricky questions about how exactly a tortoise travels between two points.'

'Well that doesn't sound very interesting,' said Hoo Hoo. 'I don't think I'll study that.'

'You are a haughty hound, and difficult to please! You don't seem to want to study anything. Still, let's try something else. What about austerities and asceticism.'

'What does that involve?' Hoo Hoo sounded doubtful.

'Disciplined restraint of all appetites, no, or little, eating, quiet contemplation, and a fondness for all vegetables.'

'Not eating?' said Hoo Hoo in disbelief. 'What kind of joint is this? No way! I'm not doing that!'

'Divination, then?!' snapped the Proteanimator.

Hoo Hoo could tell her new teacher was angry. She was also frustrated with him, but, in this moment, she thought she could detect a faint flicker in his eyes. It was like something inside him had moved. Without thinking about what it meant or why she was doing it, she raised her tail and stuck out half her tongue.

Then she said:

'Divination? What's that?'

'Well,' replied the Proteanimator, 'divination involves staring for a long time at the bones of dead animals. After which time, you must roll your eyes, and proclaim in a low monotone the secrets of the future. It might sound morbid, but it can be very fulfilling.'

'Divination – pah! I don't want any of your grimy animal bones!'

'Well, what on earth can you possibly want?!' asked the Proteanimator.

Then, in total exasperation, he picked up a candle holder with his teeth, and hit Hoo Hoo over the head with it three times.

Hoo Hoo was quite surprised.

The Ponderous Proteanimator steadied his nerves by murmuring a line of verse:

What knowledge begins with nothing?
What sight can see the void?
What sounds begin with silence?
What life from life destroyed?

The two creatures stood in silence for a while, until

the Proteanimator spoke:

'You are a troublesome and testing pupil. And I feel sure that such remarks will follow you wherever you go and no matter what you do. But…'

He hesitated.

'What is it, oh Sage?' asked Hoo Hoo.

'… but something stirs quite naturally in you.'

'I saw something in your eyes just now,' said Hoo Hoo.

'You would not have known, but I saw it in yours, too. *It* does not belong to either of us. *It is one. We are many.* You saw the secret signs that we should all respect. This, alone, tells me that I must take you as my pupil, and let those secrets speak through you, however much your mischievous and infuriating disposition might stand in the way. So, as of this moment, you are my pupil.'

'Excellent!' cried Hoo Hoo.

'But all my pupils must have a spirit-name. And I have decided that it is only fitting that yours should be Bald-but-difficult.'

*

So, from that day, Hoo Hoo studied in the burrow and learned the ways of proteanimation.

Hoo Hoo was a quick learner, and her natural intuition for the Bald meant that she made good progress.

But, just as her teacher had predicted, she found that she would all too easily lapse into old ways and habits. When reworking the materials of a pencil, she couldn't always resist the temptation to turn it into a pig's tail and stick it onto the bottom of one of the other pupils. Hoo Hoo was, in every way, Bald-but-difficult.

This disrespectful tendency came to a head when she was not far from perfecting her skills. She could apply proteanimation to most things. She could even, if she concentrated hard, see through herself and recreate her body in another form. Her teacher impressed on Hoo Hoo that this was the most difficult and dangerous part of the art.

'To lose yourself is one thing; but, if you enter into the wrong attitude of mind, you might find yourself in your transformed state *permanently*.'

Hoo Hoo, even with this warning, found that whenever she practised self-transformation, she was even more tempted to fool around. The thought that she could turn herself into other things toyed with her imagination. How, for example, would the other pupils react if they all came into dinner and she was on the table disguised as a bowl of soup?! Suppose someone went to eat from the bowl, and at that moment, she transformed back into herself. It would be quite a practical joke, she thought.

At the end of one day, just as they were all about to go to bed, an Airedale called Juniper goaded Hoo Hoo.

'I heard you can even transform yourself now,' he said to Hoo Hoo.

'It's taken a lot of practice, but, yes, I've got the hang of it.'

'Really! Are you sure? Self-transforming is really very hard, you know!'

'Are you calling me a liar?' said Hoo Hoo defensively.

'Calm down, calm down! No one's calling you a liar. I was just envious, that's all. All of us are.'

He paused. This seemed to placate Hoo Hoo.

'Of course,' he continued, 'if you really want to put the matter to rest, you could always give us a little demonstration.'

Now this suggestion stoked Hoo Hoo's pride.

'Okay,' she said boldly, 'I will.'

She took a few steps backwards. Before the other dogs knew it, she had disappeared, and a large pineapple plopped onto the floor before them.

'A pineapple!' cried Juniper.

Then the pineapple grew legs. It made a loud farting noise as it grew a mouth and stuck out a tongue. It began to dance around on its little legs, doing something like a can-can.

'Pooh!' cried the pineapple. 'I'm no ordinary pineapple. I can sing and dance. Look at me – I'm a dancing pineapple!'

The other pupils enjoyed the spectacle of the dancing pineapple and were soon cheering it on. One or two of them even formed a line with it. The whole scene caused such a ruckus that it disturbed the Prote-animator. He burst into the room.

'What is this brouhaha? What is the meaning of it?!' he roared.

All the pupils hung their heads and tried to hide behind each other. They fell silent. Hoo Hoo tried to change discreetly back into the form of dog but found that she couldn't do it. Was she stuck as a pineapple? She did her best to stand sheepishly at the back of the crowd, looking – as far as this is possible for a pineapple – ashamed.

'This is a place of quiet contemplation and ponderous reflection. Whatever you are doing, it was not quiet; and I can't imagine it was very contemplative!'

Deeper silence overcame the assembly of pupils, until Juniper the Airedale stepped forward.

'Oh Sage, we all lost our senses. Hoo Hoo, you see, told us that she had learned the art of self-transformation. So, she gave us a demonstration. As you can see,' he said pointing at Hoo Hoo, 'she has become a dancing pineapple.'

The Proteanimator's eyes were far from ponderous and serene.

'I would like you all to retire – quietly – for the evening,' he said.

Hoo Hoo tried to tiptoe out on her little legs, while searching her pineapple head for a way to change back.

'Not you, Bald-but-difficult!' said the Proteanimator. 'I want a word with you.'

The Proteanimator looked her up and down once the others had left.

'You can't change back,' he said, 'can you?'

The pineapple, tearfully, shook her head.

'Oh Hoo Hoo, best and worst among pupils, I knew it would come to this. How many times must I tell you, these special skills you have are not yours to do with as you please. They go beyond your desires, so you cannot use them selfishly.'

'But Sage, please! I am a foolish dog, I know. And I can't help myself, but surely there must be something you can do? I can't stay like this forever!'

The Proteanimator considered the matter.

'I'm afraid, I have only one choice. Which means that you have only one choice. You must leave our community of learning and go back into the world. The nature of things means that you must learn to bear your insights and skills in the right way, challenged with all the threats and temptations of nature.'

*

So, the Proteanimator helped Hoo Hoo change from a dancing pineapple back into a dog, but only as he guided her out of the burrow.

Hoo Hoo didn't know where else to go, so she decided to return to her cave. On her travels, she wandered up into some gentle hills, and found herself strolling over the moorland. The heather shivered in the wind, and grouse garbled under its cover.

She trudged to the edge of a ridge and looked down on a valley. She could see a cluster of farm buildings. She didn't know it at the time, but this was Long Dale Farm, one of the largest and most powerful farmsteads in the region.

'Got an apple?' came a voice from behind her.

She turned around. A large piebald horse was bearing down on her.

'An apple?' asked Hoo Hoo.

'That's what I said!'

The horse was very blunt.

'No. No, I don't have an apple.'

'Oh. That's, like, a shame. I'm starving.'

'I'm sorry about that,' said Hoo Hoo.

'I guess I'll just have to, you know, eat you instead.'

'Eat me?'

'Yeh.'

'Do horses eat dogs?'

'Sometimes we do, you know,' replied the horse. 'Anyway, whatever. You're trespassing.'

'You own this moorland?'

'Yeh.'

'So, you're going to eat me?'

'That's the penalty for trespassing. I'm going to eat you. With marmite.'

The horse bared his teeth at Hoo Hoo.

This was a very strange horse. Hoo Hoo didn't quite know what to make of it, but she had the feeling that the horse was just trying to pick on her.

She decided to turn into a hippopotamus.

The horse blinked to confront a trick of the eyes. The dog had disappeared and, in its place, stood a giant cow-like creature with a large bulging belly, a neck like a barrel, and a nose like the front of a bulldozer. What on earth was going on? Had he been talking to a dog or this peculiar creature? Had his brain gone soft?

'Oh…' stammered the horse, and finally managed to blurt out, '… w… well, who are you?'

'I,' said the creature in a deep voice mellowed by an ample digestive system, 'am a hippopotamus.'

'A what?'

'A hippopotamus!' bellowed the hippopotamus.

'But… but…' said the horse, 'I…'

'And if you don't trot off right now, I'm going to seize you between my mighty jaws and snap you in two like a twiglet!'

'What…? But you was just, like, a… you was…' the horse's mind fluttered about faintly, 'how can you be… and what's a hip…?'

The horse continued to falter, until it summoned a little more courage.

'Why should I pay attention to you? You're just, like, a fat heifer, yeh!'

The hippopotamus, in a flash of impatience, held the horse in its eyes. Then its mouth opened to reveal a jaw, almost the full size of its body, and two extremely sharp teeth that were long enough and sharp enough to make the horse's guts tighten. If the hippopotamus took a few steps forward, it could easily snap off the head of the horse whole, in a single bite. Then came the roar. It gurgled up from somewhere in the boggy belch-hole of the hippo's stomach with a mixture of violence and hunger.

The horse was now staggering on its legs, stunned into inactivity. Only when it finally came to its senses did it turn and run as fast as it could. He ran over the moorland, down the hillside, and didn't stop until it reached Long Dale Farm.

'Run for your lives! There's a fat killer cow in the mountains!' it yelled.

The farm descended into uproar. He galloped about, whinnying hysterically about *a monster cow* and *a fat hippyhoppymus with enormous teeth.*

The more the horse cried out his shrill warning, the more the creature morphed into a spawn of his imagination. It was quickly crossed with a giant pig, had grown horns, and overpowered its prey with unwholesome body odour.

*

Long Dale Farm was run in a very orderly way. At least the farm animals liked to think it was. They had created committees to run everything.

Overseeing these committees was the Board for Agricultural Action (BAA). A bossy cockerel, who threw his weight about, chaired the committee, but a collection of sheep did the heavy lifting. Except they usually just treated committee bleatings as an opportunity to get together and grumble.

The committee was designed to set out clear actions which could be put into practice. But since most of the decisions it managed to take only annoyed the many animal communities on the farm, it spent most of its time worrying and moaning about how to please everyone. It set up more committees to represent different farmyard groups: the Duck's Committee for Kindness and Inclusion (DUCKI), the Barn Owl Executive and Leadership (BOwEL), the Pig and Ordure Review Committee (PORC).

Before the BAA could pass a motion, it had to, so to speak, get it through the BOwEL. But since members of the subcommittees very often raised objections, this could easily result in a blockage.

All the same, when news reached the farm of the horse's treatment and Hoo Hoo's unusual behaviour, it shook everyone into a shiver of panic. A special emergency session of the BAA convened to discuss the matter and agree a response.

Still, *emergency* didn't have quite the same meaning for the BAA as for other creatures. BAA bleatings usually lasted for several days. This one lasted a day. For two-thirds of it, the members discussed what to include on the agenda and whether they should ask the chicken corps to keep minutes. After chewing it all over thoroughly, the BAA recommended to its subcommittees that there was only one sensible course of action: they would send a strongly worded letter.

After she had seen off the horse, Hoo Hoo had found a place to shelter, and settled down for the night. She was surprised to be woken by a barn owl. She was even more surprised to see it drop a letter before her, and say, in a clipped tone:

'I am to return with your reply.'

Hoo Hoo was baffled by the bird's behaviour. She studied the missive and was still more surprised (and secretly amused) to be addressed as 'Dear Dog/Hippopotamus'.

The letter read:

Dear Dog/Hippopotamus,

I write on behalf of the Board for Agricultural Action (BAA), its properties, lands, and citizens (excluding moles). It has come to the attention of the BAA that there is a certain creature on the moorland with the skill to 'proteanimate' or, in more common language, a capacity to change the visible aspect and form of their person in a manner that includes (or does not exclude) a complete range of animals, wildlife and general objects of the world. We have come to understand, not without qualification and allowing for the available evidence, that you are this certain creature.

The BAA makes no comment on the provenance of this certain creature (hereafter 'you'), or how it came to acquire such a portfolio of powers. Without wishing to prosecute or condemn the holding and performance of such powers, and yet noting that it is within its right to do so, the BAA sees fit only to observe that farmland jurisdiction requires all citizens to obtain a practising licence for all 'special and/or aux-

*iliary powers', including, but not confined to, the art (or arts)
of proteanimation.*

*In a spirit of leniency, the BAA deems it sufficient to issue
a formal warning to you (the creature), and to require that
henceforth you assent to the following terms of reference:*

A frown had settled across Hoo Hoo's forehead, like
a light layer of snow. When she had read this far, she
exclaimed to the owl:

'What in the name of charred chickpeas is all this
guff?!'

'Am I to understand that as your formal response?'
replied the owl.

'Who wrote this?' asked Hoo Hoo.

'I believe it is quite clear.'

'It's as clear as a coal-coloured cloud covered by another cloud!'

'I am to return with your written reply,' said the owl
tersely.

'I'm not going to chew through this trough of treacle!
Take me to the windbags who produced this mashed
marrow of words!'

'Oh no, I couldn't possibly do that.'

But Hoo Hoo refused to take no for an answer, and
the hapless owl had to flutter down the hillside and
through the valley with Hoo Hoo until they came to

the edge of Long Dale Farm.

News that the hippopotamus had arrived spread like wildfire. The stamping of hooves could be heard inside the stable, four chickens wobbled at unnatural speed across the farmyard, and a small company of ducks tried to hide by ducking under the water. Only Big Barry, a large St Bernard, was untroubled. He curled up behind the door to a barn.

'Doesn't look much like a hippopotamus to me,' he said.

As it happened, that morning Long Dale Farm was preparing for a special festival. Balder, the wisest of all creatures, and his faithful servant, Avebalderheda, were paying a visit to the farm, since they had heard all about how orderly and well run it was. The farm creatures had spent many days preparing for it and had gone to some lengths to cook up a feast.

When Hoo Hoo marched out of the hills, it caused so much panic that most of the creatures ran for their lives, leaving a large part of the farm deserted, except for a few chickens and a nervous-looking lamb with an eye patch. Even the owl who had brought Hoo Hoo the letter seemed to have fluttered off somewhere.

Her nose, meanwhile, led her towards the big barn, from where delicious and quite unusual smells were wafting. On entering the barn, she blinked in amazement. A long trestle table stretched its full length. Plate after plate of pies, platters, roasted vegetables, assortments of cakes, glass decanters of wine, and many more things festooned the table in an eye-goggling assembly.

'They are having a feast!' said Hoo Hoo to herself.

Then a look of mischief seized her.

'I know! I'll teach them to send me flab-filled letters!'

Coiling the spring in her back legs, she jumped onto the table. There, she started working her way through the dishes and delicacies and helping herself generously to the wine.

By the time she reached the end of the table, she had left behind a trail of destruction, and half-eaten pastries. She was also starting to feel quite drunk! In the grip of a sudden idea, she half ran, half staggered out of the barn and into the offices of the BAA. She found a pile of letterheaded paper and wrote a memorandum for immediate issue, instructing the pigeon corps to deliver a bombardment of droppings over the barn.

Pleased with her ploy, she wandered into the farmyard, where she amused a small family of field mice by turning herself into an exploding mushroom.

The company of the farm only dared to return to their home when they met their esteemed guests (Balder and Avebalderheda) on the road.

'What's going on?' asked the black dog. 'Why are you

all running away from your home?'

One of the sheep explained that they had been invaded by a dog who could turn into a hippopotamus.

'Oh, I don't think you have much to fear,' said Avebalderheda. 'Follow me!'

As it happened, the aerial bombardment of bird poo which Hoo Hoo had order arrived at the same time as the farm animals returned. The droppings rained down, and in a flash, Hoo Hoo turned herself into a chicken, laid a few eggs and started throwing them at the company. One egg landed on Balder's nose.

'What's the meaning of this!?' demanded the cockerel, as he entered the farmyard.

They soon learned what had happened.

'So, not only have you eaten our food, got drunk on the special wine reserved for this occasion, and sported yourself with no regard for public decorum, but you have issued a counterfeit instruction from the BAA. This is outrageous!'

The cockerel seemed to have discovered twice as much plumage.

'There is nothing left for it,' he intoned. 'Seize that hound!'

'Just you try, pen-pusher!' cried Hoo Hoo.

First, she turned herself into a basket of rotten apples and pelted them all with maggot-ridden fruit. Then she turned herself into a muck-spreading machine and sprayed them all with silage. And finally, she turned into a butterfly and made her escape by fluttering up to the roof of the farm buildings.

Balder, although mildly amused, could see what was going on straight away. And Balder could see further and deeper into the nature of things than any Ponderous Proteanimator. And, as soon as she saw Hoo Hoo escaping as a butterfly, she formed a butterfly net and used it to catch the fugitive. Through her own feat of deep insight, she forced Hoo Hoo to take her natural form. With the help of Avebalderheda, she constructed a cage around the rogue dog.

Balder didn't say very much. But when the ruckus had died down, she approached Hoo Hoo in her cage, looked her in the eye, and said two simple words:

'Old tricks.'

Then she turned her back on Hoo Hoo and winked an instruction to Avebalderheda.

'You are a lively and spirited creature,' said the black dog. 'And you have clearly developed insights and put them to use. Even if they are ignoble and corrupt. But you are a flame burning too brightly. So brightly that it burns out. You are an arrow without a target. You are a wild horse, untamed. But just as an arrow forgets its purpose without a target, you are a counterfeit proteanimator. You perform cheap tricks for amusement or your own gain, where true proteanimation peers into the limpid pool of nature. It sees beyond itself, and there discovers beauty, compassion. It sees the *truth*, which settles, quietens, and chastens a spirit turned restive with too much concern for material things.

'I don't know where you have picked up your hodge-podge of skills. But it's very clear that you don't know how to use them and are not fit to do so. Your punishment is just as clear: from today, you will be taken high up into the mountains, and imprisoned in a cave. There you will stay until, many years from now, a traveller on a journey to discover the truth will find you. Your task will be to accompany him and use your powers to aid his quest. Only that way can you find your true character.'

Porker

'So now you see, Master,' continued Hoo Hoo, 'how I came to be imprisoned in the mountain and why I must accompany you on your journey.'

Cloud looked doubtful. He didn't completely trust her. Neither did he completely believe the story. Some of it seemed a bit over the top.

'Well,' he said reluctantly, 'I think that was much longer than you needed to make it. We have wasted most of the afternoon. But I can begin to see why you think I am your master. Even so, I would prefer not to be called *Master*. I also realise what this journey means for you. But if you have told me the truth, then it means I must always keep an eye on you. So be warned – you are on trial!'

'I understand, Master,' replied Hoo Hoo. 'You know best, of course.'

'Well then, I think we must get moving, or it will be dark, and we'll be at the mercy of all the wildlife the night can throw at us.'

'Fear not, Master!' said Hoo Hoo. 'If the powers that be saw fit to make me watch over you and your journey, I am sure they will have other creatures in their service. So even if we do find ourselves in a few tight corners – and I would be amazed if we don't – then there is a good chance someone will come to our aid.'

'Nevertheless,' said Cloud doubtfully, 'I think we should get moving.'

So, finally, Cloud and Hoo Hoo picked up the road to the west. The track only led them higher into the hills. It wound through a long sunken valley, flanked on both sides by steep slopes, patched with scree. Lonely ash trees poked up through the stones. They hit a sudden ascent, and emerged into another valley, which rose eventually to high moorland, ruffled with heather.

The light was fading. They were starting to worry that they would not find their way down into more sheltered terrain before nightfall, much less chance upon someone who might offer them hospitality.

So, they were relieved when the path took them on a clear and marked descent. They were even more relieved to see the outline of two barn buildings just visible in the dusk, at the edge of a pine forest. But they were also just a little surprised to make out the shape of a creature climbing up the path towards them. They could see, at a distance, that the creature was a fellow dog, but only when he drew near that he was a King Charles Spaniel. The spaniel was well groomed. He carried a satchel of belongings on his back.

'Ho there!' called out Hoo Hoo, flagging down the young dog. 'Do you know if anyone lives in those buildings?' she asked. 'We are humble and weary pilgrims looking for shelter.'

'Speak to them yourself,' said the King Charles in a surly tone. 'I have had it up to my coiffured ears with that place and its problems.'

'Now hang on, young dog,' said Hoo Hoo. 'Is that any way to greet strangers who need your help? And why are you so suited up for a long journey, and in such a hurry at this time of the evening?'

'What business is it of yours?' replied the spaniel. 'All you need to know is that those two buildings are possessed by a fiend who has pushed my father to the edge of his wit and sanity. And it seems that I'm the only one who can do anything about it. Still, I have my doubts.'

'Now, steady on,' said Cloud, 'and tell us everything. We might be able to help. A fiend? What do you mean by that?'

'Well just that! About a year ago, a giant St Bernard

showed up at our home. At first, he was polite and pleasant enough. In fact, his manners were impeccable, and he was fun company to be around. So much so that my father agreed he should marry my youngest sister. But not long after we embraced him to our family, he lost all his charm and just ate! He ate all the bread, the vegetables, the pasta, the chocolate – you name it, he ate it! My poor father has been driven to distraction and despair. So, we have scraped together what little gold and silver we have. I am on my way to hire a minister of justice from Long Dale Farm. With any luck they will bring the monstrous dog to account. Don't delay me anymore.'

Hoo Hoo's ears had pricked up, and her eyes glimmered in the light of the early evening.

'A fiend, you say! Well, that's just the ticket! I can soon sort him out. I'll tell you what, if I can boot out this big buffoon, will you give me and my master shelter for the evening?'

The spaniel's eyes shifted between the two travelling companions.

'I don't know,' he said. 'I doubt you can do much good, but really it's not for me to say. You'll need to persuade my father. Come, I'll take you to meet him.'

The three dogs trotted down the path, over the hillside, until they came to the barn buildings. Before they reached the doorway of the first building, a sturdy King Charles, leathered with age, bounded out of the door.

'You charlatan!' he shouted at the younger dog. 'I told you to hurry as fast as you could to Long Dale Farm. Instead, you climb all the way up the hillside only to stroll back down. What happened? Did you forget your nose warmer?!'

The old dog's son explained hastily what had happened. The father, when he learned that they were travelling pilgrims with special powers, gave a sort of muffled howl, and ran into the barn. He returned wearing his best waistcoat and a tricorn hat. In the eyes of farm law, such hats distinguished the wearer as a respectable creature.

'How now,' he said to his guests in a very formal way. 'My name is King Cone. I am the master and lord of these buildings, and the land that surrounds. This is my son, Big Boy Cone. We are called 'Cone' because we live on the edge of a pine forest, and there are many pine cones about. In fact, if you look closely you will see that the roofs of these buildings are made of them!

'But never mind about that – so you are holy pilgrims with special powers? And you say that you can overcome the menace who has made all our lives miserable for so long?'

'Oh yes,' said Hoo Hoo confidently, 'I can deal with

that porker in no time at all. You just need to let me at him.'

'You!' said King Cone in surprise. 'You're a little wisp of a thing. This creature is a huge oaf, with very large teeth, and wobbling thighs. He would make a small pot of pâté out of you!'

'Don't you know anything, Cone-Head!' cried Hoo Hoo. 'You have to see beyond appearances. I have learned how to do that, and that's the source of my special powers. That's how I will deal with your fiend – I'll see right through him!'

'Well, we shall see,' said King Cone, a little flustered, 'but I'm forgetting my manners. Won't you come inside? Then I can tell you everything you need to know. At the very least, I can offer you shelter for the night.'

'You're very kind,' said Cloud, 'and we're very grateful.'

'That's funny,' said King Cone, as Cloud entered, 'I can smell rosemary.'

Curled up on a rug by the hearth in King Cone's house, they were presented with a plate of cheese and a platter of cold meats. King Cone even offered them home-brewed ale. Cloud said that he wanted to keep a clear head, and Hoo Hoo explained that she had taken a vow never to drink alcohol again. But King Cone filled a large wooden dish with ale, and lapped from it thoughtfully as he told the story of the family's misfortune. He stopped only to nibble at a piece of cheese.

Cloud noticed that King Cone was not only named after a pine cone and had a roof made from them, but that he also had a head shaped like one. Cloud mused. Had the King Charles spent so much time around pine cones that his head had adapted? Or had he been born with a pine cone head and so naturally was drawn to a place like this? The shape of King Cone's head was certainly rare and irregular.

'Until a year ago,' said King Cone, 'I had never had any trouble. This has always been a quiet and peaceful place. I brought up three daughters, and my only son, whom you see before you. The first two daughters married local dogs and settled down very well. My third daughter – we call her First Freshness – was hoping to follow her sisters, when last year a St Bernard came strolling down the hillside. As you have just done. At first, he was polite. He was well turned out and educated. And when we invited him to take lodging with us, he proved to be very helpful and diligent. So, he seemed, at the time, a very good match for my daughter. More fool me, I gave my blessing to their union.

'Then, not long after, he started to change. You might even say that he revealed his true colours. How did he do that, you ask? It's simple – he started to eat.

And eat. And eat. He ate the carrots. He ate the potatoes. He ate our entire crop of tomatoes. He devoured pastries, pies, puddings. He munched through cheese and biscuits. And he ate *endless* sausages.

'So, really, it was not surprising that he should turn into a monstrosity with a bouncing belly. My daughter, you'll understand, was distressed by his greed. Her mate has lost all affection for her, and she feels neglected.'

'This over-eating creature sounds very inconsiderate,' said Cloud.

'Inconsiderate!' cried Hoo Hoo. 'Master, that hardly gets between the paws of it. I'd say this creature is totally lost! His appetite owns him!'

'But I'm interested to know,' cut in King Cone, 'how do you expect to bring him to justice? You said something about special powers.'

'Quite right, Captain Cone-Head. I do have special powers. And I think I have already started to see through this prize nuisance.'

King Cone and Cloud didn't look convinced.

'What's your plan?'

Hoo Hoo's plan was simple. She would go over to the other building, and hide behind a tree, until the St Bernard showed some signs of life. She would then transform into First Freshness and get into the building. When she was inside, she would bash him over the head with any large object to hand.

'What good will that do?' asked King Cone.

'Well, once I have knocked him out, we can lock him up and keep him locked up until he can show a bit more control and promises to behave a bit better.'

'Oh, very well,' said King Cone, a bit reluctantly. 'It's worth a try.'

'There's just one thing,' said Hoo Hoo.

'What's that?'

'I'm responsible for the well-being of my Master. He enjoys discussions about elevated things. His mind is very lofty. You look like a dignified fellow – perhaps you could keep him company with some suitable conversation while I attend to the task at hand?'

'Well, what sort of thing should we discuss?' asked King Cone.

'Oh, you know, what does a single leaf tell us about the nature of the universe? That sort of thing.'

'Oh… okay,' said King Cone.

Hoo Hoo dashed out of the first farm building with a smile and ran into the woods near the second farm building. Hoo Hoo peered through the window of the second farm building, where she could see First Freshness. She made a quick study of her and transformed into her perfect likeness. She sniffed around the roots of the trees, which were thick with the smell of rabbits and squirrels.

Hoo Hoo could hear the intruder coming a long way off. Twigs cracked; the ground almost shook. When she saw the St Bernard, she was shocked because she recognised the dog from the brief time she had spent at Long Dale Farm.

'That's Big Barry! What's he doing here?' said Hoo Hoo. 'Oh, my darling!' she cried, approaching the St Bernard.

She trotted up to meet Barry, all the while looking like First Freshness.

'Thank goodness you have come home.'

'Darling?' said the St Bernard, taken aback. 'Since when have you called me 'darling'?!'

'There is no time to talk about it. You must hurry. You are in danger. We all are. Your father-in-law has recruited the help of some foreign wizard creatures so he can get rid of you.'

'Wizards!' laughed the St Bernard. 'I hardly think so.'

'You must believe me. There is a spaniel, and a collie-dog. The collie-dog is wise and learned (but a bit high-minded). The spaniel is fearsome. She has magic powers. She has vowed to turn you into a pot of pork fat for all your misdoings.'

'Really,' scoffed the St Bernard, 'I think your father has let his imagination run away with him this time.

But, if what you say is true, I would have thought you would be pleased to be free of me. Aren't you always saying that I'm good for nothing?'

'But, my darling, nothing frightens me more than magic. I would choose you a thousand times, rather than risk being turned into something… unpleasant. Please, let's go inside before it's too late.'

The St Bernard rolled his eyes a little before ushering Hoo Hoo into the second of the two farm buildings.

'Very well, in you go,' he said.

Once inside, he had a shock. He saw two dogs who looked exactly the same. They both looked like his wife. On closer examination, he saw that both were his wife.

'Ahhh!' screamed the St Bernard. 'I am seeing double! I knew I shouldn't have eaten those mushrooms!'

Then the real First Freshness stood to attention.

'Ahhh!' she screamed. 'I am seeing another version of me! I must be dead! Or dreaming!'

'But this is too much for me!' cried the St Bernard. 'My brains must be all scrambled and mashed. I can't cope with it – I'm off!'

And shouting these words, the St Bernard hurried out of the front door in a panicked wobble, before Hoo Hoo had a chance to hit him over the head with anything.

Feeling pity for the distressed daughter of King

Cone, Hoo Hoo quickly resumed her shape as a spaniel.

'It's all right,' she said to First Freshness, 'I'm helping you and your father be free of this fiend! I am here with a holy hound from the East. We are travelling west in search of meaning. I have special powers, as you have just seen. I'll soon knock some sense into your husband!'

Hoo Hoo took a moment to look pleased with herself.

'Okay...' said First Freshness, who was startled out of her wits. She didn't have time to respond. Hoo Hoo hot-footed out of the room, on the trail of Barry the St Bernard.

*

It took Hoo Hoo a while to find her quarry. She tracked the paw marks and found the wretched creature asleep in the hollow of a tree. He was so exhausted by his exertions that he could no longer keep his eyes open. Loud, guttural snoring came from the hollow. Inside, Hoo Hoo saw the fatigued face of Barry propped against the inside of the tree.

'I know,' said Hoo Hoo to herself, relishing the opportunity, 'I'll have some fun.'

A broad grin swept across her face. She lowered her nose to the ground, and in a few seconds, she had turned herself into a woodlouse. She scurried up the inside of the tree, over Barry's shoulder, and into his ear. Then she yelled:

'Oi! Barry, wake up!'

Barry stirred with such a spasm that he smashed his head on the inside of the tree. His legs skidded about in the mud and leaves inside the hollow, as he tried to bring himself to attention.

'All right, all right, calm down!' said Hoo Hoo. 'First of all, I just want to have a little talk. Then I'll decide whether I'm going to eat your brains out from the inside!'

'Wha... who are you? And *where* are you?' stammered Barry.

'Never mind about that now. Let's get down to business. Let me make it clear, I know who you are. You are no ordinary rascal roaming the country to terrorise and intimidate people into giving you food. You come from Long Dale Farm. I don't know how you ended up here, but I strongly suspect you were up to no good!'

'How can you know this?' said Barry. 'You must be some sort of magical spirit, particularly since I can't see you.'

'Don't fret over that now. I am no 'spirit'. I, too, have met the authorities at Long Dale Farm. I know its ways, and I know higher authorities who would make you pay dearly for what you have done to these poor dogs.'

'Who are you? Show yourself!' cried Barry.

'Yes, I think the time has come for me to reveal my-self.'

Hoo Hoo climbed out of Barry's ear. (Barry looked very puzzled.) As she jumped onto the leaves at the bottom of the hollow, she turned herself back into her true form.

'There!' she said with something like relief, shaking off the ear wax.

'You!' said Barry, recognising her at once.

'That's right. It's me. Hoo Hoo!'

'But you were expelled from Long Dale Farm. You got drunk and sprayed Balder and all the company of the ethereal world with horse manure!'

'Well,' said Hoo Hoo with a twinge of guilt, 'these days I'm on the straight and narrow. I have paid for my sins. I have taken a vow to help my master to travel west and bring back the Thumbald to his land.'

'What's the Thumbald?'

'Who knows! It seems to matter to him.'

'West? Did you say you are travelling west?'

'That's right.'

'But hang on, you don't smell of rosemary!'

'What?'

'I was thrown out of Long Dale Farm for eating chicken eggs that didn't belong to me! Avebalderheda – that black wastrel! – kicked me out and made me take a vow. She made me swear solemnly that I would help a pilgrim traveling to the West as he searched for a great and mysterious prize. But she said I would know this pilgrim because he would smell of rosemary. You don't smell of rosemary!'

Hoo Hoo snorted.

'I wouldn't put it past you to make anything up just to get your sticky paws on a sausage sandwich. Rest assured, I don't smell of rosemary, but my master does! Even so, if what you have told me is true, then you must swear before my master, and the dogs you have abused.'

'I will, I will,' cried Barry. 'You have no idea. It's true. I do like my food. But when you have eaten as much of it as I have, you realise that it doesn't bring you happiness. You have no idea how much I long to be free of my appetites. And Avebalderheda has promised me that if I accompany your master on his journey, on my return I will be free of them. Show me their faces, and I will swear whatever you want!'

Hoo Hoo and Barry returned to the barn buildings, where they found Cloud and King Cone deep in conversation about whether a nose could ever pass straight through a solid object, like a tractor.

'I think it is, at best, only theoretically possible,' Cloud was saying.

'Master, Master!' cried Hoo Hoo, as she entered the

barn building. 'Look who I have caught! You may find him a changed and repentant creature.'

'So, you are the humble pilgrim set to travel west,' said Barry. 'Please, I too want to call you 'Master', if you will let me. I vow to help you on your quest or die trying. I am overpowered by the smell of your rosemary!'

'Well, now steady on!' Cloud stammered sharply. 'And I don't want you to call me 'Master'. One of you is enough!'

The St Bernard and Hoo Hoo managed, in their garbled way, to explain everything to Cloud and King Cone. Everyone was pleased. Fat Barry apologised for the way he had behaved. King Cone was delighted all his food wasn't being eaten. Big Boy Cone was pleased that he didn't have to travel over the hills to Long Dale Farm. And even Cloud was pleased, if a little cautious, that he had one more companion to help him travel in search of the Thumbald.

That night they lit a fire at the edge of the pine forest and toasted each other's fortune.

'Perhaps,' said Big Barry, towards the end of the evening, 'perhaps, if and when I return from our journey west, and I rediscover my better nature, perhaps then – and only then, you understand – I could be reacquainted with my wife.'

Hoo Hoo pricked up her ears and growled at him.

'You fool!' she cried. 'Have you learned nothing? Pilgrims don't have wives. I can see we're going to have to watch you, and make sure you don't succumb to your old temptations. We will have to be vigilant and remind you of your vow. Let me see… I know! Until you have fulfilled your vow, we will all call you Porker. And only at the end of our journey will you be allowed to take a different name.'

But, despite these words, Barry (or Porker as he was now known) thought he saw First Freshness smiling at him for the first time he could remember.

Which made him wonder.

Mouse

Cloud was glad of his new company. He no longer felt quite so lonely, and the conversation helped keep their minds from tiredness.

Hoo Hoo and Porker came to see that Cloud was a very thoughtful dog. They would trouble him with difficult questions, myths or problems no one had ever managed to solve. Why, wondered Barry, would a hare always outrun a sheep when its legs are so much shorter?

Even so, Cloud sometimes wished for a bit more solitude. His two disciples had their annoying habits. Hoo Hoo couldn't sit still and was always darting off to disturb the peace. Porker was the opposite. He was always tired. And he was always hungry. At least three times every hour, he would ask how long it was before lunch or dinner. His stomach growled so loudly that it displaced rocks on the hillside.

'Careful!' Hoo Hoo would call out. 'You'll start a land-slide!'

After a full week of walking, they began an ascent towards a pass through the mountains. They spent the morning zigzagging up a switchback path until they reached a high plain, edged by a sheer cliff. The plain was empty except for a wide stream. On one side of the stream stood a small wood cabin. A tendril of wood-smoke trailed from its chimney.

Porker was out of breath. His stomach rumbled and the echo rattled around the hills.

'Can't you belly-belch quietly?' cried Hoo Hoo.

'Wait a minute,' said Cloud.

'What is it?' asked Hoo Hoo.

Cloud frowned.

'That's funny, I could have sworn I saw something.'

'What did you see, Master? I see a hut. Is that what you saw?'

'Well, I mean it wasn't some*thing* exactly. More some*one*. Another dog, in fact. A very small one. It was gambolling about near the hut. But... I mean this can't be right... it *looked* like it just disappeared before my eyes.'

The three companions strolled up to the wood cabin cautiously. They saw a sign nailed to the main entrance.

It read:

Roam and bored for fried animals only.

The three dogs looked at each other.

'I wonder who lives here?' said Cloud. He called out: 'Hello there! Is anyone at home?'

In reply there came something like a squeak. A small, squashed creature crawled out from a hidey-hole under the cabin. It had a slack jaw, loose ears, and the air of an impending bowel movement.

Its voice seemed to float away at an uncontrolled high pitch.

'Oooh, excuse me. I was just looking for my… er… for my… ears… for my earmuffs… I have lost them… and I didn't… er… I didn't hear you coming.'

The dog shuffled awkwardly.

'That's all right,' said Cloud. 'We wondered if you might have room for us in your cabin. We don't mind being bored but would prefer not to be fried.'

'Tee hee,' tittered the dog. 'Oh yes. The sign.'

He said nothing more.

'So, as I say, we are pilgrims and looking for somewhere to stay.'

'Tee hee,' said the sausage dog, 'tee hee. Well, yes. Please, come in.'

Cloud, Hoo Hoo and Barry searched each other in surprise, as they followed their host into the cabin.

'You're very thin,' said Barry. 'I hope you've got enough food to go around.'

The sausage dog ushered them inside. As Cloud came closer, he thought the dog sniffed at him.

'I'm Mouse,' said the sausage dog. 'I mean, that's my name.'

Mouse was a sorry-looking thing. He couldn't sit still, and his eyes moved all the time.

He was frightened by everyone and everything. He recoiled every time one of the company took a step closer to him. And he was, it seemed, most frightened of the thoughts in his own mind.

'Do any of you have fleas?' he asked.

This was his first question once they were all breathing the stale air of the cabin. Then, feeling guilty, he added:

'Not that it matters.'

For a time, Mouse shuffled about, showing them where they could settle down for the night.

'I might be able to find something to eat. I expect you're hungry.'

His voice quivered.

'I'd eat a plateful of antisocial spiders, I'm so hungry,' said Porker.

Mouse considered the statement.

'Oh dear,' he said, 'oh dear, oh dear.'

And he wandered off to rummage around his cupboard.

Their host managed to find something to eat. But it involved a lot of searching, and the results were an assembly of old vegetables, some stale bread, and warmed-up tomato soup. Porker, though not ungrateful, wasn't satisfied. And Mouse, when he spread everything out for them, would take none of it for himself.

'You're not eating?' asked Cloud.

'Are you fasting?' asked Hoo Hoo.

'Are you unwell?' asked Porker.

'No, no,' said Mouse, 'I'm just... I'm just not very hungry.'

The explanation sounded hollow. Cloud tried to probe further.

'You've eaten already?' he asked.

'Mmm... no I... well, yes... that is, earlier... yes, I ate earlier.'

'Earlier. I see. Well, if you change your mind...'

'Oh,' replied Mouse, a little dreamily, 'no.'

His voice trailed away.

The company ate in silence. Then Cloud asked another question.

'How did you come to live up here on the plain?'

Mouse's eyes drowned in panic. He hesitated.

'I came here a long time ago, because... because... because I like a quiet life.'

'A little lonely, isn't it?'

'Oh, I don't mind that.'

And for the first time he sounded sure of himself.

He trundled off to wash some dishes and make a pot of tea. The pilgrims shared questioning glances, but with a bit of dinner in their bellies, they were content enough.

Mouse returned with a pot of tea. He watched them from a nervous distance, even as his eyes and nose searched about Cloud.

'Reserved sort of creature, isn't he?' said Porker.

They settled into the plump baskets laid out for them in one corner of the hut.

'I suppose some dogs just like their own space,' said Cloud. 'Still, did you notice, he hasn't asked us anything about our journey? And have you seen how thin he is? He's a tiny scrap of a thing.'

'I'd say there's something fishy about him,' said Hoo Hoo. 'If you don't mind my saying so, Master, I think we shouldn't let this host of ours out of our sight!'

'Yerrs,' said Cloud steadily, 'perhaps you are right, Hoo Hoo.'

Between the three of them, they agreed that each

would take it in turns to keep one eye open throughout the night.

Mouse settled into his own bed in one corner of the cabin, concealed by the shadow of a candle. True to their plan, Cloud pretended to sleep in his basket, but secretly he kept his eyes half open. And yet he was so tired that his mind flickered in time with the candle on the far side of the room; and the two extinguished at around the same time.

*

Cloud didn't know how long he had been asleep. He was stirred by the sensation that something was moving about his neck. Groggily, he shuffled his body about in his box, but with a faint, dream-like feeling that another nose was sniffing and tugging at the locket. An interval of time must have passed before he realised that he was awake, and the necklace was no longer around his neck. He stood up.

'Hoo Hoo! Porker!' he yelled.

His slumbering, snoring companions woke into a commotion of noise. Cloud lit an oil lamp, so that he might shed light on the midnight mischief at work.

They were all astonished. The locket was suspended mid-air on the other side of the room. It hovered, almost completely still. Mouse was nowhere to be seen.

A second after Cloud had raised the light, they all

heard what sounded like two metal objects colliding, followed by a muffled cry of alarm. The locket fell from its unnatural levitation, and they heard Mouse call out in pain:

'Oh, my teeth!'

The voice came from inside the room. They could even hear the poor sausage dog, stumbling about, apparently in some pain.

Hoo Hoo was the quickest to work out what was happening. A growl was starting to grow inside her when the door of the cabin swung open. It was so dark outside that the black coat of the creature in the doorway melted into the night. All they could see was a pair of blue eyes, sparkling in the lamplight.

'You again!' cried Cloud.

More paws could be heard scuffling about on the floorboards. The door to the cabin closed just as suddenly.

'Stay where you are, Mouse!' said the black dog severely.

'What's going on?' asked Porker.

'It's obvious, isn't it?' said Hoo Hoo. 'Our 'host' has played a trick on us.'

'Enough of this nonsense!' said the black dog.

She inhaled deeply, and then exhaled through her nose.

Mouse appeared out of nowhere and collapsed on the floor. His mouth was closed tightly. His face showed that he was in pain.

'Cloud,' said the black dog sternly, 'collect the locket.'

Cloud did as he was told. He scurried across the floor, and flipped the necklace with his nose, so that it lassoed securely over his head.

'Now then,' the black dog continued, 'I expect all of you are wondering what's going on.'

The *all of you* made it clear that even Mouse had been deceived.

'Well, I know I am,' said Porker.

The black dog could see that all eyes were on her. She paused and then, a little theatrically, shook off some of the leaves and twigs hanging from her ragged coat.

'Well, well, well,' she said, striding between the four dogs, before her eyes settled on Cloud. 'So now, at last, you have all your travelling companions.'

Mouse stood to full attention. He hadn't been expecting this.

'You can see already,' the black dog went on, 'that Mouse knows what I mean, even if you don't.'

They all looked at Mouse.

'Oh, Mouse is harmless enough. You have seen how quiet and frail he is. He wouldn't harm a fly. Or if he would, you would never know it. For a time, Mouse lived on Long Dale Farm.'

Porker and Hoo Hoo were startled.

'Yes, you might well be surprised. As it happened, he left the farm to live here some years before either of you were there. Or I should say, he was expelled from the farm.'

'Expelled?' asked Cloud. 'Why?'

'For stealing.'

'Stealing!'

'It's not quite what it seems. Mouse is, as I said, innocent enough. In fact, he is more than innocent. He is conscientious and kind-hearted. He puts everyone before himself. But he is also frightened. Of some things, in particular. But of most things, in general. So, if you take his modesty, and his fear, you get a dog that, on the whole, prefers not to be seen. And he wants not to be seen very badly. In fact, after years of trying, he has a rare ability: he can make himself disappear.

'Don't be shocked. You have just seen him *reappear* before your eyes. Some of us might know how to change the way we appear. But to disappear entirely is something else.

'You see, Mouse came to discover that, by putting others first and living in fear of everything around him, he forfeited the very basic things of life. Most of all food. And he started to wither away. He never wanted to be seen taking food when others were asking for it, which meant that he could never eat. So, he soon learned that the only way he could eat was by taking it when no one was looking. He became Long Dale Farm's invisible night thief. Pies and parkin, bread and buttercream, carrots and custard, that cake baked lovingly the day before – all went missing overnight.

'Of course, he was found out. *I* found him out. And justice dictated that he should live in this remote place. For most of the time, he can fend for himself. But the pickings are slim. So, as you have seen, he lapses into bad habits. He filches whatever he can from passing strangers. I would guess that he caught the smell of rosemary inside the locket, and that he mistook it for something edible. Even though it should have told him to join you. What happened, Mouse – did you not recognise the smell?'

Mouse looked ashamed.

'I… yes… I… but I… I was hungry.'

He hung his head.

The black dog continued.

'That's why he'll be your third companion. He was placed in exile and told he could stay here until a dog from the East came to seek his help in his search for lost Knowledge. Together you will travel west, and we must hope that you return with the Thumbald.'

The black dog took a moment to think about the case of the wretched and reticent creature huddled up in the corner of the cabin.

'Mouse's case is curious, don't you think? By wanting to withdraw from everything, he misbehaved. And yet making yourself invisible – now there's a skill that even Hoo Hoo might envy! Is it a *good* thing, I wonder? Or not?'

Mouse's expression was difficult to make out. It was caught between anguish, and interest in what the black dog was saying.

'So, there it is,' she continued. 'One of you must find a place in the world of visible things. Another must temper their greed. Still another must use their tricks for more than self-flattery. And you, Cloud, must discover the proper place for all these things. *You* must find the Thumbald.'

A dream

Cloud was deep in a dream. He had returned to Easthill, except the farm was completely empty. There were no other dogs in sight. And he was making towards the farmhouse. The front door was open. The rooms were empty. But a breeze drifted through each room. In the kitchen, he saw the back door was open. The wind swept through it, making cups and saucers on the dresser rattle.

He knew that someone else was in the room. He even knew that the unseen presence was behind him on his left side. But he couldn't turn around.

'I'm in the company of an evil spirit. That much I can see,' he said out loud in his dream. 'I can only guess who you might be, and why you have approached me in my few precious hours of sleep. On my journey west, I usually sleep rough. No doubt, you have some evil aim in mind. That's all very well, but it's important for you to know…'

Cloud was interrupted by the *spirit.*

'You don't need to go on about it.'

'Oh,' said Cloud, 'what do you mean? I only meant to… I just thought you should be aware that I'm on…'

'Yes, yes, I know all about your journey. You're going on a quest to the West. You wouldn't be the first.'

'Oh right.'

Cloud was a little put out.

'In fact, that's why I thought I would stop by for a chat.'

'Are you on a journey, too?'

'Not quite. I was carried here. Or *wafted* here, you might say.'

'*Wafted?* Are you a bad smell?'

Cloud tried to sniff the air in his dream.

'Don't be so impertinent! We might be dreaming, but that's no excuse for bad manners. I'm not a spirit. But there is one about tonight. The Spirit who Wanders by the Light of the Moon brought me here to talk to you. And he's the only ride I can get back. So, let's cut the small talk and get down to business, shall we?'

'If you say so.'

The spirit was very assertive, Cloud thought.

'If I am assertive,' said the voice, 'then it is because

we have very little time. And we are already wasting it. I would also remind you that I'm not a spirit.'

'I never said anything!' protested Cloud.

'No, but you thought it. Don't forget that this is a dream. The same rules don't apply.'

Cloud tried hard not to think about anything else.

'Who are you if you aren't a spirit? And what do you want with me? Also, it might help if I could see you. What have you got to hide?'

'Nothing at all,' said the voice.

Cloud found suddenly that he could move. He turned around to confront the voice. It belonged to a large Wolfdog with a coat of sopping-wet white hair. He looked at Cloud sorrowfully. He was standing in the corner of the kitchen, dripping water on the stone-cold tiles.

'As you can see, I'm a dog, just like you. I suppose it's true that you are talking with my spirit right now, rather than my body. But my point is that I don't want you to think I am *only* a spirit. I have a body, even if it is wet and wasting away. That, you see, is why I have come to visit you.'

'Why? What has happened to you?'

The dog tried to shake off the water on his coat. He succeeded in spraying a lot of it about the kitchen. But when he had finished, he was just as wet as when he had started.

'It's fitting that we should meet here,' he continued, looking around. 'I come from a farm like this one. But it's smaller. Easier to maintain. There weren't – there *aren't* – many of us on the farm. Still, for my part, I ran everything. I was top dog, Head Hound. I inherited the title from my father. He ran the show before me. And ran it well. For a time, I ran it well, too. We had plenty to go around. The fields were irrigated. The geese were well behaved. Then it started to go downhill. We had several poor harvests. Everyone had to go on a diet. We had beans. But everyone got sick of them and started complaining. 'Oh not more beans!' they would say. 'I'm just so sick of beans!'

'So, what with that and the inevitable farting, things started to change. The other creatures stopped respecting the place. They wouldn't look out for each other. They became cynical. Some of them even threatened to leave.

'I was very worried. I wanted to turn the situation around. We held public meetings where everyone could voice their views. We tried sowing crops in new fields. We even made a special fertiliser from lamb's wool dipped in pig's urine, but none of it – *none of it* – worked.

'And, by then, the other dogs came to a shared understanding. Once we had known the Bald. But we had lost it. This was my fault, they said. I had somehow destroyed the harmony of the farmstead. I mean, it was all ridiculous.'

The Wolfdog sounded defensive.

'One day, they even brought before me a mangy old hound with a rotten brown coat. He had the nerve to ask me for help, and then told me I was losing my grip. I had him booted out. But his words were prophetic. Because soon after we received another visitor. He looked very enigmatic. He, too, was a Wolfdog and looked a lot like me. Except his coat was silver. He said he could help us. He said he knew a lot about land management. He said he could make the land fertile again.

'We all had our doubts, but it didn't take him long to convince us. We had more rain in several days than we had had in months. The crops began to grow, and that year we had a full harvest. In no time at all, it was obvious that the new dog was a boon. And I encouraged him to join the farmstead.

'I always had some doubts, mind you. Something was just not right about him. Still, I trusted him. And he betrayed me. He promised me that we could increase the yield of our crops by using water from the streams and pools high up in the hills. So, one day he led me to a cave, and guided me up the hillside, through narrow passageways and ominous gaps in the rocks, to a deep pit with a small waterfall trickling into its dark depths.

"Just look down there,' he said. He threw something into the pit, which burst into light as it hit the surface of the water. The light rippled around in the darkness. I was dazzled by the spectacle, and in my distracted state, he shimmied around behind me. With a short and malicious shove, he pushed me over the edge.

'That was how it played out. That was his real intention. He wanted to earn my trust, so that he could get close enough to destroy me and take my place. Because ever since he pushed me into the dark depths of the mountain, I have stayed here. It's a sad, slimy existence. For a long time, I have thought that I would end my days here. Were it not for the Spirit who Wanders by the Light of the Moon, I'm sure I would have already come to grief.'

'Now wait just a minute,' said Cloud, as he thought out loud. 'This doesn't make sense. You said that the imposter has replaced you as Head Hound. How can that be? The other dogs must see that he… well, that he is not you?'

Cloud felt reasonable and sensible.

'Yes, but I also said he is enigmatic. He finds favour with the forces of nature. I believe I also said that he is a Wolfdog and resembles me. Perhaps you should pay more attention?'

Cloud felt unreasonable and stupid.

'He turned out to have powers far beyond my reckoning. He managed to make himself look exactly like me. He took my title. He took my wife. He took my home and everything in it. He is a dupe. He is a deceiver in every way.'

Cloud tried to stay calm. But, privately, he was starting to wonder if it was possible to have a sensible conversation with a dream. Dreams were always quite likely to do something unusual.

'Okay,' he said with a sigh, 'let's say everything you have said is true. Let's just take it at face value: magical dog with an interest in land management, spirit of a dog trapped in a mountain, a spirit who wanders by the light of the moon – I mean, it's pretty off the wall. But let's just say it's all true. My question is simple: why, of all creatures, have you wafted into my sleep? Why have you made the matter of my dreams?'

'*Because* I am your dreams.'

'What do you mean?'

'Don't you see – I *was* somebody. I had a role, a place. I was real. Now I'm a shadow, known only in a passing moment. Your travelling companion knows all about this sort of thing. She has mastered the art of deception. She can see the difference between what is real and what is only a disguise.'

'Well, yes, I suppose she does have a knack for that sort of thing.'

'But don't you see, she's perfect! She will see straight through this imposter and help everyone else do the same. Then I can return to my rightful place.'

'And how do you expect us to go about this task? If the deceiver is as cunning as you say, will he not expect something of this sort?'

'He is certainly skilful and tricksy. But your companion is in a league of her own. And besides, I suggest you begin by trying to win favour not with him, but with his family. Or *my* family, I should say. Start with my son.'

'Your son – how should we do that?'

'That's easy. Each morning he takes a walk in the woods nearby. You can't miss him. He is the spitting image of me at a younger age! And every time he takes his walk, he does the same thing. It's quite uncanny. He climbs up into the hills. There, he always stops by the entrance to the cave where I'm imprisoned, and he drinks from the stream just by it. Some part of him, you see, knows that something is not right.'

Cloud – in his dream – thought about what the Head Hound had told him.

'Okay,' he reflected, 'let's suppose what you say is

true. And let's suppose that we are prepared to do as you ask. If the imposter is as convincing as you claim, why should your son believe the things we tell him? Look at it from his point of view. Suppose a complete stranger were to approach you. They tell you your father is not your father because the spirit of your real father appeared in a dream and revealed the truth that he is actually barely surviving at the bottom of a mountain pool – supposing that, do you think he would believe me? Some things you might take on trust. But that's stretching it a bit, isn't it?'

'Yes, yes, I see the point you are making,' said the Wolfdog, irritated. 'I have thought of that! I have something for you.'

The Wolfdog rolled his tongue over something in his mouth. He spat it out on the floor.

It was a large tooth.

'When my son was a young pup, I would frighten him with a story. I have always had this false tooth. But I told him I lost the original by speaking out of turn, so a pixie cursed my mouth. And I would warn him to mind his manners or he might end up with no teeth at all. In truth, I think he just enjoyed it when I pulled my tooth out! But this is the one thing the imposter has not managed to imitate. Because he doesn't know about it. If you show him this tooth, it will put him in mind of me, and win you his attention.'

Cloud grimaced a little at the tooth.

'Right,' he said.

'So that's agreed then, is it?'

'Well, I...' began Cloud.

'... Oh wait a minute. Here comes the Spirit Who Wanders by the Light of the Moon. I must catch my ride. Please, take my tooth! Help me! Call your friends to my aid!'

The Wolfdog disappeared.

'Hoo Hoo!' called out Cloud.

'What is it, Master?' came another voice, stealing entry to the dream.

Cloud blinked.

'Hoo Hoo!' he heard himself say.

'Yes, what is it, Master?'

Tarnished morning light crept into the small retreat where the travellers had taken rest for the night. It silhouetted Hoo Hoo. The room was blurred.

'Hoo Hoo, is that you?' asked Cloud.

'You were dreaming, Master. I could tell from the rhythm of your breathing, and your twitches. When you called my name, I called back. You are awake now. It was only a dream.'

'Only a dream! Oh, but it was more than that, Hoo Hoo. It was more than that! A visitor came to me in my sleep with a message – he brought me a request.'

'A req… now, listen, Master, I daresay you are tired, and your head is even more full of weird things than usual. But you must learn to keep your paws on the ground.'

Porker cut in.

'Dreams are nothing more than undigested mushy peas… or is it cheese?'

Hoo Hoo continued to reason with her 'master'.

'You are always daydreaming about things, Master. And I expect that whatever fever of the imagination you experienced was nothing more than a simple wish. You can explain all dreams like that. Rest assured, you can.'

'No, no, you are quite wrong, Hoo Hoo,' Cloud retorted. 'Dreams are wayward and unpredictable, but they can have meaning. They are ways of speaking between the cracks of ordinary speech. They are soft and subtle. I'm quite sure that this dream was real. It was a dream, but it was real. Or it was real, but a dream.'

'I find that mushy peas just give me wind,' said Mouse.

'What happened in your dream, if it was so real?' asked Hoo Hoo.

Cloud told them how the Wolfdog had been wafted to him by the Spirit Who Wanders by the Light of the Moon.

'I am especially concerned,' Cloud continued, 'because where I come from, we live in fear of a new power which has been spreading faster, wider, and further than any of us would like to imagine. A spirit called Animo has been building an empire – or so we are told – and he does this by stealing the body and identity of other creatures. If I am right, the case of this Wolfdog sound just like the work of Animo! The search for the Thumbald is the search for the truth, and I will never find it, if I can't see beyond this dream to all the things that are real. I feel that I must uncover the truth in this case and find out what's *really* going on here!'

'Say no more!' cried Hoo Hoo, when he had finished. 'I can see that I'm being called to a feat of heroic action, which requires my special powers. I see the chance to prove myself!'

'I don't know,' said Porker, more doubtfully, 'it still looks like mushy cheese to me. I know I wouldn't chance my coat for a spirit wafted by the light of the moon.'

'Yes, I… ahem… I agree,' said Mouse, chirping up, 'it sounds as if there could be a lot of risk involved. And I don't see the… I mean, why would you… we do it? Besides, what makes you so sure the dog in your dream was real?'

Cloud remembered the tooth.

'But of course!' he cried. 'The dog left me something. He left me a tooth.'

'A tooth?'

'That's right, a tooth.'

Mouse wasn't impressed.

'A little careless, isn't it – leaving your teeth lying around in a dream?'

'Who says it was *his* tooth,' said Porker sharply. 'He might have stolen it. He might be a dentist.'

'Wouldn't that be difficult if he's stuck at the bottom of a mountain?'

'Well, these days dentists have flexible working patterns.'

'Now where can it be?' mumbled Cloud, searching for the gnasher.

The retreat was a draughty stone shelter with a wooden door, nestled at the edge of a wood in the mountains. Cloud cast about its small interior, expecting to find the missing tooth somewhere on the floor.

'Dentists don't generally spend their nights haunting people,' said Mouse, 'in my experience.'

'Ah hah!' exclaimed Cloud.

On the doorstep lay a dirty, white pre-molar. As far as they were all able to tell, it could have easily come from a large Wolfdog.

'That proves it, then,' said Hoo Hoo. 'It goes to show

that everything my master saw and heard in his mysterious dream was true. And that means I must help to defeat this no-good imposter – we need a plan!'

'You're right. Let's get thinking.'

Cloud and Hoo Hoo looked as if they were thinking very hard. Mouse and Porker looked as if they had woken to find a dream had delivered a Wolfdog's tooth to their doorstep.

'I've got it!' said Hoo Hoo, with a skip of her back leg. 'We need to lure this young pup away from the imposter Head Hound. Here's what we should do – we'll seek out the farmstead and when the young master goes out for a stroll beyond the farmlands, I'll turn myself into a coconut tree and drop a coconut on his head. Then we'll slap him about the face a bit, and you can show him the tooth. How does that sound? Pretty good, huh! Do you know, sometimes I think I might be a genius!'

'Ahem,' said Cloud, 'I like the general idea. But perhaps we could fine-tune the details.'

'Oh details, details,' said Hoo Hoo, 'I'll leave those up to you. Just let me throw those coconuts!'

*

It was agreed, as they marched towards the farm, that Hoo Hoo would square up to the son of the duped Wolfdog. She would bring him before Cloud, who would overpower him with persuasion.

The company followed a path down the hillside, into a high valley cupped closely by the curvature of the terrain. The farm stood on its own, with a couple of outbuildings, overlooking a short drop to a stream, which slipped politely around the rocks, roots and point bars of the land. At the edge of the wood, they had a clear view of the smallholding, and were surprised to find so many creatures hanging about it. A small army of dogs stampeded, trotted and bounded over the open ground. They had the care and custom of dogs about to go on an outing.

Cloud called his brain to attention.

'Master, Master,' said Hoo Hoo, 'look at all these long-eared, drooling dimwits. I think I need to turn into a forest of coconut trees, so I can bombard them into the ground. Oh, please, please, let me turn into a forest of coconut trees!'

'Now listen,' said Cloud very seriously, 'we are only interested in the Wolfdog's son. We need a plan to single him out. I suggest that we follow the party at a distance, try to pick out the son, and look for some way to get his attention.'

'Perhaps I could turn into a giant mongoose – I bet that would get his attention!'

'It might get *everyone's* attention.'

'Okay. Yes, I see your point.'

'I'll tell you what, on our journey here, I noticed a birdwatchers' hut at the end of the path set off from the woodland trail. Why don't we try to lure the young son to that location? If we manage it, Porker and Mouse can lock the door behind him. Then we will have him at our disposal.'

'Good idea, Master,' called out Hoo Hoo. 'There's clearly more to you than a peculiar smell of rosemary and a lot of cryptic poetry. And your flash of inspiration has stirred the ingenuity in old Hoo Hoo's brain!'

Cloud didn't like to ask.

They agreed the rendezvous with Porker and Mouse, then started tracking the hunting party. It didn't take them long before they thought they could see a young-looking Wolfdog surrounded by a retinue of retrievers. Cloud and Hoo Hoo couldn't believe their luck when the young dog sallied up to the foot of a forested slope to relieve himself.

'I've got it!' said Hoo Hoo and made a dash for the trees.

'Got what?' asked Cloud.

'No time to explain,' she said, disappearing into the woodland, 'but I'll meet you with our prize at the birdwatchers' hut. Just see if I don't!'

Meanwhile, the young Wolfdog had happily watered the roots of an old elm. He sniffed around a toadstool. Then he heard a rustle. Followed by a bark. But it was not the bark of a dog. Eyes met him out of the wood. They were cunning. They were criminal.

The fox jumped out straight in front of him. The creature was not the tawny colour of tradition. It was completely white.

'Oi, wolf!' said the fox. 'What's the matter? Is it arthritis of the brain?'

The fox watched the blood rise behind the Wolfdog's eyes, before the fox hightailed it into the rough terrain of the upland wood. The Wolfdog snarled and set out in hot pursuit of the fox. He could see it darting about between the trees, no more than a few metres ahead. He was sure that if he really tried, he would catch it, or at the very least, trim the spruce from its tail. But even as he strained every muscle to half the distance to the fox, somehow his quarry managed to keep an even lead. In fact, the Wolfdog strained so hard that he tripped on the root of a tree and tumbled forward. That was it, he thought. If the fox continued at the same pace, he would never catch it.

But when he picked up the pieces of himself, he saw that the fox stood before him at the same short distance. And it stared. He couldn't figure it out. Was the fox waiting to see if he would continue the chase? Was it trying to say something? The Wolfdog began to sense some sort of trap.

'Feeling tired, are we?' asked the fox.

The Wolfdog growled and took up the chase once more. Between them, they kept up the pursuit for several minutes more. The Wolfdog became more frustrated. No matter what he did, and no matter how far his anger released extra reserves of energy, he could not gain ground on his opponent.

A wooden hut with shutters for windows came into view. The fox made for its entrance. The Wolfdog was confused. Why would it retreat to a hut? Once again, the thought that this might be a trap made him stop. The fox, too, stopped just outside the door of the hut. It turned on its tail and sought the eyes of its pursuer. This look meant something, thought the Wolfdog, but he couldn't work out what.

The fox slipped quietly into the birdwatcher's hut.

The Wolfdog stopped to think about his options. Was there something unnatural at work? He had, after all, never heard of a white fox before. Still, he knew these lands and, as heir to their governor, he saw no reason why he should be intimidated by a simple birdwatchers' hut, home to a scavenger.

The hut was dark inside. Only one of the shutters had been opened. A dim shard of light cut across the floorboards. The Wolfdog couldn't see the fox anywhere. But sitting on its hind legs, he could just make out the shape of another dog. At least, he thought it was a dog. He could see the tip of its snout. The dog spoke:

Misfortune plucked my ire
It led me to a wayward cloud
Where we talked free-floating nonsense
And I found respite from the world.

'Who are you?' asked the Wolfdog. 'What happened to the white fox I saw run in here?'

Faint laughter came from voices somewhere in the room. Then one of the voices urged the others to 'Shhh!'

The Wolfdog cast about in circles, but he could see no one else.

'Who's there?!' he demanded. 'Show yourself!'

'A *white* fox?' asked the dog in the corner. 'What makes you think you saw a white one? They must be very rare, if they exist at all.'

'I saw one, I tell you. I saw it come in here. It taunted me!'

The same titter came from somewhere.

'Well, I know about something I have never seen, and yet it exists. Perhaps you have seen something, and yet it doesn't,' said the dog in the corner.

'What kind of nonsense is that?'

'The kind they talk in the clouds.'

'Well, we aren't in the clouds, so please don't talk nonsense when I ask you a sensible question. And why don't you step forward, so we can speak plainly and face to face?'

'We can't speak face to face in the darkness,' said Cloud.

'Now listen to me, you gibberish-talking nose-in-the-dark, I'm a very powerful and influential creature in these parts. I can swat my tail where I like. And I detect fiendish fox-logic at work. It's all very… *foxy*.'

Cloud responded in verse:

Today I sit in darkness
My head about the sky
But you think you see a father
When, in fact, you see a lie.

'You are nothing but a babbling buffoon. You talk so little sense it makes me think your brains are made of black pudding and bilge. What on earth are you trying to tell me?'

Quick as a flash, Cloud replied.

'Perhaps we need a little light – then you might see some teeth sparkle!'

'What?! Teeth – what can you mean?'

'No?' said Cloud. 'You don't know what I mean? Then it's easy enough to set you straight. Why don't you meet my friend?'

Cloud gave a short, sharp bark.

An object landed on the floor. It landed in the path of daylight, which beamed through the window. The Wolfdog looked at it. He couldn't quite work it out. Then it started to look familiar.

'What's that?' he asked. 'Is it a…?'

'I'm a pair of false teeth,' said Hoo Hoo, who had turned into a pair of false teeth.

The Wolfdog looked stunned. Then angry. Then stunned again.

'Teeth,' he stammered, '*your* teeth?'

'They're not really *my* teeth,' said the false teeth, 'because I'm just a pair of teeth. I don't belong to anyone. And I'm false.'

'False teeth.'

'You can learn a lot from a pair of teeth.'

'Why are you talking to me, teeth?' asked the Wolf-dog in a disbelieving sort of way.

'Because you need to learn the difference between true and false. We might as well begin with something simple. Like teeth.'

The Wolfdog looked thoughtfully at the talking

teeth.

'Are you some sort of sign? Are you a magical creature talking to me in symbols?'

'Why would I do that?' asked the false teeth. 'If I want to talk to you, I just use my tongue.'

The false teeth appeared to grow a tongue from nowhere, then waggled it about between its incisors.

The Wolfdog turned all huffy.

'You are a rude and offensive pair of teeth! And you talk tongue-tangling tosh, which even a halfwit would think was half-witted. Do you not know that I'm heir to the land all about you? I'm really important!'

'Now don't get all hoity-toity,' said the pair of false teeth, 'or I might get annoyed and nibble at your nose. Believe it or not, I'm trying – we are trying – to help you!

'Answer me a few questions. Not so long ago your father had some trouble managing his land, didn't he? You had a poor harvest, and everyone complained because they had to eat beans, which made them fart a lot – isn't that right?'

'Yerrs,' said the Wolfdog.

The false teeth were certainly well informed.

'But then your father embraced a stray dog – one of your own breed – who performed magic tricks to fertilise the land. Again, am I right?'

'You are. Go on.'

The Wolfdog was becoming more curious.

'What you don't know is that the performer of apparent miracles deceived your father. He led him to a remote place, and pushed him into a dark, wet cavern, where he remains to this day. Then this scheming and serpentine creature stole your father's identity and took his place as Head Hound. The dog you call your father is as false as the teeth talking to you right now!'

The Wolfdog weighed everything up. Then he started to laugh.

'Ah ha ha ha!' he roared. 'You expect me to believe all that cobblers? You are priceless. What a hoot!'

'And why do you find this such an unlikely notion?'

'Why? I'll tell you exactly why, teeth. I have known my father for as long as I can remember. Since I was a young pup. I think I would recognise him, if he put on a wig and started strutting about, like a bogus Head Hound. I know my own father – I think I would notice! But even more ridiculous is that you expect to believe this based on the testimony of talking teeth! They would push *me* down a dark, wet cavern if I came out with that sort of tripe!'

'I see,' said the talking teeth.

'Yes, and to tell you the truth, I can't see why I shouldn't have you thrown down a cavern for trying to hoodwink me.'

'Do you believe your dreams?' asked the talking teeth.

The Wolfdog had to halt his thoughts.

'My... what do you mean?'

'If you were to receive a message in your dreams, would you believe it?'

'In a dream? Dreams are nothing but poorly re-membered impressions bent by the mind at rest. Why would I believe anything in a dream? Only a fool would do that!'

'You should mind your manners,' said the talking teeth. 'Don't you remember the pixie who cursed your father's mouth?'

The talking teeth vanished into thin air. The same tooth which had come to Cloud in the dream lay in their place.

The young Wolfdog stood staring at the tooth.

Cloud spoke out from the corner of the room.

'Go ahead,' he said, 'take a closer look. Examine it.'

The Wolfdog sniffed at the tooth, pawed it, then grasped it between his own front teeth.

'Do you recognise it?'

The Wolfdog searched across the room. His eyes were wild.

'But how could you...?'

'Your true father brought me that tooth. So that together we might avenge him. He brought it to me in a dream.'

'In a dream,' muttered the Wolfdog.

But his words were a thoughtless echo.

Then came anger.

'But how do I know you haven't... what have you done to him?'

'Calm down, calm down. I see your thought. There is one way to test the truth of my story. I will even come with you. We will come with you.'

Hoo Hoo stepped out of the darkness to meet the gaze of the Wolfdog.

'That way, if we are lying, you can mete out justice in your own way.'

The Wolfdog turned his eyes back to the tooth.

'Yes,' he said, 'let's see.'

*

'Mother,' said the young Wolfdog.

He entered the small walled garden set to one side of a dilapidated grand house, which formed the centre of the small farmstead.

'Son,' said the Wolfdog's mother. She turned on her hind legs. 'Though I might as well call you 'stranger'. I see you so rarely. Why have you come to see me? And yet the strange things I have just seen might mean that your visit is no coincidence. And who are these other dogs you have bought with you? They're a motley bunch.'

Just as the father Wolfdog had described in Cloud's dream, the farmstead was obviously flourishing. The grass was lush. The flower beds were neatly spruced and burgeoning. Beyond the walled garden, crops grew in areas measured to meet the ambition of a future harvest. Everything was well organised.

Even so, Cloud thought there was something *artificial* about it all. It was like a thin dusting of magic gave the impression of order. He imagined that if he were to only uproot a foxglove, then the whole polished performance would fall apart. Somehow, it was all unnatural.

'They are, indeed, a motley bunch. Don't I know it! They have come to practise a form of wizardry which will help us.'

'Oh son, what wastrels have you befriended? Why do you talk of wizards? I bet they're just tramps who haven't eaten for days and are appealing to your better nature.'

'Normally, I would have said the same thing, Mother. But they have impressed me. Perhaps it's all just a trick. But I will find out. I need your help.'

Hoo Hoo piped up. She sounded just a little indignant.

'Now listen to me, you spoilt ruler of well-tended cabbages, I resent some of your remarks. I'm Hoo Hoo, High Lady of the Mountain-Tarn Cave for the Deliverance of Lost Creatures. I'm no ruffian vagrant. And I like to think I take good care of my appearance. I have even heard it said that I am dazzling and resplendent!'

Hoo Hoo brimmed with steady self-satisfaction.

'My companions might look like scruffy no-hopers who have been combed by the rough edges of a hedge. But I'm different. And I thank you to note that I don't practise cheap tricks. I'm as ponderous and proud as they come!'

'So I can tell,' said the Wolfdog.

Hoo Hoo was still a bit huffy, but she made way for the conversation between mother and son.

'Mother, I was about to ask you a question. But I heard you say just now that you have seen some strange things. What did you mean?'

The son was visibly concerned for his parent.

'And now that I take a closer look at you, I can see that you have been crying. What's the matter?'

'Oh child,' said the mother Wolfdog, 'it was nothing more than a dream. And only one half of which I can remember. It upset me, as you can see. And I have been straining my mind to remember it. But, please, I would rather not talk about it now. Let's turn, instead, to your question. What did you want to ask me?'

The son took a breath.

'Do not be any more upset than you are already, Mother. My question is: who is the Head Hound of this farmstead?'

'Heavens, child!' cried his mother. 'Your mind must have gone mushy in the company of these delinquents! Who else but your father?'

'And how have you found my father lately? Have you noticed any change? Speak truthfully, Mother!'

The poor creature was clearly conflicted, but she couldn't bear to conceal the truth.

'I think it's strange that you should ask these questions. And it makes me think that there must be more to all this than meets the eye. But, for the life of me, I can't see how it all hangs together. How have I found your father, lately? Ordinarily, I wouldn't say this, but the warmth that was in him has disappeared. He plots and plans the business of the farm all day. He is good at it, I admit. But all he does is make cold calculations. It chills me to say it, but I don't know him any longer. He is a stranger to me.'

The son nuzzled his mother gently, to offer her some comfort.

'Please, Mother, don't be upset. If what I have to say is true, then your feelings do you credit.'

'What can you mean?' asked his mother.

'Today I was out hunting when a white fox approached me from nowhere. It taunted me, and was
very disrespectful, in the way that foxes are. I chased after it. It led me to this odd-looking company of travelling dogs. They told me a story. At first, I thought it was
nonsense. Or unlikely. But then they showed me something which made me think twice. The story they told
me was about my father – your husband.

'This shabby-looking Border Collie,' said the young
Wolfdog, referring to Cloud, 'claimed that my father
came to him in a dream. And in the dream his coat was
all wet.'

The Wolfdog's mother gasped.

'And in this dreary state, he said that he had been betrayed by the magician who came to fertilise our soil.
He said that the magician tricked him, led him into a
cavern, pushed him to a deep pool, where he remains.

'Now, I expect you will tell me, Mother, that this
sounds far-fetched. And you would be right. I rebutted
their story in the same way. Until they showed me
something.'

The young dog produced the tooth which Cloud had
received in his dream.

'As you can see, it is a false tooth we both know well.
It's my belief that we must confront your husband with

this tooth to find out if he really is your husband. First, we must… but, Mother, why do you look so stunned and silenced? You look like you have seen a ghost!'

True enough, his mother's eyes switched on circuits of fear.

'Let's hope, my son, that it was not a ghost. Not yet, at least. Before you arrived with your new friends, I, too, was passing the late afternoon with a nap, when I was met by a dream. And my dream was the same as you describe, but less vivid, somehow. I saw the likeness of your father, dripping with water. And I heard how he had been deceived. But I can't remember the rest of the dream. I was trying to recall it from my memory when you arrived.'

'But Mother,' cried the young Wolfdog, 'don't you see that this appears to confirm what I've been told, and what's borne out in the hard matter of this tooth?'

His mother managed her son with a look.

'Yes, I agree that we must distinguish true from false, one way or another.'

*

The young Wolfdog, Hoo Hoo and Cloud all retreated to the birdwatchers' hut. There they found Mouse shifting about quietly, and Porker snoring in the middle of the room.

'Who's this large one?' asked the young Wolfdog.

'He's a greedy guzzler. But he may be useful,' said Hoo Hoo.

'How?'

'Never mind that now,' said Cloud. 'We need to cook up a plan of action.'

The group plotted a plan. First, they would rescue and resuscitate the drowned hound in the mountains. Then the young Wolfdog would confront the imposter with the tooth. This, they expected, would cause a chaotic kerfuffle, at which point Hoo Hoo and Cloud would deliver the true Head Hound to the farmstead, and oust the imposter with a crowd-pleasing wave of righteous indignation.

'I like the sound of that!' said Hoo Hoo.

The young Wolfdog went back to the farmstead. He was told not to confront his false father until he had received word that his true father had been rescued.

'Well, that's a patch of pickles you've got us into, Master,' said Hoo Hoo.

'Why do you say that?'

'How are we supposed to rescue this cavern-entombed Head Hound? I mean, I know I'm good, but this is a challenge, even for Hoo Hoo!'

'There are ways. And means,' said Cloud dreamily. 'It reminds me of a verse…'

'Now don't go all woolly-minded on me!' upbraided Hoo Hoo. 'We have a tough task ahead of us. What shall we *do*?'

Cloud was called to attention.

'Yes,' he said, 'I'm sure you're right. But, really, Hoo Hoo, I would have thought that with all your skills you would be able to sort this one out yourself.'

'Oh don't doubt my skills,' said Hoo Hoo, bristling a little. 'Sometimes they just need a little push in the right direction, that's all.'

'I see,' said Cloud smiling, 'well, how about this for a 'push'? This Head Hound we need to rescue is hidden away in a difficult and dangerous place that is hard to access. We need someone who is good at imposing themselves, even where they aren't wanted.'

Clouds eyes turned to the heaving stomach on the floor before them, and the rasping snores which grunted and gurgled from its mouth.

'Who did you have in mind, Master?' asked Hoo Hoo excitedly.

'Our porky friend has plenty of experience throwing his weight about where it isn't wanted. I would say he's ideal for the task.'

'Him!' exclaimed Hoo Hoo. 'He won't even move unless you dangle a doughnut in front of his nose! Really, Master, if that's the best your elevated brain can come up with, then we are in a tight spot.'

'Now don't be hasty,' said Cloud. 'I agree that it's not in his nature to risk his neck for others. But we must show him the way. And what if we were to cook up our own – harmless – porky pie. The truth of the matter is that only Porker has the strength to heave the body of the Head Hound from its watery resting place. So why don't we tell him that he is going on a mission to find a treasure trove of chocolate eclairs, rather than a damp Wolfdog. Would that not stir him into action?'

'Ahh!' said Hoo Hoo. 'I see your cloud-covered mind, now. Yes that might just work.'

Cloud bowed his head modestly, but secretly felt very pleased with himself.

'Okay then, let's get to work!'

Hoo Hoo trotted around the snoring bulk of Porker.

'Oi! You foolish fumbler – wake up!'

Porker had a weak brain and a very full belly. He didn't stir.

Hoo Hoo jumped onto his stomach and bit him on the nose. The St Bernard scrambled, tumbled and circled about, until the two dogs stood face to face in the centre of the birdwatchers' hut.

'It's time to get up. We have work to do.'

'What work? Isn't it the middle of the night? I was asleep!'

'One doesn't have to follow from the other. You are

always asleep when you aren't eating! In any case, didn't you hear what that young Wolfdog had to say?'

'No, I was asleep!'

'He let us into a little secret. The Head Hound of this nearby farm has a secret stash of chocolate eclairs!'

'Chocolate eclairs!' Porker blurted out, suddenly standing to full attention.

'Yes, I thought that might interest you. Come along – why don't we check them out? He keeps them at the bottom of a pit in a cave up in the hills.'

'Show me the way!' said Porker. Then he thought about it. 'Isn't that a bit of a strange place to keep chocolate eclairs? Also, I suppose you'll want a share of them if we do this together,' he continued, his brain keeping pace with his stomach.

'Ah well. I'm all about fame and celebrity rather than eating. Think of this as a favour to you. And this Head Hound doesn't trust those around him not to pilfer from his foodie fund so he has to keep them well concealed. He knows that the creatures about him have been underfed for years. The rogue!'

Porker was persuaded. His stomach growled with excitement.

They set off together.

Hoo Hoo led the way out of the forest and towards the escarpment cut into a sudden rise of hills.

'This looks like a likely place for a cave!' she said.

They spent some time hunting about. All the while Porker complained that he was tired, and that he hoped the chocolate eclairs were worth it.

'That loafer is all stodge and no stamina,' Hoo Hoo muttered under her breath.

Finally, they came across the entrance to a large cave, inset from a natural rise in the land above the path. Water dripped from the ceiling, and pools had formed across the uneven floor.

'Well, this is a damp and cheerless place,' said Porker.

'It's a good place to hide treasure, then!' returned Hoo Hoo.

As they peered into the dark interior, they could see a wide crack in the back wall, just wide enough for them to enter.

'That's it!' gasped Hoo Hoo, and she trotted forward.

One behind the other, the two followed the wandering course of a passageway as it threaded through the hillside, widening, narrowing and bending, much like a river.

'We will never find our way back!' complained Porker. 'And I can hardly see. And I'm starving.'

The passageway was dark but not pitch black. A dim, rusted light seemed to filter into the tunnel from somewhere, though neither of them could work out from where. Hoo Hoo imagined that there was a blazing light somewhere at the centre of the mountain, which broke into a thousand different crevices, holes and passages, becoming dimmer and dimmer as it diffracted.

Then they came to a cavern. At once they saw the pit, and a waterfall coursing into its depths. The same splinters of light sparkled all around the chamber.

'It's down there,' said Hoo Hoo.

'Down there!' cried Porker. 'You can't be serious! We can't go down there. I can't even see the bottom!'

Hoo Hoo had expected this response.

'*We* are not going down there. *You* are.'

'I am?'

'Yes. Come, I will help you.'

'I'm not jumping down there. It's quite likely I'll just go splat at the bottom.'

'Then we'll make sure you don't.'

Hoo Hoo had backed up to the edge of the cavern before she said these words. Then she ran at full speed towards the pit and jumped straight into its darkness. The explosion of light flashed in the darkness, and a rope ladder rose up from the descent.

'Hurry,' said the rope ladder, 'climb down. Do you think this sort of trick is easy?'

Porker rescued his mind from its stunned state.

'Are you sure about this?' he asked.

'Just get on with it!'

'Well, don't drop me!'

'As if I would,' said the rope ladder.

The ladder swayed about and groaned.

'Oh Balder! How much do you weigh, Porker?'

'My stomach is expansive,' was all Porker could manage.

The pit went down deeper than either of them had imagined. But, after several minutes, Porker could just hear the waterfall gushing into a pool. This spurred him on, and after a further five minutes of exhausting work, he could see the pool, and the light, beaded and broken by the splashing and rippling of water.

'I can see the pool now!' cried out Porker. 'I'm just above it.'

'Thank goodness for that!' said the rope ladder.

The ladder, with a sort of tangible relief, vanished into thin air, leaving Porker with nothing to hold onto. He only realised what was going on a moment before he hit the water. He panicked. Then he smacked into the water, like a rough-cut slab of stone.

'You hideous nose of a dog!' he cried out, just before his head was submerged.

Hoo Hoo was peering down towards the pool from the cavern. She gave a neat little laugh.

Before long, Porker bobbed like a barrel to the surface.

'Chocolate eclairs!' he called out in the darkness. 'What sort of wet-headed charlatan would hide chocolate eclairs down here?! This is just one of your floppy-eared practical jokes. I know you well enough by now. No amount of do-gooding will reform your bad nature.'

'Stay calm,' said Hoo Hoo, chuckling a little. 'The eclairs are under the water. You must dive down and have a look around. See what you can find.'

'Under the water! Who ever heard of keeping chocolate eclairs underwater?!'

'It keeps them well preserved,' replied Hoo Hoo trying to sound convincing, then added, 'improves the flavour, too.'

Porker took a deep breath.

*

Meanwhile, a baby eel was slithering about. Since he had been born, he had learned how to take a turn around the pool. He did this two or three times a day, just to keep watch and see if anything unusual happened. But it never did. Sometimes a fish swam by. Sometimes a stone or rock fell into the water. More rarely still, he would hear two or three sheep meeting in secret to talk about going to the toilet. Generally, it was pretty quiet.

The only exciting event in the life of the baby eel had

been the time a large Wolfdog fell into the pool. This event had become so momentous that the creature was now preserved in a secret underwater chamber. Eels even came together at open meetings to discuss the meaning and significance of the falling Wolfdog. Some thought he was the original creator of the pool. Others thought he was the son of the creator of the pool. Some others claimed that he had been, at one time, an eel, but had managed to slither out onto open land, where contact with the strange and benighted world above transformed him into a grotesque dog-like form. Since then he had been trying to find his way back to the pool.

The theories kept coming. *Wolfdog lore* had become a serious and compelling field of study. Only a minority thought that he was a dog who had got lost and fallen in the pool. That just seemed a bit boring.

So, it is difficult to convey just how electrifying it was for the baby eel to witness another dog fall in the pool, and then start heaving about under the water with its clumsy paws. The baby eel couldn't contain his excitement. He slithered off to tell his father.

'Father, Father,' he shouted in a blurring sprint of words, 'I-have-just-seen-a-dog-fall-in-the-pool-and-he-is-swimming-this-way-but-he-looks-lost-and-swims-like-an-enormous-elephant-with-stubby-little-legs-what-should-we-do-Father?-what-should-we-do?'

'Now be calm, my son,' said the father eel. 'Good governance values a clear head above an excitable manner. Am I to understand from what you have told me that a dog has fallen into our pool?'

'Yes. A very big one.'

'Now, there's a thing. There's a thing. I will say that this is an interesting, if not unforeseeable, development. Where one dog falls in your pool it is probable, if not certain, that another will follow. I think we can expect to find a connection between this hefty one and our prize Wolfdog. Let's go out to meet him.'

Porker was still flailing about under the water, trying to find his way around. But he was dazzled by the strange beam of light, pearling from different places and casting shapes and shadows all about him. Then he saw two strange snake-like creatures glide towards him. They moved quickly and came too close for comfort. One of them was a lot bigger than the other and looked very stern.

'Who are you?' asked Porker.

'We might ask you the same question.'

'Never mind about that. Just tell me where the chocolate eclairs are, and I'll be off!'

'The what?'

'The eclairs. You know, the treasure.'

'What treasure?'

The baby eel whispered something in his father's ear.

'Perhaps he means the other dog, Father.'

'Oh, I see. The *eclairs*. Yes. Well, come with me and I'll show you. Perhaps you can help us. There are many here who would be interested to know more about it.'

'Really?' said Porker.

'Have you come far?' asked the father eel.

'I was leading a wicked life in the hills. I had married the daughter of a dog with a cone-shaped head and eaten all his food, when a couple of do-gooding pilgrims came along. They couldn't mind their own business, so they forced me to renounce sausages and a life of crime. Instead, they have made me travel west with them in search of the Thumbald. This is just a detour, really.'

'Ah,' said the father eel, as if he understood.

'What are you, then?' asked Porker, but he sounded a bit disdainful and impatient. 'I expect you're some sort of earthworm who has lost their way.'

'We are eels.'

'Oh, I see,' said Porker, even though he didn't.

The eels led Porker into a chamber down at the bottom of the pool. At the back of it laid out on a slab of stone was the body of the Wolfdog.

'We keep the treasure in here so that our citizens can pay their respect when they choose.'

'Very nice,' nodded Porker. 'So where are the chocolate eclairs?'

Porker was just starting to wonder why there was a dead dog in the chamber.

'As you can see, they have been laid out respectfully before you,' said the eel.

'Behind the dead dog, you mean?'

Bubbles punctuated the conversation.

'Erm,' said the eel, 'the eclairs are the dog.'

'What?' cried Porker. 'What kind of weird wiggling water-worm are you? Do you really think I have somersaulted through the darkness and endured the company of a long-eared trickster just so I could wrap my undernourished chops around a dead dog rotting at the bottom of a mountain pool?'

The eel stammered an apology.

'I'm… I'm sorry. Surely, there must be some mistake… I only hope we haven't offended you heavenly bodies. I assure you we have treated him… it… them… with the utmost respect. And the body of the dog is not rotten. We have preserved it in our own spittle.'

'What?!' cried Porker again. 'And I suppose that gobbing all over the body makes it more tasty for you, does it? I'm partial to a little food, but I'm not perverse!'

'I'm sure there must be some sort of misunderstanding. We have treated your treasure very seriously. He is honoured and worshipped by everyone. And if you are offended by the spittle, you should know that it has kept him alive. Oh, yes. His heart still beats. All you need is a little eel urine to rub all over him, and he will be as right as rain!'

'That does it,' barked Porker. 'I've had enough of this. There are no chocolate eclairs down here. This is just another trick that hairy-brained hooligan is playing on me. She's probably rolling around on the floor in hysterics as we speak!'

Porker stormed out of the chamber and swam back up to the surface of the pool.

'Oi – nose-poker!' he called up to Hoo Hoo. 'I've had enough of your mischief. It's not funny. Get me out of here.'

'Have you found the chocolate eclairs?' called back Hoo Hoo.

Porker nearly popped with rage.

'There are no eclairs down here, as you well know, you deceitful loose ear of a dog! There's just a drowned dog who has been preserved in eel spit!'

'You pork-filled puff pastry! That is the treasure. I mean, it's true I did trick you (just a little bit). I mean, there are no chocolate eclairs down there. But did you really think that would be a good place to keep them? So why don't you just haul up the drowned dog and we'll be on our way?'

'Oh no you don't. I've had it up to my water-filled ears with you and your treacherous bent of mind. I'm not moving another muscle.'

'Fine! You stay down there. I'm sure the eels will enjoy spitting on you, too!'

'You swine! Just send down the rope ladder and get me out.'

'Not on your nose! Not until you fetch up that dog.'

Porker muttered and grumbled. He splashed about in a noisy way for a bit.

Finally, he took another deep breath and took the plunge.

'You've come back!' said the father eel. 'Did you forget something?'

Porker didn't quite manage to look apologetic.

'Er... well, yes. I can see how a dog covered in eel spit might be quite a find, after all. So, if you don't mind, I'll take him and be out of your... skin.'

The eel lowered his head dutifully.

'He is one of your kind so who are we to interfere with the affairs of Heaven? We are grateful even for the smallest glimpse of the bountiful order you bestow on us. But, please, you must take this with you...'

The eel passed Porker a sachet.

'What's this?'

'That's our urine.'

Porker took the sachet warily.

The eel hesitated.

'And I believe you should know something else. Some of us were born to live and survive in the darkness. But some creatures were born to experience the light, and yet they are trapped in the darkness. The dog you are about to take is one of them. But there are many others. These shards of light you see gleaming about our pool are the spirits of lost creatures. All of them are seeking out the light. At least, that's what some of us have come to believe. I expect it's right that you should take this dog and return him to the light. Down here he is trapped in a world of shadows, flickering images and illusions. He's not real. And when a piece of reality is missing, something false often takes its place. You must restore this piece of reality, and hope that it will help the other fragments of light to find their way back to a brighter world.'

Porker had no idea what the eel was talking about.

Bowing politely to the two eels, he slung the Wolfdog over his shoulder, and made his way out of the chamber.

Porker and Hoo Hoo cursed, banged, slipped and pulled hair. Eventually, they managed to heave the body of the Wolfdog out of the pool, through the passageways of the hill, and back to the birdwatchers' hut. They put the body down and collapsed in exhaustion. Porker went straight to sleep.

Cloud approached the body. He looked over the dog's features, which were familiar from his dream. He looked over the layer of slime in which the poor creature had been wrapped. He thought he could see a few flickers and sparkles of light twinkling off the coat of the deposed Head Hound.

'I know this dog,' muttered Cloud.

He had, of course, seen the creature before in the dream, but by saying these words, he meant something more. He felt something strange, which he didn't quite understand. He felt connected to the dog.

He squatted on his paws before the body and cried.

*

Once they had all recovered enough to think clearly about it, they discussed how they could bring the Wolfdog back to life. They had an argument about who should smear the eel urine on the spit-covered body of the Wolfdog. Porker said that he had experienced more than his fair share of eels. Hoo Hoo said she thought it might impair her powers. And Cloud was just a bit uncomfortable about sticking his paws in eel urine.

'I'll do it,' said Mouse.

Everyone else suddenly felt very guilty.

The resuscitation didn't take long. The saliva slipped away from the Wolfdog's body. Twitches and ticks of movement signalled the stirrings of life. He turned on his side, raised his head, and opened his eyes. Mouse looked back at him, frightened as usual. The Wolfdog sniffed at the sausage dog, then showed his teeth in a smile.

'I don't know who you are,' he said, 'but I have never been so pleased to see and smell a fellow of the species as I have been to see and smell you. You make me feel good to be alive!'

It's hard to describe the effect these words had on Mouse. They worked like a spell. For the first time, Mouse felt something like self-worth.

Out of the stunned silence came the first cries of happiness. The Wolfdog had returned to reality. The four pilgrims gathered around. They introduced themselves and explained what had happened. The Wolfdog thanked each in turn by rubbing noses.

Finally, he said:

'Why do I smell?'

They all hatched a plan to give the Wolfdog a bath.

'But wait a moment,' said Cloud, as they soaped the Wolfdog's paws. 'This won't do. The plan was to make you look like a travelling pilgrim, not like a sweet-smelling Head Hound.'

'What are you saying?' said Porker. 'I'm not going back for more eel urine!'

Cloud mused.

'Perhaps we just need to make you look a bit more… dishevelled.'

*

Having tidied up the Wolfdog, they ruffled his coat with hawthorn, and sprinkled him with a smattering of dust and leaves from the road. But to make him look even more inconspicuous, they even cloaked his head in a hood, and told anyone who asked them on the road that he had taken a solemn vow to shield himself from the world's sight.

Before they set off, Cloud looked into the trees. There he saw a wren, so he spoke kindly to it. He asked the bird to fly down to the farm and tell the Wolfdog's son that his father was alive and well, and about to return home.

The Wolfdog's son had been waiting impatiently for news of his father. He was overjoyed when the wren flew in at the window to tell him that the final reckoning with the imposter was at hand. In a whirl of energy, he asked the bird to rouse a royal ruckus, and bring all the creatures of the farmstead together.

'Tell them I'm holding a special ceremony of celebration for my esteemed father.'

When this news got about, everyone was thrilled to find themselves invited to a surprise celebration. Squirrels, chickens, sheep, a lonely goat, a chorus of birds, and of course, a small workforce of dogs who kept the farm running, all assembled in the walled garden. At the centre of them, prowling about, was the false Head Hound, shadowed by his wife. He pretended to be as excited as everyone else by the shock celebration.

Has he finally worked it all out? thought the imposter. *This day may require all my craftiness!*

'Father!' called out the young Wolfdog. 'I'm glad to see you. And I hope you don't mind my calling this little ceremony at such short notice!'

'I would hardly call it 'little'!' laughed the imposter Head Hound. 'But who could object to a son applauding his father?!'

'My thoughts exactly! And that's the point. That's the reason I've brought everyone here today. You are under-appreciated, Father. By me, most of all! Not long ago we were all in dire straits; but your effort and skill have turned everything around. We all, I believe, owe you a debt of thanks.'

'Son, you are too kind. It's my *duty* to consider the welfare of you all.'

'And you, Father, are too modest. Now, now, it's true. And as a token of our appreciation, I want to give you a special present. Others here may not grasp the meaning of this, but I'm *sure* you will remember.'

The younger dog dropped the tooth on the patch of grass between them.

A collared dove with poor eyesight was perched high up on the wall. She swooped down to get a closer look. Then she cried out for the benefit of everyone:

'It's a tooth!'

The younger dog noticed that the imposter dealt a hard, lingering look at his 'son'.

'Show your true colours,' whispered the young Wolf-dog. 'I dare you!'

But the imposter would not speak. The son had expected to see a flash of anger in the eyes of his onlooker. Instead, he was unmoved.

'But, Father, surely you remember this tooth? You have frightened me with it since I was a child!'

The assembled farmstead could tell that something was not right. Then came a brouhaha. Five strange and unruly dogs strolled into the proceedings. They all looked very scruffy and arrived through the entrance to the walled garden with a group clatter. The Border Collie at their head gave a loud sneeze when he passed the flower bed; the overweight St Bernard at his side belched loudly, and the sprightly Springer Spaniel farted. The hooded figure at the back tittered.

The farm animals clamoured with objections. Muttering turned to shouting.

'How rude!'

'Who are these dogs?'

'I don't know them!'

'That's no way to treat a Head Hound.'

'That one just farted!'

'How rude!'

The Border Collie trotted forward to reach the centre of the crowd and meet the gaze of the imposter Head Hound. Like the younger Wolfdog, Cloud could see immediately that the imposter knew the game was up. But he could also see that his mind was at work on an inscrutable reply.

'Good creatures, please don't be alarmed!' called out Cloud. 'As you can see, my companions and I are paw-worn wayfarers. We do not know your manners. But we hope that you will treat us kindly.

'You should know one thing – I am a pilgrim! I come from a place like this, a little further east. But our land has been forsaken by the Bald. It's my task to travel west and seek it out once more. You see, at one time, we followed our tradition, which was to revere and celebrate the presence of the Bald in our lives. We called it the Thumbald. But it has now gone missing, and no one in my community knows what's what anymore.

We don't really know good from bad, the difference between pleasure and happiness, the love of natural beauty above its cheap imitation – in a nutshell, we no longer see true from false.

'Now, I have a wayward, wandering mind. I dream, I think, I study. But that's not enough for a quest like mine. I need skills and energy to keep me going. For that I have Hoo Hoo…'

Hoo Hoo skipped lightly up to the centre of the circle and did a little circular dance. Then she, too, caught the eye of the imposter Head Hound. Curious, she sniffed at him.

'And I need an appetite to sustain me on my journey and give me strength. For that I have Porker.'

Porker wheezed forward slowly and bowed his head.

'And, of course, the truth is both seen and unseen. For that I have Mouse…'

Mouse skipped forward quickly. He bowed too, but nervously.

'Together,' continued Cloud, 'we are hunting for the truth. When we hunt, we smell. Which means we have learned to smell out true from false. So much so that when we reached your farmstead we were overpowered by the stench – that's right, the stench – of falsehood! Your land is engulfed by a hue of lies. You may not know it, but there it is! We have peered through the mist and haze of a dream, to see the fabrication right at the heart of this, your home.'

Hoo Hoo huddled up to Porker.

'Master certainly likes to go on a bit on these sorts of occasions, doesn't he?'

As if he had heard the whisper, Cloud summoned his companion.

'Hoo Hoo, will you tell this crowd what we have learned and witnessed in the last few days?'

'Gladly, Master.'

Hoo Hoo stepped forward.

'It is as my master says. The first night we stayed in your land, he was visited in a dream by a passing spirit of the night. It told how, until recently, your farm had suffered. Crops would not grow. Management of the land was inefficient. That sort of thing. But then a magician arrived and managed to help out. The well-being of the land appeared to be restored. But I am well schooled in the art of trickery and deception. I can smell it a mile off, even with my nose tied in a plastic bag and a pleasing smell of fried mushrooms to distract me! And I tell you this magician was using cheap tricks. Yes, he managed to improve the way the crops grow. But it was out of no respect for the land. His methods will soon have plundered and destroyed every natural resource and good-growing thing you have. Then, he will leave behind him only a wasteland.

'But you must not fall under his spell. You must all learn to listen to the world around you rather than rely on tricks and magical systems. The world has plenty to offer, if only you are open to it!

'And, worse still, this 'Wolfdog' not only cast your land in a sickly spell, he plotted his way to the highest seat of power. This hound who stands before you is not the rightful Head Hound of the farmstead, but the same magician who tricked his way into the lives of you all!

'Unknown to you all, this magician led the true Head Hound up to a cave in the mountains and drowned him in a deep pool. Then, using his wily deceit, he assumed the guise of the Head Hound. He even stole the true Head Hound's wife!'

The crowd started to mutter and exclaim.

'But that's not all! Oh no! We even think this imposter is a spy working for a deceiver-in-chief, a mountain spirit, who hates the world and takes his revenge by stealing the body of other creatures. I speak of Agent Animo, of course! And I say – be warned! If you let this imposter get his way, he will destroy everything that you hold dear and imprison you all!

'How do I know all this? Because this was the story told to my master in his dream. And how do I know the dream was true? Because my companion and I went into the mountains to recover the true Head Hound. And because the true Head Hound is standing right before you!'

The hooded Wolfdog stepped forward and removed his hood.

The crowd cried out in shock.

'Enough!' called out the fake Head Hound, breaking his long silence. 'These are just high-minded words!'

The false Head Hound vanished before everyone's eyes. In his place, they saw a small robin redbreast flutter away over the garden wall.

'I knew it!' cried out Hoo Hoo. 'This magical malefactor has all the powers of a Proteanimator! Quick, we must be after him!'

So saying, Hoo Hoo transformed into a giant tawny owl. She spread her wings and beat her way into the sky on the tail of the fugitive robin redbreast. Hoo Hoo saw it disappear into the branches of a tall beech tree. Following it, she landed on one of the branches. She twisted her head to see what she could see. The robin had disappeared.

'Another trick, I expect,' she muttered.

Then something hit her on the back of the neck. She turned around. Something hit her again, this time right between the eyes. She looked up and saw a squirrel prancing about on one of the branches. It was pelting her with its nuts!

'Why, you naughty nutter!' she said, and took off towards the squirrel.

The squirrel fired a barrage of nuts at Hoo Hoo, jumped over a few branches, then leaped into the open air, where it transformed in mid-flight into a paper aeroplane. To Hoo Hoo's surprise, it sailed back towards the walled garden.

By the time Hoo Hoo had landed on the wall of the garden with the other birds, she could no longer see the aeroplane.

'What has he done now?' she thought.

Then she caught sight of something which made her wings flutter. Standing in the centre of the walled garden she could see Cloud – twice! Two versions of the Border Collie were standing next to each other.

She flew down to rejoin her companions and transformed into her true self as she landed.

'Porker! Mouse!' she called out. 'Which one of these two versions of our master just appeared?'

Porker and Mouse were as surprised as Hoo Hoo to discover two Clouds.

'Well, I'm Cloud,' said Cloud.

'That's nonsense!' said the other Cloud. 'I'm the real Cloud. This one's the magician.'

'Porker? Mouse?' said Hoo Hoo sternly. 'Did you see?'

'No, Hoo Hoo,' said Mouse. 'We were all watching you as you flew about in the trees.'

'This is ridiculous,' said Cloud. 'I know who I am.'

'And I know who I am,' said the other Cloud. 'The identity crisis is all yours!'

'This is going to be difficult,' said Hoo Hoo. 'And this is a very clever trick. The magician has serious powers. He knows I can't hurt my master without jeopardising our quest and my own duty. It's very clever! I don't know how to sort this one out. We're in a fix!'

Mouse's eyes flitted thoughtfully between the two Clouds. He had a brainwave.

Slowly, he approached the two Border Collies. He gave each a little sniff. Then he returned to Hoo Hoo, and whispered in her ear:

'It's the one on the left. He doesn't smell of rosemary!'

Hoo Hoo's hackles shot up, and she went to attack the version of Cloud on her left. But before she could seize him, he had transformed once more, this time into a tortoise.

Hoo Hoo couldn't help it – she just laughed!

'Haha! A tortoise! How is that going to help you escape? Call yourself a Proteanimator!'

'Now that's enough of that!' said the tortoise, crawling along slowly. He was making for the centre of the assembled throng. 'Can't you see that I'm making a mockery of you all?!'

'Don't think that tack will get you out of it. I'm going to crush you in your shell. It's time for tortoise escalope!'

'Keep your paws to yourself, dog! You may have learned a few clever manoeuvres, but you are no match for me!'

Looking at the tortoise, Porker suddenly thought that he looked familiar. Then his memory worked it out.

'Holy ham hock!' he cried. 'You're Balder's pet tortoise!'

The tortoise sighed visibly.

'So, one of you playthings of the wind has finally worked it out!'

'This,' explained Porker more urgently than he had ever done anything, 'is one of Balder's closest and most trusted friends. It's said the tortoise spreads his wisdom wherever he goes.'

'True, true,' said the tortoise.

He sounded just a little smug.

'But I don't understand,' said Cloud. 'Why would you mistreat this farm? It doesn't make any sense.'

The tortoise quoted:

I talk gibberish,

But I still talk.

'So, hounds, wayward clouds, and boastful springing spaniels, you begin to see things in a new light! You thought you had it all figured out. But I'm no magician, or even a rogue tortoise! And I am not working for Animo! I have been acting on the instructions of Balder. Balder is compassion itself. She is wisdom itself. She is beauty itself. And she wants to help you in your quest. The Thumbald wants you to find it. I was sent here to help you!'

'Now, I don't understand that at all,' pleaded Cloud. 'How has what has happened here helped our search for the Thumbald?'

'You said it yourself, just now. The search for the Thumbald is the search for truth, beauty and justice. It's the search for reality. To the Wolfdog, I say this: I imprisoned you in a dream because you didn't respect the world around you. You did not see its potential. You once turned out a brown-coated dog. Little did you know it – but that dog has tremendous power and potential. And you chose to have her cast out! Instead, you fell for the dupes and counterfeit prosperity I brought to you in the guise of a magician. But now, you have returned to reality. You have become real again.

'But to you, Cloud, I say this: I come to you as a warning. I may not be working for Animo, but you are right to be concerned. His influence is everywhere! And my trickery is a lesson designed to match his. You are right to seek out the truth. For these dogs, for your home, but also for *yourself*. You were born alone, an orphan. Your mind is adrift, 'in the clouds', because you have never had anyone to ground it for you and give it meaning.'

Something twinkled in the tortoise's eye.

'You have seen how this young Wolfdog lost a family through deception. But he is not the only son to lose a family...'

A dream

The festival of
light

Cloud and his companions set out on the road. They felt a mixture of triumph and doubt. They were pleased that they had rescued the drowned Wolfdog. The Wolfdog was even more pleased. He had thanked them publicly and made them honorary citizens. And yet they were unsettled by the words of Balder's tortoise. They had left them with a sense of a mission only half accomplished. They trotted along paths, dirt tracks, old, faded ways through mossy woodland. Their curiosity about what was expected of them led the way.

Their journey followed a long, slow descent from the highest terrain, into a vast glaciated valley. They sheltered in old stone buildings, highland barns and disused huts. Streams trickled out of higher crags, peaks and solitary passes. Some disappeared underground. But as they made their way through the valley, the water converged to form a stream, and then a small river. Trees had grown appreciatively on the banks of the water, where only birdsong broke the silence.

When they stopped by the stream for a drink, Hoo Hoo caught Porker staring into the water. A roach was gliding just beneath the surface. A hungry bulb of drool had formed out of the corner of Porker's mouth. It was quickly gathering weight.

'Porker!' called out Hoo Hoo sharply.

Porker jolted to attention. The drool fell and splattered. The roach darted off to find shelter.

Porker didn't say anything. But his stomach complained loudly.

'There's no need to take that tone,' said Hoo Hoo.

'Where are we?' asked Mouse. 'Are we lost? We haven't seen anyone or anything for days. I wonder if we have reached the edge of the world.'

'We're in a wild and remote place. That's for sure,' said Cloud. 'But if we stick to our course, we'll find shelter eventually.'

'Let's hope so,' grumbled Porker. 'We seem to be living off fried mushrooms and roots. What kind of life is that?'

The company of dogs settled on a silt beach, which was hidden by a sharp drop from the riverbank. Hoo Hoo was about to upbraid Porker for being permanently hungry and remind him of his vow, but she was interrupted by a distant noise. A clip followed by a clop was coming towards them at a canter. The clipping and the clopping were so close that it sounded like two horses. All the dogs froze. The track on which the horses would soon pass by was only a few paces away. Should they approach the horses? Or stay hidden?

'Master, should we…?' asked Hoo Hoo.

'Ssh,' said Cloud.

The horses drew nearer.

'They're just horses,' whispered Porker. 'What harm can they mean?'

Even so, the dogs sensed danger. They kept quiet.

As the horses reached the shelter of the trees, they could be heard speaking. This was, at first, little more than a neighing jumble of sounds. But, before long, they could hear everything.

'They wouldn't know olives from oatmeal,' said one horse, 'or carrots from crudités. So, it hardly matters.'

'But you're missing the point. They wouldn't know what to do with an olive because all they know is oatmeal. Given them the opportunity, and they'll not only appreciate olives but oysters and okra!'

The horses didn't see the dogs when they went by. But the talk of food was too much for Porker. His stomach growled loudly, which caused a small field mouse to scurry across the track. The eyes of the horses traced the journey of the mouse back towards the riverbank, where they just caught the sight of Hoo Hoo's long ears jiggling about in mirth.

'Well, now who are you, sneaking about secretly across our land?' cried out one of the horses.

The four dogs clambered out from the riverside. They were a little ashamed. And a little frightened.

'Please, we mean no harm,' replied Cloud. 'We're only pilgrims on a journey west. We don't want to cause any trouble.'

'Pilgrims!' called out the other horse. 'Well, that's hardly innocent. You'll be begging and cadging food – or worse, stealing. And at a time when we have seen a noticeable downturn in productivity!'

'What my friend is trying to say is that we do not recognise the idea of 'a pilgrimage'. If you want to pass through our land, you must make a contribution. Either you must pay a toll or contribute to what we know about the world.'

'What do you mean?' asked Cloud. 'We only believe in the Bald.'

'Ha!' cried one of the horses. 'The Bald!'

'Ha!' said the other horse.

'The Bald makes no hay with us! No, we said goodbye to that silly claptrap a long time ago.'

Hoo Hoo was starting to get annoyed.

'Some years ago, the community of animals in these parts were banging on about the Bald. Or some peculiar version of it. They adapted it to the fit and feel of the land. But it didn't do them any good. If they had a bad harvest the Bald didn't do them much good. So, they mustered their resources. A few of our kind had studied abroad under the influence of some wise and powerful creatures, and there they became exceptionally learned and clever! Three horses, one after the other, put forward new ways to manage the land and its creatures.

'The first horse, Arouet, said that running things was a very special skill, and that only certain well-educated creatures were suited to it. He said that an elite should run everything.

'The second horse, Bobbs, didn't necessarily disagree, but he thought that the main aim of the elite was to ensure order. Without order it's impossible to manage the land!

'But a third horse, Lark, said that all of this was unfair and unequal. He thought a small elite should run things, until everything was shared out equally.'

Cloud was very interested.

'Venerable vegetation!' he said. 'This sounds like a very unusual place. Are all the creatures so open to new ideas?'

'All the creatures?' asked the horse, a bit confused. 'What do you mean?'

'Well, all the creatures who live in these lands.'

'All the...' stammered the horse, and then he burst into a fit of laughter, 'nah nah nah... dear me no... what an idea!'

'Why do you laugh?' asked Cloud. 'I don't understand.'

'So I can see, so I can see! Oh, I'm sorry. I can see you don't know how these things work... and why would you? No, no, if there's one thing that our enlightened horses agree on – and believe me there's plenty they disagree on – it's that managing the land takes... well, how shall we say, it takes a certain amount of skill. The right training. The right ability. Of course, it also helps if you have the right creatures, too! And let's face it, most creatures don't pass muster! They don't have what it takes.'

Cloud had thought, at first, that this land was a refreshingly modern and open place. Now he had doubts.

'As we have told you, we have no money. So, we cannot pay your toll. But now that you have told me a little about your land and the creatures in it, I think we might be able to contribute in some way.'

'Excellent. I'm sure the First Minister will be very interested to hear what you have to say.'

'Before we meet your First Minister, do you think we could meet some of the creatures who live in these parts? I mean, the ones who don't run everything.'

'What a coincidence you should ask! We were just on our way to speak with a warren of rabbits. They haven't been pulling their weight, and we want to set that right! Why don't you come along?'

The warren was only a short walk. It was hidden away at the edge of a sparsely populated area of downy birch. The ground was thick with rabbits. They popped up from nowhere and got in each other's way. They went down one hole, came up another, expecting to find themselves somewhere else entirely. It gave a chaotic impression. The two horses were irritated.

'Now then, now then,' said one of the horses sternly, 'let's have a bit of order, shall we? Call it to attention!'

The visible population of rabbits turned from a state of sheer chaos to distant curiosity.

The horse embarked on a long (and long-winded) speech about the cost of labour. None of the rabbits understood. They kept fidgeting about.

'Who are these dogs?' asked a young bunny.

'Never mind that now,' replied the horse.

Hoo Hoo, perhaps because she didn't like the horses, took a shine to the rabbits. She liked their restlessness, and it made her even more restless than usual. She set about them with a bit of chattering and harmless gossip.

She soon learned that almost all the rabbits were contracted to act as couriers for a local family of pigs. The pigs were too fat and lazy to dart about the countryside, so they paid the rabbits. It wasn't bad work, the rabbits said. And it kept them in lettuce. But they had received complaints. Some rabbits had lost their package, or spent too long delivering it, or fallen asleep in a hedge.

She pulled Cloud to one side.

'Master, what do you make of all this? It's like nothing I've ever known. These horses seem to think they live in a new kind of paradise. But I'm not so sure.'

Cloud had been mulling it over, too. He had spent a little time talking to the rabbits. It was a curious situation. Partly they got something out of it all. Some of them even enjoyed it. But he noticed that many of the rabbits looked a little forlorn. The bounce had gone from their little legs and their ears flopped with less vigour.

He also found that a lot of the rabbits were having help sessions, where they sat down in their burrows for an hour to talk about the way they were feeling. It was clear enough: the warren had resorted to counselling.

This way of running things had produced a lot of depressed rabbits!

'I agree, Hoo Hoo. I could be wrong, but it seems that the horses think the rabbits are a load of idiots, who are nothing more than drones! I think we need to shake things up a little!'

'Master, I like the way your tongue talks! What shall we do?'

Cloud furrowed his brow gently.

'Now, don't mistake me. I don't want to take advantage of your special powers. But I wondered... I mean, I thought you might find your way to... not that I want to do any *harm*...'

'What is it, Master? Tell me!'

'Well, I thought you might *do* something to these horses.'

Hoo Hoo's eyes channelled electric current.

'You want me to turn into something, don't you?'

'Only if you find it agreeable.'

'Oh, I do, Master. I do. What did you have in mind?'

'Let's just see what comes to your mind, shall we?'

Hoo Hoo and Cloud approached the horses to have it out with them.

'Now listen to me, horses,' said Cloud. 'Isn't it obvious what's going on here? You're forcing all these rabbits to behave in one way, and you have made them unhappy. You have a lot of depressed rabbits on your hands! What are you going to do about it?'

The horses laughed.

'I can see you are from an uncivilised part of the world. What am I going to do about it? Nothing. No one forces these rabbits to behave as they do and I don't hear them complaining about the extra lettuce and radishes their way of life brings them.'

Cloud turned this over in his mind but found little to reply with.

'Ha!' said one of the horses. 'Hadn't thought of that, had you! But that's the nub of the matter: you can't eat a lettuce without digging up the chicken wire! That's what progress is all about.'

Hoo Hoo couldn't think of an answer to the horse either, but she was very annoyed. It looked as if her eyes might explode. But, instead, she exploded in a different way. First, they could hear her body buzzing. Then little flies started to pop out from beneath her coat.

'Hoo Hoo, are you all right?' asked Cloud uncertainly.

Before he could receive a reply, Hoo Hoo erupted into a swarm of angry horseflies and rounded on the horses. The horses let out a loud neigh.

'Oh my!' cried one of them. 'What just happened?'

They had no time to find out, as the swarm of horseflies descended on them. Cloud later discovered that

Hoo Hoo chased them so far that they got lost in an unfamiliar part of the world and were forced to make a living washing dishes with their tails.

When she returned, Hoo Hoo addressed the rabbits.

'Friends!' she said. 'We have liberated you from your slave labour. You are free to hop about the countryside!'

'Hooray!' said the rabbits.

Then the rabbits thought about their situation.

'Hang on,' said one of them. 'This is no good. As soon as the village learns about what has happened here, there will be uproar. We will be punished and treated very cruelly. Oh, what have you done, dog with the unusual power to turn into a swarm of horseflies?! What have you done to us?'

'Village? What village?'

Her blood was up.

'The village is home to the three horses who have introduced all sorts of weird ideas into these lands. They will stretch our ears and make us eat terrible things, like houmous! Oh, what shall we do? What shall we do?!'

Hoo Hoo became more indignant.

'I'm not afraid of any village. They are no match for Hoo Hoo, High Lady of the Mountain-Tarn Cave for the Deliverance of Lost Creatures!'

'Don't be so sure,' returned the rabbit. 'They are very smart over there in the village. It's very modern. They even have a toilet!'

'The day I am terrified by a toilet-trained thorough-bred is the day I would be ashamed to call myself a spaniel with floppy ears. That day will not come! You show me these commode-coveting cowards, and then you'll see what's what!'

The rabbits sensed Hoo Hoo's determination.

'It's now very clear to me,' said Cloud. 'We must go to the village and have firm words with the three horses.'

'Well said, Master!' echoed Hoo Hoo. 'But I think we will need a bit more than 'firm words'.'

*

The village was only a few hours from the rabbit warren, but by the time they reached its outskirts, the light had begun to fade from the day. They decided to spend the night in the ruins of a barn pitched at the foot of a barren hillside. They could see the village before them: a burnished glow in the dusk.

After a busy day, Cloud settled down to sleep. The others were about to do the same, but Hoo Hoo was too eager. She couldn't sit still, much less sleep.

'Oi!' she whispered over Cloud's heavy slumber. 'Porker! Mouse! I've got an idea. Wouldn't we be in a better position if we knew a bit more about this village before we got there?'

'I suppose,' said Mouse, 'but how's that going to happen?'

'This is just our chance. All those potty-trained ponies will be asleep. So why don't we shoot off now and scout about the place. I'm sure the master will thank us in the morning!'

'I don't know,' said Porker sleepily. 'I'm tired, and in any case, what do you expect to find at this time in the evening?'

'I'll tell you what I expect to find, Porker – food! And plenty of it. I overheard one of those oppressed rabbits talk about a festival the village is holding. Imagine the spread they will lay on! Just imagine!'

'I suppose we could sniff around a bit.'

Hoo Hoo, Mouse and Porker pattered out into the night.

They found their way into the village without much trouble. All the horses were asleep. The night hummed with the soft snore of horse nostrils. Hoo Hoo, Mouse and Porker crept about the deserted streets. Or, at least, Hoo Hoo and Mouse managed to creep about. Porker stumbled about, trod in a large pile of horse manure, and swore loudly.

'Shh!' hissed Hoo Hoo. 'Can't you go anywhere without making a racket? Look, the village hall is over there. I bet that's where we'll find out more about the festival.'

The three dogs trod carefully towards the village

hall. Above the porch way they could see a banner. It read *Festival of Light*.

'If I know anything about anything (and I like to think I know pretty much everything about everything), I'd say the best time to upstage a festival of light is under cover of darkness,' said Hoo Hoo.

But when they tried the door, it was locked.

Hoo Hoo was not fazed.

'This is a small matter.'

She disappeared into the keyhole, then popped out as its key.

'Turn me!' said the key.

Mouse did as he was told. The door gave way. The key disappeared into the keyhole and, on the far side of the door, reappeared as Hoo Hoo.

It was dark inside the Festival of Light. So dark they could only just make out the faint outline of objects in the hall. Even so, they could *smell* the contents of the hall without any trouble. A rich, delicious aroma filled their noses. Porker, impulsively, took a step forwards and trod on something. Mouse yelped.

'Ow! That's my paw!' he cried.

'Watch where you're going, Mr Big!' said Hoo Hoo. 'We don't want to wake the full trap of ponies!'

'But I can't see anything,' protested Porker.

'We'll soon fix that.'

Hoo Hoo turned into a lantern, suspended in the air.

With the extra light, the dogs could now make out the rows of empty troughs on either side of the hall. Then, against the back wall, they could see three neatly presented tables with layered pyramids of food, pinnacled by pictures of horses.

'Wait,' barked Hoo Hoo, 'we need to see more clearly.'

The lantern cast its light about the room until they came across a three-point light switch on the wall. Mouse flicked each switch with his nose, and three fluorescent tubes of lighting flooded the room. The tables of food were mouth-watering.

They could see now that the pictures of each horse were suspended from the ceiling by wires. Coloured ribbons of cloth hung beside each picture, emphasising the high status and importance of each portrait. They looked like venerable teachers in a cult of worship.

'Oh my!' said Hoo Hoo.

But Porker was already eating. He had sunk his chops into a large puffed-up pie, steaming with the joy of its juices.

'Make sure you leave some for the rest of us!' said Hoo Hoo.

Hoo Hoo trotted after Porker and Mouse, who looked over his shoulder nervously.

Between them, they worked hard at the food on the three tables. But the tables hadn't really been designed for dogs. They could only reach the lower steps in each tier of food.

'I know,' explained Hoo Hoo, 'it would be much easier if we moved those silly pictures and climbed up to the top of each table. Then we could eat what we want!'

She climbed up and unhooked each picture. Then she threw them on the floor and jumped up and down on them for a bit. As she went about this insult, she noticed something else on the wall of the village hall, which led through to some sort of annex. On the door was written Toilet, then, in brackets, (PLEASE RE-MEMBER TO FLUSH!).

Discourteous cunning spread across Hoo Hoo's face.

'I have another idea,' she said.

'What's that?' asked Mouse, his nose covered in a mixture of puff pastry and cream.

'These horses are clearly full of themselves. I think it's about time we brought them down to earth.'

'How?'

Hoo Hoo didn't bother to explain. She simply tore up each picture, rolled up the remnants into a ball, pushed open the toilet door, and stuffed everything down the loo!

'There! Oh, and I mustn't forget to flush!'

Hoo Hoo flushed the pictures of the horses down the toilet.

Except Hoo Hoo had never used a toilet before. She didn't know that the flush could only cope with so much waste. In a moment, the U-bend was blocked, the flushing mechanism was stuck, and the venerated contraption was leaking water all over the floor.

Hoo Hoo returned to eating.

*

Meanwhile, a pony was struggling to sleep. He and some other ponies had been responsible for laying on the festivities in the village hall. And he was worried. He was worried that something was not right. The festival was celebrating the three visionary horses and their great contribution to modern life. Except the horses were quite difficult to please. They all had quite big egos and thought they were very important. If the festival didn't go well, it wouldn't look good for those who had organised it. The pony decided he would get up and, for one last time, check everything he and his colleagues had prepared.

When he stepped out into the street, his heart froze. The lights were on. He shook his head, blinked, and snorted a little. Then he looked again. The light was still on.

'That's funny. I thought I had turned the light off,' he

said to himself.

He decided to investigate.

The closer he got to the hall, the more he thought he could hear noises coming from it. Laughter. Occasional talking. And, more persistently, guzzling. Yes, there was the distinct sound of guzzling.

The pony peered into the porch way. The door was open.

That's funny. I thought I had locked the door, the pony thought. *In fact, I'm sure I did.*

Just as the pony was about to poke his head through the door to see what was going on, Porker stopped eating. Then he let out a roaring fart. It echoed all the way around the hall.

'Porker!' cried Hoo Hoo.

The pony couldn't help himself. He whinnied, and in sheer panic, ran back into the street to raise the alarm.

*

'It can't have been anyone from the village,' said Arouet. 'I mean, look at the mess they have made. They clearly have no manners!'

'I don't think we are dealing with a bunch of common vagrants. This was a deliberate act of sabotage,' said Bobbs.

'In that case, we should think about what this means,' said Lark. 'Perhaps we are witnessing a structural conflict in our system of political economy. Yes?'

'Shut up, Lark!' said Arouet. 'These interlopers have clearly committed crimes against us. The only thing that matters now is that we catch them and show them the full force of the law.'

'We should convene a tribunal,' said Bobbs gravely.

'And what has happened to our pictures? This is an outrage!' cried Arouet.

Arouet, Bobbs and Lark, the three horses who had done more than any to reform the village and its lands, were very upset that someone could show them such disrespect.

The pony who had discovered the outrage stumbled out from the toilet. He looked, if possible, even more dejected. He dragged in his mouth the torn remnants of Arouet's picture.

'What?! What is that? Is that...?'

Arouet neighed loudly. The pony hung his head in shame.

'All three pictures were torn up.'

'What?!'

'They were flushed down the toilet.'

'What?!!'

'The toilet's blocked and flooded with toilet water.'

'You see,' piped up Bobbs, 'this is why we must all agree to a strong assembly with the power to manage the violent tendencies of most creatures.'

'Shut up, Bobbs!' exclaimed Arouet. 'Look at my picture! We need to catch the criminals straight away before they do any more damage. You!' he called out to the hapless pony. 'You say you discovered this… this… *travesty*. I have some questions. First, how on earth did they manage to get in? Surely, the door was locked?'

'Yes!' said the pony desperately. 'I locked it. I remember locking it.'

'Then how could they have got in?'

'I don't know, Arouet! I swear, I don't know.'

'This is quite ridiculous. And it's a perfect affront to any reasonable explanation. If the door was locked, how could they have got in? What did you do with the key?'

'I have it,' replied the pony more calmly. 'I carry it with me everywhere.'

'This is absurd. It's just absurd!' cried Arouet.

And he wasn't finished.

'But you say you saw a light on in the hall when you went to investigate. You heard noises… laughter… merrymaking… that sort of thing. But you didn't bother to actually look?!'

'I… I became frightened, Arouet.'

'Why?'

'I heard a very loud… *growl.*'

'A growl?'

'Yes, a growl.'

'What sort of growl?'

Hoo Hoo, Porker and Mouse had been hiding all this time behind the ledge of a balcony at the back of the village hall. Porker, who had eaten more than his fair share of the food, was doing his best to contain his digestive rumbles and gurgling noises. But he could contain them no longer. He let free another loud fart, so loud it made the windows shake.

The three horses and the pony looked shocked.

'That sort of growl,' said the pony.

Hoo Hoo could see the game was nearly up. She would have to do something.

'Who's there?' called out Arouet. 'Who are you? Or what are you? Show yourself!'

'Me? Who am I?' replied Hoo Hoo. 'I'm a beggar. A starving vagrant.'

'Show yourself immediately!'

'Are you sure you want to see me? I'm quite unsightly, particularly for high-ranking horses like you.'

'I will tear you apart with my teeth!' said Arouet.

'That's a bit drastic. After all, I told you, I'm a passing beggar. I was poor, cold and hungry. I walked through your village. You left this hall open, and there was all this food. So I... well, I ate it. I just assumed...'

'Quite an assumption!' said Bobbs.

'This is outrageous!' said Arouet again.

'What about our pictures?' pitched in Lark.

'Oh yes those,' replied Hoo Hoo, with a little chuckle. 'Well you see, I ate so much that it made me need to use your toilet. And since I had no toilet roll...'

'Barbaric!' cried Arouet.

'Or just necessary,' replied Hoo Hoo. 'But I have to hand it to you. You are very clever horses. You managed to create all this food. What I don't understand is why you're upset when someone very hungry and needy comes along and eats it all.'

'Enough of this. Show yourself! We will make a mash of your intestines – just as you deserve!'

'Really?'

'Yes!'

'I see. Well, I would show myself, but the reason I'm lying down out of sight is that I have eaten so much of your delicious food that I now have very bad stomach ache.'

'I don't care if you have become as fat as a cream-filled elephant!' declared Arouet, trotting forward with purpose.

'Okay, but first let's see if this helps.'

Hoo Hoo could hear Porker's stomach still grumbling, so she pressed hard on its cavernous pockets of gas. Porker let out a cry. Then he farted so loudly that it caused a breeze throughout the village hall. The smell was unbearable, but Hoo Hoo turned herself into a fan and wafted the overpowering odour towards the horses. The smell made them cough and choke so much that they had to retreat into the fresh air.

Before the horses could work out what had happened, Hoo Hoo, Porker and Mouse had escaped into the night.

*

'I've had a thought,' said Cloud, when he woke up the following morning. 'I don't think it's sensible to annoy the horses who run this village too much. Not needlessly, anyway. First, we should get the lie of the land.'

Hoo Hoo's eyes widened, but she kept silent. Porker burped. Mouse looked guilty.

'I think we need a pretext. And I have thought of one. We should go into the village and ask for directions. Which, after all, might be helpful, since we don't really know where we are.'

The others observed a moment of silence, apparently so they could think.

'An excellent plan, Master. Let's do that,' said Hoo Hoo.

Mouse nearly said something, but he spent so much time thinking about it and hesitating that it was soon too late – his companions had already made it out of the door.

When they entered the village via the main road that ran through its centre, they were soon greeted. A bull stomped up to them and asked what business they had in the village. There had, the bull explained, been an act of public vandalism the night before.

'We're many things,' replied Cloud, 'but we aren't vandals. We've only stopped here to get some help and directions. We heard you have a First Minister. Could you take us to them?'

The bull thought. Then, grudgingly, he guided them to a big manor house at the centre of the village. This was the home of the First Minister.

'What's your business, then?'

The First Minister was a large, athletic Connemara pony, with muscly legs. He had agreed to meet the four travellers in the garden at the back of the manor house. He padded about with authority.

'We are humble pilgrims,' explained Cloud, 'on our way to the West. I have come from a smallholding called Easthill. Once we knew and respected the Bald. But no one really understands it anymore, so it has become forgotten and misunderstood. I'm travelling to the Lake of Gifts and plan to return with Knowledge.'

The First Minister shuffled about impatiently.

'The Bald?'

'Yes.'

The First Minister blinked.

'So, how can I help you?'

'We're sorry to press your hospitality and goodwill, but we wondered if you could point us in the right direction?'

The First Minister suddenly looked pleased. In fact, he was barrel-chested with pride.

'I bet we can. I'm sure we can. I *know* we can. We can do better, as a matter of interest – and it is a matter of interest. *Considerable* interest. It so happens I despatched a team of cartographers to the western lands, and they have returned with the first ever maps of the territory. They chart everything: from the mightiest river to the tiniest path, from the highest peak to the smallest pile of mouse droppings. I can give you a copy, if you like. What do you think of that, then?'

Hoo Hoo turned up her nose at the offer, but she didn't say anything. Cloud looked a little shocked.

'Oh,' he said, 'well, thank you. That would be very... *useful.*'

'Exactly!' neighed the First Minister. 'Useful. It would be very, very, very... useful. Get you there in no time at all. No more getting lost. No more coming down the wrong valley. No more straying sorely into a badger sett. No, no, none of that. The path all the way. Clear, simple, *logical*. Except I wonder if we would have ever seized the initiative to create a map like that if we had trusted the Bald? To produce a map you need to observe the world. Carefully. Methodically. Could you say the same thing about this 'knowledge' of the Bald? I wonder. Mmmm.

'Mind you, I would find it pleasingly ironic, if you were to get to this place you're heading by using my map. You would get there. But you would realise that your journey was completely pointless! Ha! Yes, quite ironic! And quite pleasing!'

Hoo Hoo couldn't hold her tongue any longer.

'Master, I don't need a map to find my way about the land. My nose is more reliable than any careful calculation. I would sooner blow my nose on this moose-headed map!'

'Steady on, Hoo Hoo! Steady on. Don't be so hasty. The map sounds like a very useful thing. And it will make our task a lot easier.'

'Indeed,' said the First Minister brightly, 'it even comes with annotations, so you can see where the dangers lie. Things like 'this river has savage trout' and 'hereabouts the beetles are thoughtful'. Lots of wonderful detail!'

'What about restaurants?' asked Porker.

The First Minister ignored the question.

'Our surveyor will give you one of our best copies. I'm quite sure you will find it 'useful'.'

Hoo Hoo had more to say, but they were interrupted.

The three brainbox horses, who had been smelled out of the village hall the night before, stood defiantly on the First Minister's lawn with hot nostrils of vengeance.

'What is this?!' thundered Arouet.

The First Ministered turned in surprise.

'Arouet, I had no idea you were here.'

'What's going on? What can this possibly mean?'

'What can *what* mean?' asked the First Minister.

'You are conversing with these… these… there is no word too foul… these barbarians… these degenerates… these putrid, pestiferous pilferers.'

Hoo Hoo leapt to the defence.

'By Ponderous Proteanimation, that's an outrageous slur, and a slight on our character we shan't forget! Who are you to go about making big-banging insults like that?!'

Arouet ignored Hoo Hoo.

'I see you don't know. You don't even know that you are being deceived at this very moment!'

'Arouet, please explain yourself,' said the First Minister earnestly. 'As you know, we are an open and inclusive community. We welcome foreigners!'

Arouet came back with a crack of lightning.

'That you should show any hospitality to these pro-faners of progress is beyond a joke! What can they have told you? Has no one told you about what took place in the village hall last night?'

'No,' said the First Minister.

'Let me explain, then. When one of my assistants locked the hall for the night, you will remember that it was crammed with a feast of foods to celebrate the leaps and bounds we have taken under our new systems of management. But my assistant, ever prudent, returned to the hall so that he could check things over. There he found these intruders guzzling all the food!'

'Guzzling?'

'All the food, yes! I mean look at that one,' said Arouet, pointing at Porker, 'he's really fat! And my worthy assistant was frightened by a frightful noise one of these miscreants made, so he took flight and raised the alarm. Naturally, I, Bobbs and Lark went to investigate. The filthy fiends, exhausted no doubt by their reckless gorging of our product, were hiding behind the balcony in the hall. From there, they taunted and abused us in a very unreasonable way. Then, to cap it all, my assistant discovered that they had torn up our icons and flushed them down the toilet!'

'For shame!' muttered Bobbs.

The First Minister was about to speak.

'It doesn't end there, First Minister! It doesn't end there! We were about to apprehend the criminals when they overpowered us with a horrendous stink. In our disoriented state, they managed to escape.'

'It was nature at its most brutal,' chipped in Bobbs.

'Quite right, Bobbs. Quite right. But even that's not the end of it. This morning news reached me that two of our most accomplished regional managers were attacked by these saboteurs and forced to flee for their lives. An entire community of rabbits has revolted. I tell you, these malfeasants are enemies of the village. They want our destruction. They will stop at nothing less. Hospitality! You should have them executed publicly!'

It was easy to see that the First Minister was shocked. He turned to the pilgrims, unsure how to treat them, as if he had willingly let a tick grow fat on the diet of his own blood.

'First Minister,' said Cloud hurriedly. 'We must be allowed to defend ourselves against these charges. I have travelled a long way. I have been mistreated before, but I have never been quite so unfairly bad-mouthed.'

'Go ahead!' snorted Arouet. 'Lie! I wouldn't expect anything else.'

'Of course, I deny everything you have said. None of it is true. It's only fair that I should have the chance to reply.'

The First Minister weighed the matter judiciously.

'Something is not right here. That's for sure. But I can only get to the bottom of the matter if I let you speak. So, speak – defend yourself! But if I find that you haven't told the truth, then the punishment will be severe!'

Cloud was slightly panicked. He couldn't quite connect all the accusations. Secretly, he suspected that Hoo Hoo might have had something to do with the village hall, but he wasn't sure.

'First of all, I think it's important to know the facts. My companions and I reached the edge of your lands yesterday. There we met two horses – these must be the two horses you have mentioned. They explained some of the new and innovative ideas you have developed here. We were impressed. They sounded very modern and clever. But then, it's true, we became less impressed. They took us to see the rabbit warren which you just said rebelled.'

Cloud paused to catch his thoughts. He also knew he would have to start lying a little.

'Now it's also true that the rabbits rebelled. Just a little bit. I mean, I wouldn't call it a revolution. It was more of a gentle protest. It's true, there was also an unfortunate episode with some horseflies who were sympathetic to the plight of the rabbits. But we were innocent bystanders. We are, I submit, being used as scapegoats for a problem you don't want to face.'

Arouet neighed with haughty disdain.

'That's a lot of pungent manure!'

'What d'you mean?' the First Minister asked Cloud.

'Those rabbits were not goaded into rebelling. By us or anyone else. They were unhappy. They were forced to endure an unnatural life. Yes, it brought them advantages. But it also made a lot of them unhappy. Their rebellion was just waiting to happen. You can't force creatures to go against their natural instincts!'

Lark had been looking more and more excited as he heard Cloud speak. He couldn't contain his thoughts anymore.

'I knew it!' he cried out. 'What have I told you all these years?! It's exactly as I thought. As I predicted! Fascinating! Quite fascinating! Oh, do go on, young dog!'

No one really understood why Lark was so excited.

Cloud continued.

'I know nothing about the village hall. That's news to me. But, from what I have seen of the way you manage things, I can guess what might have happened. If you treat everyone in the same way you treat those rabbits, then it wouldn't surprise me at all if some of them have rebelled. That's how you should explain whatever happened in your village hall. Not by blaming innocent travellers.'

The First Minister was thinking.

'So, you are saying that there are other creatures who were so unhappy that they ruined the Festival of Light by eating all the food.'

Cloud started to feel more confident.

'Perhaps. Or perhaps they were just hungry and jealous. Perhaps your 'them and us' attitude has not worked out so well for them. Just a thought.'

'I agree! I agree!' Lark cut in greedily. 'You are very interesting, young dog. But tell me – do you accept that the events in the village hall were a symptom of the underlying conflict in the complex structure of our society, which makes many creatures feel as if they don't know who they truly are?'

Cloud didn't understand the question.

'Shut up, Lark!' said Arouet. 'I keep telling you, your theories are wacko. Nobody understands them. And those who think they do, hate each other's guts.'

Lark went quiet. As so often, he felt misunderstood.

'First Minister,' continued Arouet, 'you mustn't be deceived by these lies! These reprobates have only just arrived. They obviously want to make mischief. It can't be an accident that they showed up and, inside a day, we are dealing with this sort of disorder and disruption. We, on the other hand, are your trusted counsel. How many times have we proved our worth to you? How many improvements – measurable, outcome-based re- forms – have we made?

'Trusting *rabbits* – whoever heard of such a thing! Most authorities agree that their brains are 80% lettuce! I mean, how could they ever be trusted to look after their own interests? No, that would never work! They need guidance. They need the experience and wisdom of those who have been properly educated.'

'I don't agree with that,' said Cloud.

'What?!' stuttered Arouet.

'You seem to think that those rabbits don't know what's good for them. *That* seems pretty silly to me. And besides, it might just look as if they can't look after themselves because you never give them the chance.'

'What do you mean?' asked the First Minister.

'If Arouet, and others like him, make all the choices, how will the rabbits ever learn – one way or the other? No wonder they're depressed. You give them no sense of self-worth.'

'Are you trying to tell me that if we were to hand over the reins to a lot of hippity hoppity rabbits, they could handle the complex responsibilities which make a better life possible? You are bare-bottom, barking mad! And I'm sorry if I sound a little patronising, but I suspect that you don't really know what I'm talking about.'

'You think I don't understand?' replied Cloud.

'No, I don't think you do. Might I ask what qualifications you have? You certainly don't *sound* very well educated.'

'Perhaps you think of dogs in the same way you think of rabbits!'

'Not at all! Far from it. In fact, we were all taught by a dog – and one who looks much like you!'

Cloud was amazed.

'You were taught by a dog?'

He found it hard to believe that any dog could have devised such an elitist and uncaring way of thinking.

'Indeed. A very great and powerful dog, who has made himself known in many different parts of the world. He has come to know things that most creatures can only dream about. And he does it because he knows that to really understand something, you have to develop your mind. You have to free it from the pleasing distractions around it – food, smells, lounging about in the sun. Only then can your mind become truly powerful and take you to the sort of places that most bumbling creatures think are magical and fanciful.'

Cloud held the horse in his eye.

'What is the name of this dog?'

The horse laughed.

'What a silly question! But it says a lot about you that you ask it. This dog is so elevated that names mean very little. He has many names. I called him Citta. But I have heard him called other names. Manas. Nous. Animo. There are others.'

Cloud's eyes narrowed. Hoo Hoo's hackles began to rise. Mouse's ears flopped, and Porker's stomach rumbled.

They were standing face to face with creatures who had been trained by their enemy. What was going on?

'You are right,' said Cloud to the horse. 'I am not educated. I am a dog. And everything I know I have learned in one place. Which means that there are many things I don't know. But you are wrong. You aren't the great brain you claim to be – you are a horse! Just another animal like me, and you have no right to set yourselves above rabbits or any other creature!'

'How dare you!' cried Arouet. 'You are a prime primitivist! You are a fatuous fool and a criminal to boot!'

The First Minister broke in.

'Now, just a moment, Arouet. Let's not get carried away with an argument. You're always telling me that the true test of something is its results.'

'That's it, First Minister. I... you... we are absolutely right.'

'Well then,' the First Minister went on cheerily, 'rather than discussing it, why don't we put it to the test? Why don't we have a little competition? If I'm impressed by these wandering pilgrims, then I'll let them go free with my map.'

'But what if you aren't impressed?' asked Cloud.

'Then I'll have you executed!'

'Ha!' snorted Arouet to Cloud. 'I bet you didn't think this day would be your last!'

Cloud thought about what the First Minister had said.

'Very well, I accept the challenge. Except I'm not completely sure what the challenge is. We might agree, for all I know.'

'Okay then,' Arouet went on with the wind behind him. 'In that case, let me voice a thought and we'll see if you accept it. This thought is the essence of our approach and underpins all our hard work in the village and across its lands.'

'All right. What's the thought?'

Arouet chuckled to himself.

'It's simple. It's really very simple. 2+2=4. That's my thought. Oh, I know it's simple, but it's also profound! Take another thought – suppose there's a stick. Just lying around, like sticks do. And it's straight. Let's say you pick up the stick in your mouth – I understand that's the sort of thing dogs do – and you carry it about until you come to a pond. You dip the stick in the water, so you can see one end of the stick under the surface. What happens? How does the part of the stick under the water look?'

'It looks bent,' replied Cloud.

'Exactly. But is it *really* bent? It might look it, but is it really? You might be able to *sense* that the stick doesn't really bend, but you can only *know* it by making calculations. In much the same way that we calculate 2+2=4. We calculate the properties of wood. We calculate the properties of water. We calculate the effect that one has on the other... are you following this?' asked Arouet hopefully.

'Yes. I think so,' said Cloud.

'Yes. Good. Then we might also think about the properties of your eyes and how they respond to the wood in the water. We might think about other things (like light). But, however complex our calculation, we can only know by weighing all these things up. *That*, I'm afraid, is a skill that not everyone has.

'To cut it short, we must manage the land in the same way. We look at the land mass, the nature and properties of the terrain. Then we look at the creatures in it – how many are there? What are their capabilities? Their strengths, weaknesses and basic needs? By calculating the answers to these questions we can work out how to make the best use of the land, the creatures and the resources available to them. Like I say, 2+2=4.'

'Mmm,' Cloud muttered.

He was thinking about the argument. It sounded very clever. He could see now why Arouet thought he was cleverer than most other creatures, and better at running things than them.

'Very smart,' he said eventually, 'and I think it all hangs together quite nicely. But I disagree with one thing. Just one thing.'

'What's that?' asked the First Minister.

'That 2+2 *always* equals 4. I would dispute that – just that.'

'But that's elementary – it's absolutely basic. 2+2 *does* always equal 4. It's self-evident.'

'Then that's our competition!' interrupted the First Minister.

'You want me to... ha!' neighed Arouet. 'That's easy enough to prove.'

His eyes hunted about him, looking for any convenient object he could use to make his point.

'Lark! Bobbs! Come here!' he called out, and then

turned back to Cloud and the First Minister. 'You see two horses – one, two. That's two horses. Okay?'

'Okay.'

'You two,' he called out to Hoo Hoo and Mouse. 'Come over here, will you?'

Hoo Hoo and Mouse did as they were asked and stood in a line next to Bobbs and Lark.

'Two dogs!' said Arouet, raising his hairy eyebrows. 'Do you agree?'

'I agree,' said Cloud.

Arouet looked back at his challenger. He couldn't quite believe that anyone – even a rabbit – could be this stupid. He sighed.

'I will spell it out for you. Or rather I will count it out for you.'

The horse began to count the other horses and the dogs, beginning with Bobbs.

'One, two, three…'

Arouet stopped. Mouse had disappeared.

'But… where's the little fellow gone?' he asked.

Cloud seized the moment.

'Er, you hadn't quite finished. And, since my life depends on it, I would be grateful if you would continue. You were saying: one, two, three… or *had* you finished?'

'This is ridiculous,' blurted Arouet. 'There were four creatures here a moment ago – two horses, and two dogs. Two horses plus two dogs equals *four* creatures: one, two, three, four.'

'But – and excuse me if I'm being slow – there are only three creatures: Bobbs, Lark and Hoo Hoo. So, you brought together two horses (Bobbs and Lark) and two dogs (Hoo Hoo and Mouse), and now they add up to three creatures: one, two, three. So, *in this example*, it would seem that 2+2=3. Or am I wrong?' Cloud asked, turning to the First Minister.

The First Minister looked flustered. He thought about it.

'He's right, Arouet. You know, he does seem to be right. In this case, I mean. Only in this case.'

Arouet was growing more indignant.

'This is ridiculous. Quite ridiculous. Look, let me bring your other big-bodied companion into this, and we can soon settle the matter. 2+2=3, what a ridiculous notion!'

Arouet hurried Porker into line with the others. Then he went over the formula once more.

'So, two horses and two dogs, 2+2=4.'

Then he started to count, beginning once again with Bobbs.

'One, two, three, four, fi... ants in my apples! Where did you come from?'

Mouse had reappeared at the end of the line.

'Is everything all right?' asked the First Minister.

'Er…' Arouet stalled, 'er… yes. Quite… quite all right.'

He couldn't quite believe what he was seeing, so he kept looking at Mouse as though he might disappear again. Then he asked the sausage dog in an accusing sort of way:

'Where did you come from?'

Before Mouse could answer, Cloud took the floor.

'I'm afraid I was never very good with numbers, but aren't there five dogs standing before us now? One, two, three, four, five. So, you took two horses (Bobbs and Lark) and two dogs (Hoo Hoo and Porker), and now you have *five* creatures. So *this time* 2+2=5.'

Cloud turned again to the First Minister.

'Or am I wrong?'

The First Minister hesitated.

'Er… no, no… you are… you are correct. He is correct, you know, Arouet. In this case, 2+2 does seem to equal 5. Yes. Though it does seem strange, I have to say.'

Cloud quoted:

There is more at work in heaven and earth
Than any mind can reckon.

Arouet turned angry.

'This is a fix! It's a fix! Those… these… you lot… you

dogs, you are playing one of your notorious tricks and deceiving us! 2+2=4, I tell you! All intelligent and respectable creatures agree it is. It's as plain and simple as oatmeal.'

'Ahem,' said Cloud, 'all I claimed was that 2+2 does not *always* equal 4. I'm sure it does some of the time. But, as we have just seen, at other times, it equals other things, like 3 and 5.

'And I suppose, if you think about it, that makes it harder to make the sort of calculations you were talking about earlier. After all, those calculations must be much harder! Which also makes me wonder if you are taking quite the right approach to the way you manage rabbits.'

'Nonsense.'

'If you look at what just happened, I would think about it differently. If your calculations aren't so watertight, maybe it's just as well to place a bit more faith in the judgement of the rabbits – even if their brains are 80% lettuce?'

The First Minister wasn't comfortable with this suggestion, but it was also clear that Arouet wasn't about to give up on his claim that 2+2=4. The First Minister tried to bring the competition to an end.

'It seems clear to me, that I should not – for now – have the dogs executed. Perhaps this is a matter we should return to when Arouet has had a bit more time to think about it. It might be best if he spends a week or so out in the fields, so he can gather his thoughts.'

Arouet was, for once, without words. His tail no longer swished. His head drooped. He dragged his hooves from their sight, trotting slowly towards the fields.

'That showed him!' said Hoo Hoo to Mouse.

*

After Arouet had left, the First Minister was unsure how to deal with the four pilgrims. They had shaken his faith in the powers of progress. Had he been governing his lands poorly all this time? Had he been seeking advice from the wrong places? Should he just let the pilgrims go on their way? Should he even help them? He didn't know what to do.

Bobbs saw his leader's indecision and the lightly powdered look of worry which concealed his crisis of confidence. Bobbs was more nervous than Arouet. He had spent a lot of time in his shadow, but now was the time to step up.

'Might I remind you,' he said, 'that we don't run these lands on arithmetic. It's important, that's true. But, as you know, First Minister, I think it's more important to observe the way animals behave. We need to take a good look around and use what we can see to reach our judgement. That's a different way of doing things.'

The First Minister was buoyed up.

'Yes, Bobbs. Yes, you are right. Of course, you are. There are many different ways of doing things.'

'Are there?' asked Cloud.

'We use different techniques,' explained the First Minister, 'and we are improving them all the time. Now that I think about it, it's not right to call into question our experiment with modern methods just because of one competition. No. The competition is far from over. I'm not even sure if I'm impressed. You have made me think *twice*. But you have not made me think *again*.'

Cloud was unhesitating.

'In that case we should definitely keep the competition open until you are impressed. It's not 'game over' yet!'

This sounded like fighting talk, thought the First Minister.

'My thoughts, too. And the same penalty still stands!' he added with relish. 'If I'm not impressed, then I'll have you all executed!'

'That goes without saying,' said Cloud.

The First Minister was a little disarmed.

'Well, Bobbs, perhaps you'd like to set things out.'

Bobbs was not as confident as Arouet. He had to compose himself before he spoke.

'My learned colleague, whom it seems you have

managed to baffle and perplex, has many interesting things to say. He and I agree on many things. Many, many things. But I start from a different place. I start by looking at other creatures. I start by studying how they behave. I look at how they behave now. I look at how they have behaved in the past. Then I ask an important question – is there a common pattern in their history of behaviour? To cut a long story short, there is.

'Some say that, deep down, creatures are compassionate and kind. They like to think about other creatures and do nice things for them – like send them on holidays or cuddle them with a hot-water bottle. Sadly, this view is mistaken. If you look long and hard at the history of the way animals behave – as I have done – you will see that this is not true at all. We have to be honest about it, whatever we might want to believe. The truth is that animals are ruled by their appetites. They only ever behave selfishly. Careful study of the past shows us that animals are cruel, callous and calculating. And life is often over in little more than a swish of the tail, cut short by the grim cut and thrust of competition.

'You might find examples of compassion and kindness. But often, if you peer beneath the surface, animals just use it to get on top.

'What do I conclude? The only way we can stop selfishness and violence tearing us all apart is if we all agree to accept a single authority, who will keep us all safe.'

Bobbs nodded at the First Minister when he said these words.

'This might mean we have to sacrifice some of the things we like. We won't get everything we want, but we will get some of it. This is the price of our security and safety. A long and prosperous life depends on a strong leader!

'Those rabbits you and your fellow travellers met yesterday, may have lost some of their freedom, but they have more of it by submitting to the First Minister than they do without him. Without the First Minister, they might be totally free, but their lives would be fleeting and painful. Whoever has set them free – whether it was you or someone else – they have done them more harm than good!'

The First Minister was pleased with Bobbs. So far.

'Hang on! Hang on!' said Cloud. 'You're jumping ahead, aren't you? Isn't this supposed to be a competition? All you have done is tell us what you think. You say that this is all based on watching animal behaviour. Where's your evidence? Where's your proof? I strongly disagree that creatures are always cruel and unkind. Sometimes they are like that. Sometimes they aren't. And some creatures are nastier than others. I have seen kindness and compassion. I have felt it.'

Bobbs came back on the beat.

'But was it *really* kindness and compassion? I'm not saying you won't find creatures who appear that way. I'm saying that you need to think about their motives. Some creatures use kindness and compassion in the same way that others bare their teeth or use their claws. Kindness is a kind of *indirect* aggression for weaker creatures who are not strong enough to fight with their bodies.'

'Prove it,' challenged Cloud.

'What?'

'Prove it! Where's the evidence?'

'The evidence comes from many places – our records of the past, experiences which I have put to the test. I don't rely on just one piece of evidence. I have done lots of tests. With rats, for example.'

'Rats?' asked Porker.

'Yes.'

'You mean rodents?' asked Cloud.

'That's right, rodents – rats. They are very easy to observe. If you put two rats together in a confined space and give them some food, they will fight viciously over it, with no concern for each other. I know it's just one example, but you will find the same thing with other creatures. And, in any case, that simple example tells you everything you need to know about the way creatures behave.'

The First Minister shuffled about on his hooves and, animated by approval, shook his head.

'It sounds very convincing to me!' he said.

'I'd be very interested to see that experiment,' Cloud said. 'You're right; it does sound convincing, but I don't think I could be completely convinced, or prepare myself for execution, until I have. It sounds as if this should be our competition, don't you think? Even if I'm bound to lose!'

Bobbs hurried off to collect some rats. While they waited, the First Minister kept quiet, but eyed Cloud suspiciously; he didn't trust him out of his sight.

Bobbs returned. He was flustered with excitement. He carried an object, which looked like a cat basket made from metal, and which contained rats. He dropped the basket on the ground between Cloud and the First Minister, then circled around it, unsettled and serious.

'Rats,' he said, gesturing towards the basket.

He skipped a little closer to his moveable laboratory and inclined his head towards some sort of vertical drawer.

'There are two compartments,' he explained. 'Each houses a rat, which has not been fed for several days.

I will remove the barrier between the compartments. Then I will drop into the chamber several cuts of raw meat. I submit that, if the rats act out of kindness and consideration for the other, we can expect them to divide the meat equally. If they don't, one will bite, scratch – even kill – the other so they can keep the food for themselves.'

The First Minister hesitated.

'Very good,' he said.

He looked at Cloud to make sure he also had no objections and wasn't about to do something unexpected.

'Yes, very good,' said Cloud.

'Okay then,' said Bobbs.

'Very. Good,' muttered Hoo Hoo under her breath.

Bobbs, very studiously, removed the barrier between the two compartments. The small assembly of horses and dogs could hear scuffling about on the inside. Removing the barrier had, like a scientific starting pistol, awakened the life within. Bobbs collected a few slender cuts of raw meat between his front teeth and dropped them into the basket through a small opening. More silence, then scuffling, came from the interior.

Bobbs stepped back, satisfied that his work was done.

'Now we just have to wait,' he said.

'Well, we'll wait then,' said Cloud.

'Yes. No hurry,' said the First Minister.

Everyone was so mesmerised by the basket and what they imagined was taking place inside it, that they didn't see Hoo Hoo transform into a fruit fly. Neither did they notice an apparently harmless fruit fly gently glide through a small opening in the basket.

It was dark on the inside. Only a few cracks of light gave any outline to the drama ready to erupt. The meat Bobbs had thrown into the basket was lying on the floor. A large black rat twitched its nose and inched towards the food. A clacking mutter came from a dark corner at the other end of the basket, but it was too dark to trace the shape at its source.

'I'm starving!' mumbled the voice.

The visible black rat, scenting the food, said nothing.

'Nothing to bloody eat in days!'

The black rat was stubborn. He gave nothing. All his energies went towards the food.

'And caged too! Imprisoned! What did I do to deserve this, eh? But you – you don't care!'

The voice of the shrouded rat had no other target than the black rat.

'You're just interested in that thing. That piece of food. You know your trouble. D'you know what your problem is? You don't think. That's what it is. You don't stop to think! Here we are, in this box. You, on your side. Me, on mine. Then lo and behold, there is no 'your' side, or 'my' side. We're on the *same* side. You don't stop to think about that, do you? No, you're straight in there.'

The big black rat didn't interrupt his careful study of the meat. Without looking up, he replied:

'You think too much and *talk* too much.'

'One of us has to.'

'Fine, you think. I'll eat.'

'And what about me?'

'What about you?'

'You're just going to eat it? I'm hungry too!'

The black rat shuddered with veiled laughter.

'Don't make me laugh! When have you ever done anything for me? D'you know what you do? All you do is give me ear abuse! Droning on and on. That's what you are – an abuser of ears! You talk like a toad and your tail smells of goat's cheese!'

'Ha!'

'Now be quiet. This looks tasty. And if I don't get to eat it, then I'll eat you. Count yourself lucky that I don't do both!'

The other rat cast about in the dark desperately.

'What if it's poisoned?'

'Then I'll die well fed.'

The hidden rat couldn't take any more. He charged out of his corner, baring his teeth and snarling. As the light caught his body, Hoo Hoo could see that he was a smaller brown rat but, starved to distraction, large enough to cause his cellmate some trouble.

'You sour-smelling patch of vole vomit! Leave that feast for me!'

The two rats fell on each other in a savage skirmish. They rolled on top of each other, in a scrap of gouged fur and flesh. Hoo Hoo could see that this would be a fight to the death. She needed to act quickly.

She settled on the wall of the basket, clearing her throat, so she could project her pronouncement into the scuffle of flesh and bone before her.

'Stop it at once!' she cried.

The black rat was about to bite the ear of the brown rat. He stopped.

'Was that you?' he asked.

'I thought it was you.'

'Don't think like a field mouse! I didn't say anything. It must have been you.'

'But I didn't say anything, either. I was going to bite your belly with my bare teeth. Why would I say, 'Stop it at once!' if I was about to do that?'

The black rat snarled at his enemy.

'You're a coward and a con artist. I see your game – this is a cunning sleight of hand. You're trying to distract me so you can gobble down the goods before I notice. But I won't fall for that sort of trick. I'm going to scratch your eyes out and boil them into a broth!'

'Stop being so insufferably selfish!' called out Hoo Hoo. 'Neither of you spoke. It was me – Biurus!'

A wild pulse of fear broke through the body of each adversary.

'Bi… Biurus,' stammered the brown rat, 'but that's not possible.'

'Of course, it's possible,' snapped Hoo Hoo. 'I'm a god. Gods can do anything.'

'Show yourself!' spat out the black rat.

'Wicked creature!' shouted Hoo Hoo.

She managed to hurl a spark of fire between the two rats, singeing the pieces of meat.

Outside the basket Bobbs raised his eyebrows at Cloud, in a way that said, *Told you so.*

'Don't you know anything?' said Hoo Hoo. 'It's sacrilege to tempt me into sight! I'm your god, not a poster boy!'

The two rats had scurried to opposite ends of the basket in fear.

'What is more, can't you see what's going on here? This meat that has been tossed your way is no chance act. How and why do you think you were caught in this basket in the first place? This is a test. Let's face it, rats have a pretty bad reputation.

'You have been starved and cooped up like this, just to show the world that rats are bad through and through. If you tear each other apart over this meat, you'll confirm every thought everyone has ever had about rats. And the creatures – horses of all things – who have set up this trick will use it to exterminate our race for good. So, you see, one of you might satisfy your hunger for a short while, but you'll harm our whole species for good!'

'Oh Biurus, we didn't know this!' whimpered the brown rat.

'Of course not! That's why I'm a god and you're just a rat!'

'Then what should we do?' asked the black rat.

Hoo Hoo doubled down on her message.

'You must show them that you are reformed creatures. You have to show them that you can see beyond your base animal instincts of survival and self-interest. You must show them you understand that you are part of a bigger world in which interests can coincide – that by sharing and considering other creatures, you become stronger! If you don't understand what I mean, here's what I think you should do...'

Outside the basket, a slightly awkward silence had occupied the air. The First Minister shuffled about uncomfortably. Bobbs stood, smiling and just as unsure what to say. He leaned in to hear what was going on inside the basket. Cloud, Porker and Mouse stood politely in a line, waiting to see if they would be executed.

Finally, Bobbs could take no more.

'It seems to have gone very quiet in there, don't you think?' he said. 'I'm guessing one of the rats has done for the other. I'll lift the lid off now, but don't be shocked by what you see.'

Bobbs went to remove the lid. Just before he did, a small fruit fly flew out.

Bobbs, despite his warning to the others, was so shocked by what he found inside the basket that he spent a whole minute just staring at it. He tried to say something, but the words wouldn't come.

'What is it, Bobbs?' asked the First Minister. 'Is one of the rats dead?'

'Yes, what is going on in that box?' asked Hoo Hoo, who had suddenly popped up from somewhere.

'I...' stuttered Bobbs, '... I... but... I... where on earth did they get a table?'

All the horses and dogs looked over the rim of the basket. Inside, they saw two rats – a large black one and a smaller brown one – seated at a miniature table, laid out with a miniature tablecloth, plates, knives, forks and glasses. The pieces of meat Bobbs had thrown into the basket had been properly cooked, and the rats were sharing it between them. They also appeared to be having a pleasant conversation.

'It was very good of you to cook this for me,' said the black rat.

'Not at all, not at all. I always enjoy your company. The company of good friends draws out the flavour – that's what I say! You're very welcome. I only wish we could have invited a few others. When you think about all the rodents who are scavenging about for food, it really is heart-wrenching.'

'A toast to that!' said the black rat, raising his glass.

'Oh, hello,' said the brown rat, looking up at their observers. 'You must be the one who locked us away together in the basket. D'you know, I think, at first, the pair of us didn't like it very much, but it really gave us the opportunity to get to know each other. We were just sharing an enjoyable dinner. Perhaps you'd care to join us? After all, we want to include everyone!'

'But... but...' Bobbs couldn't find the words, 'but... you're rats.'

This was the most he could manage.

'You sound like very friendly and considerate rats,' said Cloud.

'Thank you,' replied the black rat, 'very kind.'

'You're welcome.'

Bobbs continued to stare at the rats.

'I don't like to say it, particularly after you have done us such a good turn,' said the brown rat to Bobbs, 'but it isn't really polite to stare.'

'These rats don't sound evil and selfish!' called out Hoo Hoo. 'They are lovely, kind and very well brought up! It looks to me as if all that evidence you said you had collected was a bit inconclusive. Maybe you should be a bit more thorough in the future!' she said, admonishing the horse.

'That's right,' said Cloud, 'and I suppose that means we can't say that creatures are *always* selfish and uncaring. Maybe they are some of the time. But not always.'

Cloud turned to the First Minister.

'Wouldn't you say, First Minister?'

The First Minister looked as if he was trying to swallow a whole pumpkin.

'I… I… yes… I… must admit that… it's very…'

'Which makes some of the other things you were saying a bit harder to swallow, too. About the rabbits. And the need for a strong leader. That sort of thing.'

Bobbs hung his head in shame. He turned on his hooves.

'I don't understand it,' he muttered to himself.

He retreated to the stables, where he thought about the miserable and mean nature of existence.

*

The First Minister was, if anything, even more dumbfounded than when Arouet had left in a sulk. He had no idea what to do. This sort of thing had never happened before. In the past, he had always been able to rely on his counsel. Confusion engulfed and overpowered him. He could no longer speak. He could no longer think. In fact, he could barely move. Instead, he just smiled at his guest dogs. It was a smile sketched into his face by fear and madness.

The dogs found it a bit unnerving.

'Is everything okay, First Minister?' asked Cloud.

The First Minister didn't reply. He just smiled.

As things descended into silence and insanity, Lark saw his chance.

'First Minister,' he said, 'you have known about my ideas for a long time, but you have ignored them because Arouet and Bobbs had a stronger claim to your attention. These curious wayfarers have managed to show you that their ideas were all bunk – or at least, they had not carried their insights to the most logical and scientific conclusion! This is what I always thought. (You wouldn't listen, but never mind that now.) So it's imperative...'

This was all too much for the First Minister.

'Enough!' he cried. 'Yes, yes, you can have your go.

Prove to me whatever you want!'

Lark was interrupted, but not wrong-footed.

'Right. Well then. In that case I hope I can show you another way. A new way. Perhaps, even a way that these foreigners might know and understand.'

'Perhaps,' said Cloud, who still found Lark curious, 'what is your new way?'

'Both my friends were right in some ways, but wrong in others,' replied Lark. 'Like them, I believe that we can create a better life for our animals. We just differ in our methods.

'Arouet believed that there was a way to manage the interests of our animals by cleverly measuring and calculating everything. He thought that if creatures paid other creatures to produce everything more efficiently, everyone would benefit. Instead, he just enslaved all our rabbits and made everyone selfish! Bobbs, on the other hand, thought that being selfish was natural, and – because he was nervous – thought that all the creatures would see the need for a strong leader, like the First Minister, who would make things safe for everyone.

'But the truth of the matter is that, if you want to benefit everyone, you have to involve everyone, not just a few creatures. Like Arouet, I think we can all be more productive – but that doesn't mean we have to enslave our rabbits! Everyone can benefit if we all work together, if we co-operate and share it out equally.'

The First Minister was a bit concerned about this idea.

'How would that work?'

Lark's eagerness reached a new pitch of fever.

'Let me show you, First Minister. Let me show you. The really good part is that you won't need to do any more ruling. You can be equal to everyone else in the village and across its lands. Give me a few minutes, and I'll collect as many of the village animals as I can find. Then, we'll put the idea into practice. I may need to use a little force, at first – but you'll see that all I'm doing is helping the creatures to see the truly *logical* and *just* result of all the work they have seen in the village.'

The First Minister was reluctant, but almost past caring.

'Oh, all right then,' he said.

Hoo Hoo sidled up to Cloud.

'Something tells me that we won't need to do very much for this competition.'

Cloud was still trying to understand Lark, but his mind was moving in the same direction.

'I think you might be right, Hoo Hoo.'

Twenty minutes later Lark returned with a long line of village residents in tow. Rabbits, sheep, dogs, cats, a few toads, cows, goats, pigs, more horses, a fat hamster, a family of roe deer, two Peruvian alpacas, and a self-important but very stupid peacock, all assembled on the First Minister's lawn.

The crowd made a hubbub, which altogether sounded like moaning.

'There we are,' said Lark. 'I have managed to get a broad spread of creatures. But to make this real, you must take part in the exercise, too, First Minister.'

Again, the First Minister was reluctant.

'Oh… okay,' he said.

'Right, so if you just stand there,' said Lark, ushering the First Minister to stand among the other creatures. 'Now everyone, this is an experiment, but it could lead to great things! Basically, I want to set you all free. Which means you need to do exactly what I tell you!'

'Then how are we going to be free?' asked one of the roe deer.

Lark thought.

'Just trust me. From now on, we're all going to accept a few things.'

'What things?' asked the roe deer.

'I didn't vote for them,' said the fat hamster.

'You don't know what they are yet!'

'That's how I know I didn't vote for them!'

'Just bear with me.'

'I thought we were going to have a say in everything?' asked one of the Peruvian alpacas.

'Well… yes, yes, you will… but you just need to accept what I am… for now… just bear with me.'

The creatures grumbled a bit, but they allowed Lark to continue.

'Right, here's the idea. We're all going to run the village together. For each other.'

'Don't we do that already?' asked the fat hamster.

'Not the way that… not really, you see. At the moment, there are a few who run things (the horses, for example), and then others who work for them. Let's face it, the horses do a lot better than you lot – and I should know, I'm a horse!'

The other horses scowled at Lark.

'But if you're a sheep, a duck, or even a beaver, yes, you might get a basic living, but all that work you put in – well, where does it go? Not to you, I can tell you that much! Things are very unequal in our little village!'

'I agree,' said a cow.

'All I want to do is even things up. We can all benefit from the clever ways of earning a living which horses like Arouet have helped to develop. But the answer – this is the really clever bit – is that we should share everything. No one should own anything.'

'I agree,' said the cow again.

'No one?' said the First Minister.

'Absolutely no one,' said Lark. 'We will own every-thing in common.'

'What does that mean?' asked one of the roe deer.

'It's very simple – take our friends the alpacas here. When they produce wool, we will share it with the en-tire community. When our friends the cows produce milk, they will share it with everyone. And not only that – we will all have a say in how things are run and organised. So that means the burden of running things won't fall on the First Minister. He can work like ev-eryone else.'

Some of the pigs began to honk in a restless sort of way.

'But we can't work in the same way as other crea-tures. We need the rabbits to run errands.'

'So you can get fat on all the work we are doing?!' called out a plucky hare.

'I don't like working for the pigs,' said a brave young bunny. 'They are bossy, unhygienic and their nasal hair is out of control!'

The fat hamster started to get worried when he heard what the rabbits were saying. It occurred to him that if the rabbits went on strike, the pigs would start looking for alternatives.

'Well, I'd be no good at the rabbits' job!' he called out,

just to make things clear.

'I agree,' said a cow.

'What about where we live?' asked a goat. 'If we're sharing everything, will we have homes to call our own? My family have lived on our stretch of the mountainside for ten generations.'

A ruckus of grumbling broke over the assembled creatures.

'You will still have your own places to live. You may not exactly 'own' it in the same way you did before,' explained Lark in a reassuring sort of way.

There was uproar.

'This is revolution!'

'I'm not sharing my pond with a hamster – never!' said a toad.

'Sheep wool and alpaca wool are quite different,' said one of the Peruvian alpacas, 'and I don't need to tell you which is better quality!'

'Peacocks don't work!' said the peacock, who was a bit slow to keep up with the conversation.

'If the First Minister doesn't decide how things should be run, who does?' asked a pig.

'We all do,' said Lark. 'We'll do it together. Through a council or something.'

'But I don't trust the cows to take sensible decisions. They're cloth-eared and really stupid! All they do is eat grass all day.'

'That's rich, coming from a pig!' said a cow.

'All you do is eat and poo everywhere.'

'At least I don't wallow in it.'

'You smell of herring!'

Lark interrupted.

'We're straying from the discussion.'

'And I'm not going to eat grass all day – what kind of life is that? It all starts like that. One day it's grass, then before you know it, you're on a diet of quinoa!'

'Grass is good for you,' replied a cow indignantly. 'It's full of nutrients.'

'Do you mean we would still be working for…?' asked a rabbit, who sounded befuddled, 'who would we be working for?'

'Exactly!' cried a pig. 'I see the way the silage is spread! You'll turn us all into cows or horses, or some sort of strange cow-horse.'

'I'm a rabbit!' said a rabbit.

'I'm a rabbit, too!' said a cat.

'No you aren't – you're a cat!'

'Really?' said the cat. 'Well, that's disappointing. Can't I be a rabbit?'

'In this new world, you can be whatever you want!' said a cow. 'That's what the horse said. (If he's still a horse, that is.)'

'It doesn't work quite…' Lark began.

'In that case, I'm a rabbit,' said the cat.

'I'm a fat hamster and proud!' said the fat hamster. 'And this is a very silly experiment, if you ask me!'

'Peacocks don't work!' the peacock repeated.

'No, no, you don't understand,' Lark tried to explain, 'you won't work for…'

'… I agree,' said a cow.

'Well, I disagree,' said a pig.

'What about?' asked the fat hamster.

'I notice the sheep haven't said very much so far,' said one of the alpacas suspiciously.

'I refuse to be a horse!' said a pig.

'Is the cat still a rabbit?' the fat hamster asked a dog.

'Here, here,' said a sheep.

'No, no, you don't understand,' called out Lark. 'I'm saying that, as a group, we must seize the means of production!'

'What?' asked a rabbit.

'Keep your hooves off my udders!' called out a cow.

'Right! That does it,' exclaimed a pig. 'I'm not putting up with this anymore. I'm raising an army of pigs and boars to put a stop to this before it goes any further!'

The pigs retreated, so they could prepare for war.

Lark could see that his experiment was failing. He was alarmed that his suggestion had caused civil war.

Increasingly desperate, he thought that words and reason were no longer any use. He decided he would have to resort to force.

'Comrades!' he called out. 'You must break off your chains and marshal your animal instincts – we must take the village in a military coup!'

All the creatures looked confused.

Lark's head drooped.

'Oh, it's no good,' he said. 'This village is too set in its ways.'

He slumped off to think about what had happened, muttering, 'Nobody understands me!' under his breath.

*

The First Minster was troubled now that his three main counsellors had come up short in the competition. Lark, he had never really trusted, but he had come to rely heavily on Arouet and Bobbs. The travellers had cast everything into doubt.

'I won't pretend to understand your ways,' he said to Cloud and his companions, 'but you have clearly had a powerful effect here.'

The First Minister stalled.

'I... don't misunderstand me. I keep my own counsel, but I wonder, if you were in my position... I mean, if you were in charge here, how would you... not that I'm... what would you *do?*'

Hoo Hoo didn't hesitate.

'First of all I wouldn't place all my faith in a bunch of horses who are full of themselves!'

Cloud was still trying to make sense of the horses and their unusual experiments. He shared Hoo Hoo's view that the horses thought too highly of themselves and had too much power over everyone. But he was even more curious now that he knew they had been trained by Animo. He had only ever heard rumours about Animo – about the hold he had over places and the creatures who lived in them. It seemed to him that he had just seen up close how the trickster spirit operated. He used creatures who claimed they possessed a secret or special knowledge, and they used that knowledge to control everyone else. Did Animo use this knowledge to bend everyone to his will? Was that his plan?

It also made him wonder about Easthill. Now that he thought about it, when Francis had arrived in Easthill he had made much of the *knowledge* he had learned on his travels. Many of the recommendations Francis had made sounded a little like the schemes of these horses.

Seeing what had happened with these horses only made Cloud more determined to see his journey through to the end.

Cloud tried to sound moderate.

'I'm sure you took their advice in the best of faith. But

Hoo Hoo's right. Why did they manage to have such a hold over you? They are just creatures, like any of us – and they have their limits and faults, too, even if they wanted to convince you that their answers were faultless. You should also treat your own creatures better. The rabbits, for example. I just don't believe you need to enslave them in that sort of work – if you help them to develop their natural abilities and interests, they will be happy and everyone will benefit. But that's just what I think. Maybe you should listen to them.'

The First Minister didn't say anything. He nodded his head thoughtfully.

'It's your choice,' he said eventually, 'and it sounds as if you have no need for it. I can also understand why you might prefer to throw it back in my face. But I would still like to offer you my map. My cartographers were meticulous in putting it together – they had many of their own adventures, I can tell you! And it shows the way to the Lake of Gifts.'

Hoo Hoo gave a disdainful low growl.

The First Minister had more to say:

'Your visit has made me think about this map in a different way. At one time I thought that with many maps like this one, we would have a complete picture of the world. Except now I see it in another light: the map isn't an answer; it's a useful tool, which shows the way, and where the way leads, no one can say.'

Cloud bowed before the First Minister.

'Then I think we should accept such a useful gift, especially when it is given with such grace.'

The bear

Cloud and his fellow pilgrims picked up their trail, on the far side of the village. A few grateful rabbits hopped about them, until the path took a sudden route up the mountainside.

The dogs followed the trail with a hint of trepidation. The weather had started to change now that they were heading into autumn. They could feel the summer retreating and sense the winter it would leave behind. Would they reach the end of their journey by then? They didn't know, but none of them welcomed the thought of treading through these hills when they were capped with snow and ice.

The path climbed. It reached a basin valley shadowed by sheer edges on both sides. The valley ended with a short scramble up to high moorland and followed a long arc with views down to another valley, populated by nothing but a minor river and occasional stone ruins.

They had said very little since leaving the village. Was it the anticlimax that followed their triumph at the competition? Or a shared sense of a journey not yet complete?

'How much further can it be, I wonder?' Porker asked eventually, voicing what they were all thinking. 'The days are getting shorter. And it feels as if we've been walking for ages.'

'We'll get there in the end,' replied Cloud.

'You always get somewhere in the end. But when's the end?!' said Porker.

They stopped, as if to consider the matter. They looked down from the ridge at the sun, which was descending for the day.

'What if there's nothing to find?' said Porker.

'You're just hungry. As usual!' said Hoo Hoo.

'No, seriously – do you never stop to think, what if *it* doesn't even exist? What if we never arrive? What if we just keep going? I don't think I could live all my life like this. I'm not at all sure I could.'

'Oh, give him a marshmallow to munch will you someone!' called out Hoo Hoo.

'It's late,' said Cloud. 'And I think we're all tired.'

Cloud set out on the path, but, in his mind, Porker's doubts were making mischief. What if Porker was right? What if they didn't get there in the end? What if there was no Lake of Gifts? What if the black dog was just a stray dog? What if there was no Balder? What if there was no *Thumbald*? These were the dark thoughts that Cloud didn't want to face up to. If they were true, what had he done? He had abandoned Easthill when it was most threatened so he could go on a pointless adventure. Far from securing himself in the only place he could call home, he had done the opposite; he had cut himself loose from it.

Cloud wanted to believe in what he was doing, but he couldn't ignore a little voice at the back of his mind which wanted to tell him he was looking for something in which to believe.

The company's mood didn't improve when they saw the way down from the ridge. The sun had little more than half an hour before it set. The path wound down into the valley below, where it snaked along the banks of a small river. Then the path and the river collided with a much larger and mightier current, which, as far as any of them could see, there was no way to cross.

They hurried down to the water, with the light fading about them. They were all slightly panicked, hoping they wouldn't have to spend a night out in the open. Then there was the river. It was vast, and they couldn't see how it would create anything other than a detour for them. They couldn't see any bridges. They might just about swim across, but the current looked very strong, and it was the widest river any of them had ever seen.

'What about the map?' Mouse asked, his voice shredded with worry. 'Won't that show a way across the river?'

They consulted the map. Their hopes were raised when they saw that it clearly marked out a large bridge, which linked an island in the centre of the river with both shores.

'According to the map, the bridge and island are only a little way to our north,' said Cloud, inclining his head in a northerly direction.

They walked for another ten minutes. Sunset had turned to dusk, and the distinct shapes of the world around them blurred at the edges and foreshadowed haunting spectres of the night.

Hoo Hoo gave a cry.

'I see it! I see it! I can see the island!'

'Are you sure?' Porker replied, squinting through the darkness.

'It's there! Can't you see it, biscuit brain?!'

They all narrowed their eyes, so they might detect through the dimness. Straining their powers of sight, they could just see the island anchored in the silence of the coursing water.

'Yes! Yes, I see it now!' said Cloud. 'But where's the bridge?'

There was no bridge.

They raced forward at a trot until they had checked from every angle available to them: no bridge ran out to the island. As far as they could see in this light, no bridge crossed the waters on the other side of the island either.

'Unless there's another island?' mused Cloud.

'There's only one island on the map,' Mouse came back.

'I don't trust that map!' said Hoo Hoo. 'Those horses didn't know their horseshoes from their hooves! I wouldn't trust them to pull a cart, let alone mark out a map! I'll soon find a way across this little puddle!'

Hoo Hoo was about to make a move when they heard a noise. It sounded like someone shushing them.

'Shh!' came the noise out of the darkness.

'Was that you?' Hoo Hoo asked Porker.

'It wasn't me,' said Porker.

'What about you?' Hoo Hoo said, turning to Mouse.

'Shhh!!' came the voice again, this time a little louder.

Hoo Hoo let the admonition wash over her.

'Well, 'shhh!' to you too!' she said loudly into the

creeping night.

'No, no, you don't understand,' said the disembodied voice. 'You must keep quiet, or you'll wake the bear!'

'What bear?' asked Hoo Hoo.

'The bear who lives on the island. He's always hungry. And if he hears your voices, then he might swim out here and eat you all. By the looks of things, some of you would make quite a feast!'

Porker tried to feel offended.

'So you aren't a bear?' asked Cloud.

'Why would I be a bear?' asked the voice.

'You could be tricking us!' said Cloud.

'Bears generally don't go in for tricks. They just eat you. That's my experience, anyway.'

'He doesn't sound like a bear,' whispered Mouse.

'How do you know? When did you last hear a bear?' said Porker.

The dogs tried to make out the shape of the voice, but they couldn't.

'I'm not a bear. Really, I'm not a bear!' said the creature who wasn't a bear.

'Then what are you?'

'I'm a hedgehog.'

'A hedgehog?'

'That's right, a hedgehog. A hog of the hedge.'

'Show yourself!' ordered Hoo Hoo.

'I am showing myself. I'm down here. You just can't see me.'

They all peered into the undergrowth, where they could just about make out the perky nose of a face escaping a ball of bristles.

'Oh!' said Mouse.

'Yes, I see you now. But with all those prickles aren't you a public hazard?'

'Believe me, I wish we didn't have prickles. I only wish we didn't.'

'Why? Don't they protect you?'

The hedgehog sounded uncomfortable.

'I do wish we could have this conversation somewhere else. Somewhere *more private*. The bear has very sensitive ears – and he loves the taste of hedgehog. As a matter of fact, he likes nothing more.'

'I'm sorry to cause you distress,' said Cloud to the hedgehog, 'but we are wayward pilgrims. We were hoping to find our way across the river before nightfall, or else find somewhere to shelter. Our map tells us that there should be a bridge hereabouts, but we can't find it. Perhaps you can help us, then we'll be out of your hair… I mean, spikes… or bristles… whatever they are.'

The hedgehog sniffed its nose and stared at the dogs.

'Oh dear,' he said, 'oh dear, oh dear.'

'What is it?'

'Oh dear, oh dear, oh dear.'

'What? What's the matter?'

'The thing is, there was a bridge right about here. It ran out to the island, and then across to the other side. But the bear destroyed it. He likes to keep his prey captive on the island, you see, and one too many of them escaped to freedom over the bridge. So, he destroyed it. Oh dear, oh dear.'

'So,' said Cloud, sensing the truth, 'is there another way across the river?'

The hedgehog shook his head or shuddered – it wasn't easy to tell which.

'Not that I know. I have never travelled far enough to find one, anyway. And hedgehogs get about more than you might think!'

Gloom swept around the company of dogs, like mist on the surface of the river. Having come so far with little to eat and facing the prospect of no refuge for the night, plus a river barring their way, it looked like their luck had run out.

'What are we going to do?' asked Mouse plaintively.

'I've had it up to my damp ears with this journey!' exclaimed Porker. 'It's just tiring and filled with root vegetables – it's no fun at all!'

Cloud thought he should show some leadership.

'My dear friend,' he said to the hedgehog, 'as you can

see, we've come to a difficult pass. We need to find a way we can get across the river. We won't do that to-night – I think that's clear. So, for now, we need to find somewhere we can rest for the night. D'you know if there are any refuges, farms, villages, or ruined cottages around here? Even a wooden hut would do. Anything like that?'

The hedgehog snuffled.

'There's nothing quite like that which you will reach in less than a few hours. But you could... I mean, you could...'

The hedgehog wasn't sure of himself.

'... sorry... I was going to say that you could stay at the Hedgehog Centre. It isn't much, but it was built to accommodate lots of hedgehogs, as well as guests. Unfortunately, we're holding a convention at the moment – this is really why I was so worried about all the noise; if the bear descends on the centre over the next few days, he'll be treated to a banquet! Still, I'm sure we could make room for you. We may even be able to provide you with a little to eat. A little. Not much.'

'Well, thank you,' said Cloud, urging the gratitude of his companions. 'That sounds like a rare treat, particularly in the circumstances.'

'A Hedgehog Centre?' asked Porker.

'That's right, it was built... though, forgive me, d'you

mind if I explain en route? I'd rather get away from Bear Island as soon as we can. We've already lingered long enough.'

The dogs and the hedgehog left the bank of the river. Hoo Hoo even agreed to carry the hedgehog on her back so they could slip away more swiftly.

The dogs learned that the Hedgehog Centre had been built in the heart of a wood, which rose up the steep banks of land in the shadow of a small gorge, cut out by the flow of the river. The centre had been completed only a few years ago, after concerns about emotionally troubled hedgehogs had grown. Many cases of hedgehogs experiencing anxiety and crises of confidence had been reported. So, the community thought it would be a good idea to build a retreat, which could be used to bring their fellow creatures together and help them overcome their problems.

The centre was tucked away inside the walls of a ruined building. Trees had collapsed on top of it, and shrubs, bushes, and bracken had overgrown the area. The hedgehogs had built a hideaway series of neatly panelled huts under the overgrown wreckage. It had a small atrium, a circular space for meditation (complete with a water feature), and a range of hospitality suites and conference rooms.

The only problem was the bear, who, it seemed, was

especially keen on eating hedgehogs. When the bear had first found the island, he had caught a hedgehog rummaging about nearby. He tried to eat it, but, with a prickled tongue, he spat it out in a cry of pain. Where other creatures concluded that hedgehogs weren't worth the trouble, the bear became more determined than ever. He ate them. And kept eating them.

More than anything, the bear enjoyed overcoming the obstacle of the bristles. He found brutal ways to shave his victims of their thorny coats, so he could get to the flesh underneath. The harder it was to consume his prey, the more he pursued it.

Sadly, this meant that the Hedgehog Centre, which had been built as a refuge from emotional turmoil, was beleaguered by the presence of a bear who would have eaten the entire convention of hedgehogs given the right opportunity.

It surprised the dogs to hear that the centre was still popular. Their host struggled to explain it, too, but he was troubled by the thought that hedgehogs, in general, were becoming more and more fatalistic. They were, so to speak, resigned to a future as the main course for a bear with a very singular bent of mind.

'What's your name?' Porker asked the hedgehog.

'George,' said George.

He had been one of the founding members of the

centre, and, for all its troubles, he wanted to preserve it.

Worry had left its mark on George, and the community as a whole. Which was sad to see because the hedgehogs were naturally gentle, peaceful and scholarly. They had their pastimes. They liked to discuss things, like art and sweetcorn. They liked to think about the welfare of other animals. So, it was a shame that they lived under a pall of gloom.

George and two of his friends (Gert and Maud) helped the dogs to settle into one of the dormitory huts, and brought them some food: roast chestnuts, sweetcorn, pepper and couscous, fried with earthworms and garlic. It was surprisingly replenishing, and the hedgehogs were good company, despite all their worries and the threat that hung over them.

'To tell you the truth,' said George, after they had been chatting for a little while, 'there aren't that many of us left. Altogether, I mean. We are even starting to wonder if hedgehogs have a future at all.'

The dogs were dog-tired, but they all felt sorry for the hedgehogs. If only by the looks they exchanged, Cloud and Hoo Hoo started to peg out a plan.

At last, they all settled down for the night. The faint, and faintly comforting, sound of hedgehog snoring came from the dormitory next to them.

'We need to do something about this bristle-baiting

bear!' said Hoo Hoo to Cloud.

'I couldn't agree more,' replied Cloud.

Hoo Hoo's eyes glimmered in the darkness.

*

The next morning the dogs gathered round a communal 'creative space' to have their breakfast. Hedgehogs shuffled about, nibbling on seeds, greeting each other with polite inclinations of the head, and for those who were still tired, falling asleep in the middle of a conversation. George sat with the dogs.

'I was thinking about your situation, so I asked some other hedgehogs, who live a little further afield,' he said. 'One of them told me that there used to be another bridge over the river, but it's over thirty miles out of your way.'

'It's all right,' replied Hoo Hoo confidently. 'We don't need a bridge. We've decided to cross the river by boat.'

The other dogs looked at Hoo Hoo. This was news to them.

'What boat, you flappy-eared fleapit!? We don't have a boat!' said Porker.

'I don't think anyone around here has a boat. Not anymore,' explained George.

'That's all right, we'll make one,' she replied cheerily.

George the hedgehog pulled a face, which, with the wrinkle of a nose, hinted that he didn't think that was a very good idea.

'You aren't the first to think of it. Let me see – there was a rabbit, a squirrel, a fox, a stoat, and a pheasant. They all tried. But it didn't go well for any of them.'

'Why? What happened?'

'They got eaten. By the bear.'

'Does anything in this neck of the woods not get eaten by the bear?' asked Porker.

'He will eat almost anything. He's a very greedy bear. We have tried to reason with him – and in a very reasonable way, too. 'Is there anything we can do for you, bear?' we call across to the island. 'Perhaps we can come to some agreement?' 'No!' he replies. 'I'm going to eat you all! Especially all the creatures disguised as hairbrushes!' We've come to think that the bear had never met a hedgehog before he came to the island. In fact, he seems to have come from a strange place. Among the little snippets he yells out at us, he often tells us that he knows how the world really is, and that he believes in nothing but eating his fill and not giving a plucked bristle for anyone or anything else. 'I believe in nothing!' he shouts at us. 'Nothing but the sating of my stomach – because there is nothing else!"

Cloud didn't like the sound of the bear. Where had he learned to think like that? This sort of talk filled him with foreboding.

Hoo Hoo was undaunted.

'Then it's about time that someone gave this bear a boot in his hungry haunches! He's got no right to go about eating hedgehogs! All creatures need a space they can call their own, where they can thrive. The rampant greed of this grizzly, spike-eating son of a manic muncher needs halting now! You hedgehogs need to be free to enjoy yourselves.'

George the hedgehog was measured. Experience had taught him to show restraint and not get too excited by anything. But hearing these words, his bristles rippled with excitement.

'I… well, I… that sounds very… I should say… that sounds… agreeable.'

'You bet it does!' said Hoo Hoo, jumping to a state of action.

An elderly hedgehog, who had been sleeping peacefully in the corner, opened his eyes, smiled, said 'Very good', then fell asleep again.

'How will you do it?' asked George, who still couldn't quite believe what he was hearing.

'That's easy!' said Hoo Hoo. 'I'll just head down to the river, shout a few insults at him. Then, when he gets annoyed and tries to come after me, I'll turn into a shoal of piranha fish, and strip him to the bone! What about that, then? Pretty good, huh! Pretty good!'

George the hedgehog blinked.

'Did you say you would turn into a shoal of piranha fish?'

Before George could fully form the thought that Hoo Hoo was a bottom short of its tail, Cloud stepped in.

'My friend has some excellent ideas, but they often need developing a little. Rest assured, though, we will deal with this bear.'

'I'm a piranha fish!' said Hoo Hoo, in a sort of crazed delirium.

Cloud was still troubled by the bear (something told him he ought to be worried), but he kept these thoughts to himself for now, and tried to build on Hoo Hoo's moment of inspiration.

'Let's think about this, shall we?' reasoned Cloud. 'This bear has done some terrible things. Eating other creatures doesn't show a strong sense of community. Then again, I'm not sure it's right to pay him back in kind. Besides, I don't know how your digestion would cope with a whole bear – you don't eat much at the best of times! I wonder, instead, if we need to reform the bear's character. We need to teach him a lesson. And who better to do that than his dinner?'

Hoo Hoo pinched her eyes.

'What did you have in mind, Master?'

'It's more a case of who I have in mind.'

Cloud turned to Mouse.

'But I'm not a hedgehog,' objected Mouse.

'It's just a question of imagination. You can be made to look like one – and a very large, sausage-shaped one. This bear likes a lot of food. He also likes hedgehogs. So why don't we give him a large hedgehog for dinner.'

'I don't want to be his dinner.'

'Don't be modest, Mouse. You'll make a very good dinner.'

'I wouldn't eat him,' said Porker dismissively.

Cloud turned to George the hedgehog.

'I guess you must have a few spare bristles?'

George was shocked.

Working together, Cloud revealed all the details in his brain. George looked slightly less shocked, but not exactly convinced. Mouse couldn't see how he wouldn't get eaten.

But they decided to give it a try.

*

After George had gathered up some bristles, it didn't take long. By lunchtime they were walking down towards the river, where they hoped to find the bear feeling hungry and irritable. George didn't say much as they walked, but he kept glancing around at Mouse. He had never seen a sausage dog dressed as a hedgehog before.

On the riverbank, looking out to the island, was a

pile cap sticking out of the undergrowth. It had once been the foundation for the bridge, but now it was often used by birds who languished about on it as they kept their eye on sources of food in the currents below. Mouse, disguised as a large hedgehog, climbed onto the pile cap in full view of the bear, and appeared to go to sleep.

'Okay, here goes,' said Hoo Hoo.

She turned into a red kite, and flew over to the island, where she started hunting about for the bear. It didn't take long to find him. He was asleep in a giant fuzzy ball under a tree, partly submerged in a blanket of twigs and wild privet. She could see his head poking up, as he snored very loudly. Hoo Hoo settled on a branch above him and threw some conkers at his head. It had no effect. She threw some more.

The bear was gone to the world.

'This is ridiculous,' she said, and flew down to land in front of him. She started pecking him on the nose violently.

'Wake up you belly in a mop! Stop snoring! Stop snoring! Can't you hear me?'

In her fury of pecking, she didn't notice the bear open its eyes.

'Snoring?' said the bear. 'Sn… snoring. Wha… I was not snoring! I do not snore! I'm a very quiet and gentle bear.'

Hoo Hoo fluttered onto a higher branch.

'You were snoring. Loudly.'

The bear ripped up the privet in a fit of rage.

'I was not snoring! I was not!'

He stomped about a bit. Then he said, a bit more calmly:

'I'm a heavy breather. That's all.'

Hoo Hoo flew onto another branch, so she could look the bear in the eye.

'I knew you'd gone soft.'

'Soft! What? Me? I'm a bear. I am not soft. Just hairy. There's a big difference! Who are you, anyway? Stop annoying me, or I'll eat you.'

'I thought you didn't like hedgehogs?'

The bear was incensed.

'Hedgehogs! Hedgehogs! I hate every last prickly pair of them! They are deceptive, mouth-stabbing, anti-eating creatures of cunning! I'm going to eat every last one of them and build a home from their stupid offensive spikes. I'm going to fashion their skin into a ball and invent a new competitive sport to bash it about. That'll teach them!'

'*Really*!' said Hoo Hoo. 'I thought you'd turned slack.'

'Slack? I eat them at a record-breaking rate of consumption! I'm a world-beating scoffer of those spike-covered cheaters!'

'Then what's that very fat hedgehog doing sunning itself right in front of your island?'

'In front of the island? What do you...?'

'... There!' said Hoo Hoo, showing the way.

The bear bounded a few steps to the riverbank and looked out over the river. He saw Mouse on the pile cap.

'He's a very large, fat hedgehog,' said Hoo Hoo, whispering in the bear's ear.

The bear took time to appreciate the moment's enormity. His eyes focused and bulged. Then his whole body fumed.

'He's the fattest hedgehog I've ever seen!'

The bear didn't know what to do with himself. He turned a complete circle, blinked then checked to see that the hedgehog was still there (or perhaps that his eyes weren't deceiving him).

'He's sitting there. He's just sitting there! What cheek! But he doesn't know what's coming, does he? I'll eat him. Ha! Just sitting there. Who does he think he is? Should I eat him whole or in bits? Should I stir-fry him with nuts or just have him plain? No, plain. Plain hedgehog is always best! Ha ha hmm. See how fat he is! He's really very fat! Ha ha brrr!'

The bear went on talking to himself like this, rubbing his paws and trying not to salivate. His mood moved between outrage at the effrontery of the 'hedge-hog', and overexcitement at the thought of eating it. He stumbled about on all fours, led by the unsteady state of his mind. Again and again, he looked over the water at the pile cap, to make sure his eyes weren't deceiving him and that a fat hedgehog really was sleeping brazen-ly in the open. Then he couldn't decide whether to just eat the hedgehog whole, then and there, or capture him and spend some time gloating over his victim before giving his stomach satisfaction.

'Yes, yes, that's it,' said the bear eventually. 'I'll put him in a bag.'

He rummaged around the island until he found an old sack he used for catching hedgehogs in batches.

'What are you going to do?' the red kite asked the bear.

'I'm going to eat it. Yes, oh yes – I'm going to *eat...* to eat it!'

The bear growled.

With his sack wrapped around his bushy neck, the bear waded out into the river and swam through the currents with all his power. His eyes were fixed on the large hedgehog.

The capture happened so swiftly and effortlessly that most of the witnesses missed it. The bear climbed out of the water, bustled urgently towards the hedgehog, threw the sack over him, and tied him up in a trap.

'Was that meant to happen?' George the hedgehog asked Cloud.

Cloud thought for a second.

'No,' he answered.

Even Hoo Hoo was slightly taken by surprise. She hadn't found a place to settle, and so she fluttered her wings mid-flight, as the bear returned to the water, carrying the sack and its hapless quarry on his back.

The bear muttered as he swam.

'Brr… big fat hedgehog… big… fat… brr… big fat hedgehog.'

Cloud gestured to Hoo Hoo that she should follow the bear and do whatever she could to help. Hoo Hoo swung about in a wide arc and flew back towards the island. The bear waded back to land with the same haste, and trotted back to his lair, where he threw the sack on the ground.

'Heavy for a hedgehog! You are a fat one,' he said.

Mouse was finding it uncomfortable dressed as a hedgehog, and even more uncomfortable dressed as a hedgehog on the inside of a sack.

'Where am I?' he called out, but to the bear's ears it just sounded like a muffled sound.

'Oh, be quiet. I wouldn't bother talking, if I were you.

There's no need.'

Hoo Hoo managed to track down the bear, and settled on another branch, this time out of sight, so she could keep watch on events.

The bear nudged Mouse through the sack with his nose.

'Brr... what did you think you were doing, you silly fat hedgehog? Just sunning yourself right in front of me. Right in front of me! Very silly. Brr. Didn't they tell you a bear lives on the island? No. No, they didn't. Well, they should have! Because I'm no ordinary bear. I'm a hedgehog-eating one. And it's not possible to eat enough hedgehogs! My hedgehog stomach is never full! And you are a very fat and juicy hedgehog. So, I'm going to eat you!'

The bear lifted the sack with his teeth, so that Mouse fell in a tumble on the ground. He looked very dishevelled and clumps of hedgehog bristle, which Cloud had attached to his back, had started to come away.

'What's this?' asked the bear, pointing out the baldness.

Mouse examined himself to discover his disguise falling apart. He thought quickly.

'The stress,' he said awkwardly.

'The stress?' bellowed the bear.

'At the thought of being eaten.'

'Oh,' said the bear, who sounded just a little surprised, 'yes… yes, well you should be stressed. I *am* going to eat you. And I will eat you uncooked, alive without any nutty garnish, thank you very much!'

The bear thought.

'Only you mustn't get too stressed. Not if it makes your hair fall out, anyway. Don't get stressed, you hear!' the bear shouted at Mouse. 'Let me tell you something; that's all part of the fun of eating hedgehogs. The hair, I mean. You hedgehogs like to make it difficult, I know. But this is what I always say to you – you taste better when it's difficult. I like scraping off the bristles to get to the meat! So, don't get too stressed. Because then I won't enjoy eating you so much.'

'I can't help it if I'm stressed,' said Mouse. 'You just said you were going to eat me. That doesn't help me relax!'

The bear thought. He thought hard.

'But that doesn't work. I can't tell you that I'm not going to eat you. Because I am. You are far too fat and tender!'

'Then you may find that my bristles keep falling out.'

'No!' cried the bear. 'Stop it! Don't let your bristles fall out! Stop it, right now! I'm telling you, hedgehog, if you don't control your bristles, then…'

The bear couldn't think of anything.

'… then what?' asked Mouse.

'Then… I'm… going… to… eat… you,' said the bear very slowly.

'But you're going to eat me anyway.'

'I… know,' said the bear, who couldn't disguise the fact that he was talking nonsense. 'I've got it! I'll just eat you right now! That way, no more hairs can fall out.'

'Oh,' said Mouse.

The bear wasn't one to waste time. He grabbed Mouse by his front paws, then licked Mouse's nose with his large smelly tongue.

'Funny,' said the bear, 'you have an unusual taste for a hedgehog.'

The bear opened his jaws. He shuffled Mouse about in his claws, so that the fake bristles were mouth-facing. He closed his eyes and bit down, trying to use his sharp, canine teeth to strip the hair from Mouse's back. His teeth snapped (painfully) together. The bear opened his eyes.

Mouse had disappeared.

The bear pressed his claws together, but there was no hedgehog between them. He inspected each paw, thinking perhaps the hedgehog had shrunk from the 'stress'. But it hadn't. It just wasn't there.

'Hedgehog?' said the bear. 'Where have you gone, hedgehog?'

The hedgehog didn't answer.

'That's funny,' the bear said to himself. 'He was here a moment ago. I'm sure he was. Here, right between my claws. I know because I was going to eat it.'

The bear felt behind his ears, on the top of his head, and looked under his armpits – the hedgehog was nowhere to be found. He rooted around in the shrubs and branches, but the hedgehog wasn't hiding anywhere. He stood on his hind legs and roared, so loudly that the trees shook and birds took flight – all except Hoo Hoo, who was giggling quietly to herself.

The bear returned his paws to the ground, and was about to start rampaging around the island when he saw the hedgehog.

'Hello,' said the hedgehog.

'Oh. Hello,' said the bear, startled.

His anger swelled, and without giving the hedgehog a second, he swiped at it, capturing it in his claws again.

'Don't run away like that! It's not fair!'

The bear, swiftly and to prevent more escape attempts, raised Mouse to his jaws, and bit down hard. He was hoping, this time, to sink his teeth into the flesh and bristle, but he had a clattering encounter with his lower molars.

'Ow!' yelled the bear.

The hedgehog had disappeared again.

'Stop doing that!' shouted the bear. 'Stop it – do you hear!? How can I eat you if you keep doing that? And how are you doing this, anyway? Hedgehogs don't usually escape. Usually they get eaten. They are things to be eaten! You are really, really annoying!'

The hedgehog didn't respond.

The bear jumped up and down in frustration.

'You know,' said the voice of the hedgehog, 'it isn't very polite to eat other creatures.'

'Where are you?!' said the bear.

'I'm around,' replied the hedgehog casually. 'We are gentlemanly and peace-loving animals, who only like to nestle in hedges and undergrowth. It's hardly polite to go around eating us.'

'Tsk. That's rich! It's not polite to go around having bristles, is it! It doesn't exactly make you easy to eat, does it!'

'Have you never thought that bears aren't meant to eat hedgehogs? Maybe that's why hedgehogs have bristles.'

'Grr… you talk like a disappearing hedgehog with bristle for brains! It's a spiteful and deceitful trick to inflict on an innocent old bear who just wants a decent bite to eat.'

Hoo Hoo had been listening closely to the conversation. She jumped off her branch, and sailed through the air, where, mid-flight, she transformed into a fetid smell of unwashed pig's trotters.

'You hedgehogs have tried to make it difficult for us, but… scrub my itchy ears! What's that smell? No nose could ever cope with such repellence!'

'That's me. Sorry!' said Mouse, who was still invisible.

'You! That's the foulest thing ever to offend my nostrils – it could cut my claws! What have you been doing?'

'You see, the thing is, you have been eating lots of hedgehogs for a long time. So, we hedgehogs got together and agreed that we were a bit miffed about being eaten out of existence. And we decided to do something about it. What you don't know is that, long ago, the humble hedgehog was a simple creature. We were quite smooth – we snuffled and sniffed among the hedgerows, brambles and thickets with no bristles at all. Then along came grumpy, hedgehog-harming animals (like bears), who thought that we would make a good afternoon snack. Suddenly, hedgehogs were endangered. We were obliged to grow bristles. You are right – we all thought this was a clever ploy, and for a long time, it helped us to survive.

'Then you came along – and you were determined to eat us, despite our bristles. Which means we have been forced to find new ways to defend ourselves. As you have seen (or *not* seen), we have learned how to disappear at will, so that when predators like you try to eat us, we can escape. Just in case that isn't enough, we also have some other tricks – we can, if necessary, emit a powerful and toxic smell, which you will find unpleasant and overpowering. Smell whets the appetite, so if a predator smells something bad, we reason that they will be less likely to eat us. I mean, do you feel like eating me now?'

'No, I do not!' the bear replied without hesitation. 'But this is totally unfair, and against the rules! You can't just go about disappearing and smelling whiffy – how do you expect a bear to live?'

Hoo Hoo, with precise timing, changed from a bad smell into an extended family of fleas. She infested the bear's coat and started to bite him mercilessly.

'There are other ways to live besides eating hedgehogs,' explained Mouse. 'That's up to you. We have learned the hard way that we need to look after ourselves. We have realised that, really, we don't live in a world that can cope with baldness – for that reason we grew bristles. Now, in this dark age, we have developed other forms of protection. We can only live in hope of a time when we return to our bald and innocent state.'

'Ow!' said the bear. 'What's that?'

The bear was scratching his arms, then his ears, then his knees, then his belly.

'Oh, that's another line of defence we have developed. We've been trialling it recently. So far it's proved to be very effective.'

'What is it?'

'If our predators start to complain about not being able to eat us, we have developed the capacity to spread fleas quickly. We can persuade the fleas where to jump. (Once you learn how to tame a flea, they are surprisingly co-operative!) You should find them, very itchy, painful and annoying!'

'Enough! Enough! I understand what you are saying – don't eat hedgehogs! No more hedgehogs for you!'

The bear was scratching madly all over.

'If this is what it means to eat hedgehogs, I'll never eat one again. Just make it stop! Make it stop!'

'I'm afraid I can't make the fleas stop. Fleas will be fleas, after all. Perhaps you should go for a swim. To somewhere else. A long, long way away. Where they don't have hedgehogs. And you can eat something harmless, like mushrooms.'

'Mushrooms! What are you trying to do to me?!'

A large flea bit the bear on his ear.

'Stop biting me! Oh, this is more than a bear can bear! It's unbearable! That's it! Hedgehogs are just one big pain in my muscular bottom! I don't know about mushrooms, but I'm not going to stick around you lot anymore! That's for sure!'

The bear ripped through the undergrowth, and leapt into the river, where he let the current carry him downstream.

'Phew!' said Mouse.

He shook the fake bristles from his back. Then, fully visible and returned to his true form as a dog, Mouse stopped to think. He had been frightened confronting the bear, but he had seen it through. A new feeling washed over him. He thought that this was what other creatures meant when they talked about *pride*. That was it, he thought. For the first time that he could remember, he felt proud of himself. Mouse no longer wanted to be invisible. Far from it. He suddenly wanted everyone to see him.

Mouse walked out to the water's edge, and looked out on his vanquished opponent, wishing the world to witness his triumph.

*

When news got about among the hedgehogs that Mouse had triumphed over the bear, spontaneous celebrations broke out. Hedgehogs who had walked about with a frail attachment to life cut loose and started to hop about with joy. Some started busting hedgehog moves, others rattled their teeth, and wiggled their bristles.

'This is wonderful – *wonderful*!!' said George.

'I feel like a new hedgehog,' said Maud.

'I can't tell you what it means to us,' said Gert. 'Suddenly, we can see a future.'

It was agreed that there should be a feast held in honour of their guests – and Mouse, in particular.

The feasting and celebrating went on well into the night. Some of the hedgehogs even got drunk and started to tell rude jokes. A young female hedgehog climbed onto her hind legs and started belly dancing (but she regretted it the next day).

'It's a shame you can't stay with us longer,' said George to Cloud. 'You would be very welcome.'

Cloud liked the hedgehogs, and he could see that his companions did too. They were kindly creatures, unmarked by too much ambition or greed. He could see how all the dogs could settle down to a new life with them.

'D'you know I think nothing would give us greater pleasure. But what can I do? I'm on a quest, and it's my duty to complete it. I must find the Lake of Gifts and return with my prize.'

George nodded his head with a little smile.

'I understand. Then I suppose you'll need to cross the

river, and we might be able to help you, there' said the hedgehog a little more secretively.

George said no more about it, until several days later. After a large breakfast, Maud guided the dogs down to the river. There, they found George overseeing a collection of hedgehogs, as they put the finishing touches to their feat of engineering: a boat (though it was more like a large coracle).

'We made it ourselves, from our own bristles! When we get together, there are plenty to go around. It might not look like much, but there's enough room for all of you.'

The dogs thanked the hedgehogs. Then the hedgehogs thanked the dogs. So, the dogs thanked the hedgehogs again. When they had finished thanking each other, they prepared to leave. Gert the hedgehog advised that they should launch from upstream, so they could ride the currents without being carried too far along past the destroyed bridge, where they could rejoin the track.

The day had turned bitterly cold, and flecks of snow were in the air. A chill wind cut across the surface of the river, which made it look colder than ever. A retinue of hedgehogs carried the boat upstream on their backs, until they reached a suitable distance from the destroyed bridge.

They launched the boat. The dogs climbed aboard. They cast off, and the currents swept them swiftly, bobbling and burbling, down the river. Porker used a makeshift oar to steer them across the water.

The currents were strong. Much stronger than any of them had reckoned. By the time they reached the point where the bridge had once been, they were only in the middle of the river. They skirted the edge of the island.

As it happened, the bear had returned, albeit temporarily. He was still determined to discover a new life (and a new diet) somewhere else, but he had left a valued pair of ear trimmers in his lair. So, he had crept back to collect them. Just as he was about to pack up for the final time, he caught an unusual scent – one that he had not come across before. It was a lovely, fragrant and powerful odour – but, more importantly, he knew in the deepest corners of his being, that the smell was edible. He didn't know it, but the name of the smell was rosemary.

The bear followed his nose, until he came to the shoreline with the water. The smell was carried along quickly. It came from a small boat full of dogs.

The bear glowered at the dogs.

'Dogs are not hedgehogs!' he said.

The bear jumped into the water and started to swim.

'We're going too far downstream!' cried Hoo Hoo.

'It doesn't matter,' called out Cloud. 'We just need to reach the other shore. We can find our way back! Keep steering, Porker!'

Porker nodded and turned to check the angle of his oar. Then he saw the head of a giant hairy creature swimming towards them.

'Bless my bowels! There's a river monster swimming after us!' he shouted.

All the dogs turned to see what Porker was shouting about.

'It's a bear!' said Cloud.

'It's *the* bear!' said Mouse, who recognised the bear.

'Row faster!' urged Hoo Hoo.

It was too late. The bear was upon them – and his nose was sniffing like a vacuum cleaner! He didn't seem to want to eat the dogs – just smell them! He sniffed all around the boat, at each of the dogs. Finally, he got to Cloud. He sniffed once. Then a second time.

'It's you!' said the bear.

'What's me?' asked Cloud.

'Never mind. I'm going to eat you!' said the bear.

Cloud hit the bear on the head with the locket. Porker hit the bear on the head with his oar. The bear, hungry and annoyed, raised his enormous paw and smashed the coracle in a single blow. The dogs were thrown in different directions into the water.

Once they had surfaced, caught their bearings and started to paddle, Porker, Hoo Hoo and Mouse saw something which made their hearts sink. The bear was swimming at tremendous speed downstream – with Cloud on his back!

In their disarray, the dogs managed to swim back to the shore from where they had set out. They were cold to the point of shaking. They were shocked. They were no further forward. And they had lost the reason for their journey, to an insatiable bear who had disappeared.

Hoo Hoo scampered down the riverbank, to see if she could catch sight of Cloud and the bear. It was no good. They had been travelling too fast.

'What are we going to do?' asked Mouse. 'We must go after them, surely?'

'It's no good. We can't chase them at the moment. We need to track down the bear in another way. Besides, I know it may not seem sensible, but something tells me we shouldn't give up on our master. He may act like a dreamy lost puppy with his head in the clouds, but there's more to him than meets the eye. Anyway, he can probably bore the bear into defeat by talking about the metaphysics of moles or something! No, I think the best thing we can do is regroup and come up with another plan. For now, let's go back to the hedgehogs. I'd like to pick their brains.'

No sooner had despair left the community of hedgehogs, than it returned with the remaining drowned pilgrims. They traipsed, tails drooping, back to the Hedgehog Centre, where they were greeted with sad eyes, and a general wilting of bristles.

'What's happened? Where's Cloud? Where's the locket?'

Hoo Hoo explained and the general mood went from sombre to sorrowful.

'There's too much violence in the world!' cried a young hedgehog, before she broke into fitful sobs.

'Now, now, I know this is a setback, but all is not lost! We can rescue my master. There's just one problem – we need to know where he is!'

'If the bear carried him off downstream, he could be miles away by now!' said George.

'There are ways to cover large distances – but what I really need is help, and lots of it.'

'What can we do?' asked Maud. 'We are hedgehogs. We move about on our little legs very slowly. It would take us months to cover that kind of distance. I suppose we could build another boat – would that help?'

'I think you can help – but we need more than your help. This is an emergency, and something like a state of war. We will need the help of all creatures who are willing. What we really need is *airborne* help. I'll turn into a red kite again, and fly out over the course of the river, but it would be more effective with some other creatures – what's your relationship like with the birds of prey in these parts?'

George stared at Hoo Hoo.

'We avoid them. In the same way we avoid bears.'

'Right.'

'Well, what about sparrows?' asked Porker.

The hedgehogs, with the help of Hoo Hoo, formed a diplomatic alliance with the sparrows in the woods. It was agreed that the sparrows would help track down Cloud and the bear, if the hedgehogs taught the sparrows elementary self-defence. The relationship was a little tense at first, but it soon settled down.

Flanked by a flock of sparrows, Hoo Hoo took flight. In tandem, the other pilgrims and the hedgehogs got together to forge their own plan of action – they found themselves eyeing a small collection of rusting wheelbarrows at the entrance to the Hedgehog Centre...

Hoo Hoo and the birds covered many miles, flying in a zigzag pattern above the meanders of the river. Soon even Hoo Hoo started to feel uneasy. They had covered so many miles that she thought it wouldn't be long before they reached the sea – and at any point on their flight, the bear might have climbed out of the river and set out over land.

'This is no good,' she said to the sparrows. 'We'll have to turn back and check the terrain again but over a wider area. Still, I have my doubts. My eyes are second to none, and I haven't seen anything.'

The sparrows did as they were told, but they also sent out two scouts to get intelligence from other birds along the banks of the river. Surely, they thought, someone must have seen something.

The aerial surveillance party didn't know that the bear had climbed out of the river, only a mile downstream from the site of the kidnapping. Despite his thick fur, he had started to feel the cold. He bundled Cloud out of the river and whisked him off to one of the many quiet and remote refuges he knew about: a small ravine in a wooded part of the hills, with a cave hidden away in one of its many stone crevices.

He threw Cloud onto the floor of the cave with a thud.

'Ow,' said Cloud. 'Watch it!'

'Don't you worry about it, tasty dog! Don't you worry about it. A few broken bones won't make much difference now. Anyway, it's the flesh that I care about.'

The bear took a long and appreciative sniff of his captive.

'Mmm, you smell expensive and eatalicious! You are flesh-flavoursome and mouth-pleasing. I might even drool on you! How did you get to smell so tasty and taste so aromatic? You're quite a find! I've come across lots of dogs before, but they usually only make you want to lick your armpits!'

'I...'

Cloud began to explain, but the bear cut him off.

'No, don't bother – I'm not really interested in the answer. What does it matter? All that matters is right in front of me... mmm, belly pleasure, I'm a lucky bear!'

'But...' Cloud tried to get in.

'... Spare yourself the effort. Why waste words? I'm going to eat you. I'm going to eat you! And that's that. The only question is how. How do I make the most of your fragrant flavour?'

Cloud couldn't quite tell if he was being asked a question or if the bear was talking to himself.

'Are you best served raw with chopped carrots or should I roast you over an open fire?'

'I don't kn...' Cloud began, but then seized the opportunity, '... well... yes... now I think about it, that's a good question. I mean it's true, I am full of flavour – you have managed to smell it. But how do you make the most of it? That's your question, if I understand you rightly.'

The bear was a bit shocked that Cloud had answered. His eyes searched Cloud for a time, as his brain worked out that his dinner was about to tell him how it should be cooked.

'Yes. It is. Out with it!' the bear said eventually.

'I flatter myself that I'm really a delicacy – and delicate flavours need to be treated carefully. You shouldn't just wolf them down. I might smell good, but I'm not in prime condition yet. Really, you should leave me to mature, if you want to get the best taste.'

The bear was puzzled.

'Mature? What are you saying?'

'I've been walking for a long time – that ruins my flavour. And the cold river will have only made matters worse. The best thing you could do is make a fire, find something like straw (or maybe even goose down) to make a bed for me, and give me three square meals each day. If you treat me like this for a week or so then – but *only* then – will I reach my prime flavour.'

All of the bear's brain went to work. No part of it was spared the effort of thinking about what Cloud had said.

'A week?'

'Yes.'

'That's a long time.'

'But worth the wait. Trust me.'

'A long time,' repeated the bear, 'and I can't eat hedge-hogs in all that time, either. Are you sure about this?'

'Oh, believe me, I know my own flavours. I'm a very special kind of meal. Take my word for it – you've hit the jackpot!'

The bear was obviously unsure but was captivated by the smell of rosemary. He didn't want to pass up any chance to make the most of it. He had never had a meal like this before.

The bear tied Cloud to a stalagmite in the cave, bounded off, and returned later with a sprung mattress, firewood and the ingredients for a bean and sausage stew. He lit the fire and cooked up the meal. Cloud thought that this was among the most hospitable treatment he had enjoyed on his journey to the West.

Later, as he was dozing on the mattress, Cloud considered the bear – perhaps it was the firelight, but his features were unusual. His face was softer and chubbier than he expected of a bear.

'Bear,' he said quietly, 'are you awake?'

'Yes,' said the bear.

'Can I ask you something?'

'Hmmm,' mumbled the bear.

'How did you come to live in these parts?'

'Hmm,' said the bear shortly, 'I don't know how. I just did.'

'Were you born here?'

'Oh… no.'

'Where were you born?'

'Somewhere else.'

'Are you still looking forward to eating me?'

'Yes.'

'And have you always had such a large appetite?'

'Hmm. I'm a bear.'

Cloud let the flames flicker.

'I suppose you must have eaten a lot of hedgehogs in your time?'

'Yes. Loads.'

'Quite an appetite. Even for a bear.'

'Why all the questions, tasty dog?'

Cloud thought.

'Do you know why I have been walking so long?'

'Why's that?'

'I'm looking for something. D'you know what I'm looking for?'

'What?'

'The truth.'

'Oh.'

'The more I walk, the more I think I can begin to see things a bit more clearly. Take this cave, and this firelight, for example. I can see you, but not as I can by the clear light of day. Nevertheless, I see you. I see you more clearly.'

'Me? What's there to see? I'm a bear.'

They both stared into the fire.

'It's funny, but when you start to see things differently, it changes the way you behave,' said Cloud. 'Perhaps, for example (and it's just an example), when you see things by the dim light of a fire you mistake your interest for those of everyone else. All you want is *more, more, more* for *me, me, me.* Never mind about the hedgehogs. Never mind about the dogs. Just eat them. And keep eating them. It's your hunger that matters, even if it's a lonely kind of hunger.

'Then again, what if you saw your hunger in the clear light of day? What would happen then, do you think? Would it reveal a lonely hunter enslaved to their appetites? Or something else?'

The bear shuffled about in the cave. He snuffled his nose thoughtfully. Then he laughed.

'Bra ha ha ha, what a brain-banged dog you are, if you think that'll work! Trying to appeal to my 'better nature' eh? I have seen the world. I was given as a pet to a wise bird of prey who taught me the ways of the world. You might like to think there's more to life than getting to the end of the day with enough food in your belly – but the only creatures who think that are the ones who have never had to struggle for survival! I've met dogs like you before – you are soft, I tell you. Filled with woolly ideas. The only 'truth' you need to worry about is the one at the bottom of my stomach – and you'll be finding out about it very soon! I will eat you. Then you will be eaten and an ex-dog. That's it. Nothing more. You lost. I'm sorry about that. (Except I'm not sorry about it, really.) Now go to sleep.'

The bear curled up in a ball, looking slightly grumpy.

Cloud continued to stare into the firelight, as it flickered and died.

Was the bear right? He had the same feeling he had experienced on the moorland the night they first met George the hedgehog. For all this long way he had believed, without any real question, in what he was doing. He *had* to believe in it. He had nothing else to believe in, so he had always believed in the Thumbald; and it was for this reason that the black dog had so easily persuaded him to go on the journey. It was for this reason that, until this very moment, he had wanted to believe that there was more to the bear than a selfish tyrant of greed.

But what if he were wrong? He would never see his home again. He was born an orphan and would leave the world one. He would never see his travelling companions again. He would end up inside the stomach of an insatiable and careless hairy monster. His future was a date with digestive juices, sloshing about in a tummy full of rancid meat and hedgehog bristles. He would never see the Lake of Gifts, if it even existed. He would never find out the truth. If the bear was right, the only truth he would find was snoring right before him.

Cloud closed his eyes, but he felt too lonely, troubled and abandoned to sleep.

*

The lingering smell of woodsmoke hung in the morning air. Cloud opened his eyes to see the bear, sitting on his haunches, looking out through the mouth of the cave. When he caught Cloud's stirrings, he swivelled his head and asked solemnly:

'What would you like for breakfast, tasty dog? Fish? Would you like fish?'

Maybe the bear was still tired, but the same relish wasn't in his voice.

'Thank you.'

The bear hesitated.

'Then you'll have to help me catch it.'

'Yes, of course,' said Cloud.

'In the clear light of day,' said the bear.

'Okay.'

The bear untied Cloud from the stalagmite. They walked out into the ravine. The bear turned to look at Cloud.

'Do you really know what it is – that thing around your neck?'

Cloud searched the face of the bear.

'Of course, I don't know,' replied Cloud calmly.

'I don't feel myself, this morning,' said the bear.

They were interrupted by a shout.

'There they are! Charge!'

Cloud and the bear gazed into the morning sunlight, as it was funnelled down the narrow walls of the ravine. Many birds were flying about, silhouetted against the glare. Hoo Hoo, Mouse and Porker stood at the top of a slope which ran down into the ravine. All three appeared to be wheeling a wheelbarrow, which, on the clarion call of 'Charge!', they lifted. Out of the wheelbarrows rolled a cluster of spiky balls. The 'balls' came rolling down the slope towards Cloud and the bear, gathering speed on the way.

The bear stared at the spectacle. Somehow, he wasn't surprised. He gave the impression of an animal emerging from a long season of hibernation.

The balls started to roll all around them. They were prickly, like little round gorse bushes. They spoke too.

'Take that!' said one.

'That's for my uncle Osmond!' said another.

'I just want you to know that I'm not naturally violent, but I have every intention of pricking your paws to perdition!' said another.

The balls, it seemed, were the entire gathering of the Hedgehog Centre, who had been called to martial action and deployed as rolling missiles.

Cloud was just thinking that they wouldn't stand up to the might of the bear, when he noticed that the bear was nowhere to be seen. The hedgehogs were unfurling on the floor of the ravine, ready to lay down their lives in battle, and Hoo Hoo, Porker and Mouse were racing down the slope into the thick of the fight with wild war whoops.

'Where's the bear?' asked Cloud.

'He's gone,' said a hedgehog.

'Where's the bear gone? The coward!' asked Hoo Hoo, a little breathless.

'He's disappeared,' said another hedgehog.

'He was here a moment ago,' said Cloud.

'What about the bear?' asked Porker, arriving late and panting.

'I'm here,' said a voice from the floor.

The dogs looked at the ground around their feet. Among the sea of hedgehogs, they saw a little bundle of fluff.

The hedgehogs formed a circle around the creature.

'You don't look like a bear,' said a hedgehog, 'or even a hedgehog.'

'I'm not a bear,' said the bear who wasn't a bear. 'I never was one. I think it's fair to say that I've been lost and couldn't remember my true nature. I was the friend and companion to Avebalderheda for a long time – she has a great appetite, but for fine and beautiful things. She perfected her appetite through me. But somewhere along the line, I was stolen by a malicious osprey working for an evil spirit and abused into a life of corruption. With Avebalderheda my appetite was turned and tempered by the truth of things – compassion for all creatures, fitted to their fleeting character. Having broken my yoke to her, and under the influence of the guileful osprey, my appetite became unhinged and gargantuan – so I took the form of a bear tied to his terrorising appetites. I had lost all sight of the truth! Last night, though, I glimpsed my true self.'

The creature looked at Cloud, then continued:

'And my true self is a gerbil.'

*

It had been an eventful morning. None of them had even had any breakfast. So, when they had all got over the shock of the bear who was really a gerbil, they had a big brunch back at the Hedgehog Centre. The gerbil took a vow to wander the countryside on a strict diet, until he was reunited with Avebalderheda. Looking shame-faced and sorry for all the harm his grotesque and distorted hunger had inflicted, he set out through the undergrowth.

The dogs stayed with the hedgehogs for another night, enjoying their hospitality and celebrating freedom. The hedgehogs also fashioned another boat for the dogs.

As Cloud sailed over the rippling surface of the river's currents, he could feel his former doubt slip away from him. The truth was a powerful and mysterious thing. It had already shown that many things are not what they seem: there was more to the world than the false claims of the three horses, and more than the empty and self-centred greed of a hungry bear. They had all crumbled under scrutiny. Did that mean he had reason to hope for all the things he had always believed?

Cloud looked ahead, eager to reach the far shore.

The bear

The lake

The four dogs picked up the trail they had lost. They walked for many months, through the winter. The snow-capped mountains dictated their route. They followed winding paths, high valleys, windswept ridges, and lapped cautiously at the edges of dark and forbidding mountain lakes. They hardly saw anyone, except lonely birds of prey, hovering ominously above them, occasional deer, and hares, which scurried from their sight at the first notice.

Which left nothing but the silence of the hills. If they stopped at the end of a sudden climb, the sound of their breathing made the silence in the background more noticeable. Their breathing, their life, sounded unusual – as though they were strange exceptions in an unbroken expanse of nothing.

Hoo Hoo and Porker took little note of it – or appeared not to. But Cloud and Mouse were, in different ways, drawn to the ethereal emptiness of the mountains. Cloud was slightly disconcerted but beguiled all the same. Mouse revelled in it – in fact, he never looked more at home than when he was *listening* to the silence.

'I like these mountains,' he said simply, as they looked down on the crescent-cut of a valley.

In time, the weather changed, and the first flourishes of spring broke through the winter-worn landscape. The scenery changed too. The hills became more dramatic, marked by sudden ascents, scrambles over scree, and equally sudden descents into shade-covered hollows patched with woodland. The map told them they were near their destination. Then, with no warning, they emerged onto the extended flat peak of a mountain, where they were confronted with a vision of lyrical loveliness. They looked down on a vast lake, which tapered into an eruption of rippling hills at its far end.

Grey clouds overshadowed the water, pierced by cascades of sunlight, mellowing the edges of the rough terrain.

'That's it! Look! The Lake of Gifts,' said Cloud.

'Prick my paws! So it is!' said Hoo Hoo.

At the nearest end of the lake, they could make out tendrils of smoke coming from a small settlement. There, they might expect to find shelter. Tracing the surface of the lake, they could see a small, coppiced island.

Wind ruffled their coats. They gazed at the island without speaking.

They moved, one by one, to begin the journey down the mountain. The track flattened as they walked towards the lake. The land undulated. The track bobbed along its surface, until it joined a river. Mountains surrounded them on all sides but kept enough distance to give the valley space. Wisps of cloud clung to some peaks and swept over patches of pine forest. The air was fresh.

The dogs barely spoke, until they reached the outskirts of the settlement. A lonely, large dog stood in their way, carrying an extinguished lantern in his teeth. He had a black coat, slightly weathered and jaded, with pointed ears that were permanently alert. The dog studied the pilgrims as they approached.

'He's a Great Dane,' Hoo Hoo whispered to Cloud.

Cloud nodded.

Behind the Great Dane, they could make out the details of the settlement. It wasn't much: a few wooden refuges, all built very simply, peppered with tents, which looked like yurts. They could also see a much larger building. Like the others, it was made from wood, but it was altogether more ornate. It had two floors, and a balcony, which circumscribed the whole building, and which formed the roof of a cloistered walkway on the ground floor below. Rising from the centre of the building was a stepped bell tower.

The Great Dane lowered his head as the dogs drew near. He placed the lantern on the ground.

Again, he stared hard at them.

'Yes,' he said eventually, 'we have been expecting you. Follow me.'

The Great Dane turned, and without looking back, walked towards the settlement. The pilgrims looked at each other. They followed.

The Great Dane guided them along the track. The place was pretty empty. They saw no more than three or four other dogs: a Labrador loitering about one of the yurts, a German Shepherd resting its head on an open window, the tails of what looked like Cocker Spaniels disappearing behind another hut.

The Great Dane led them straight to the larger building. Another large black Great Dane prowled about under the shelter of the cloister, and they saw the black dog, Avebalderheda, curled up, apparently asleep. A shard of daylight broke over her through the cloisters.

'Welcome, my friends,' she said, 'welcome to my home.'

They heard something laugh behind them, and, as

they turned, just caught the end of a shell scuttling into the building.

The black dog opened her eyes, and with a trick of her coiled limbs, stood on all fours.

'You have come a long way,' she said, 'but your journey is not complete. Tomorrow you will complete it. Today, you will rest here with me.'

'This way,' said the Great Dane who had greeted them. He used his large head to motion into the building.

'What is this place?' asked Porker.

'You will stay here, as our lady said,' replied the Great Dane.

He led each of them to their own quarters: a small, comfortable cell, with a straw mattress, a bowl of water and some fresh bread laid out for refreshment. The Great Dane also showed them a neat square room, with a pool in the shape of an inverted pyramid at its centre. He encouraged them all to take a bath.

'Tsk,' said Hoo Hoo, 'and to think Avebalderheda walks around looking like a disgrace when she has these sorts of facilities!'

The dogs, after they had settled down, took a bath together.

'So, this isn't where we get the Thumbald?' asked Porker.

'No, we must go to the island for that.'

Porker thought about this.

'I wonder if they have lots of them,' he said.

'Lots of what?'

'Lots of Thumbalds. If they're as good as you say they are, you'd think they must have a large supply of them,' he reasoned, and then suddenly looked worried. 'What if they've run out? What if we've come all this way for nothing? Mind you, I guess they must be able to get supplies, even in a lonely place like this.'

'You belly brain!' said Hoo Hoo. 'There aren't lots of Thumbalds. There's just one.'

'Just one. But that's no good. Someone will have taken it already. I didn't know things were this bad!'

'No one has taken it,' said Cloud. 'You can't 'take' it.'

'Believe me,' said Porker, very sure of himself, 'if there were just one slice of eggy bread in the world, it would go very quickly!'

'The Thumbald isn't a slice of eggy bread!' cried Hoo Hoo. 'It's not something you can eat with bacon and to-matoes.'

Porker looked confused.

'What sort of thing is it, then?'

'It's...' Hoo Hoo began, 'it's... well... you are infuri-ating!'

'And if it isn't like eggy bread, how will you know

when you've got it?'

Cloud quoted:

A mark, a brushstroke, a letter,
Are they dumb objects?
Or the visible sign of invisible things?

Porker twitched. He wanted to ask more questions, but it didn't seem right. Instead, he just said:

'I wonder what's for dinner?'

The answer to Porker's question was lentils, tomato, and sweet potato. Any concerns he had about the point of their journey disappeared as he licked the mushy mess of pulses and vegetables from his chops.

The black dog watched Porker as he ate.

'Tomorrow, I will take you down to the lake.'

'How do we get to the island?' asked Cloud.

'There's a boat,' replied the black dog.

She said no more. They spent the rest of the evening in silence.

Not long after they had eaten, a tiredness that they hadn't experienced before overcame them. Soon, they stumbled off to their quarters, where they all slept. Cool mountain spirits of the night entered their dreams and were only half remembered.

*

The light around the lake was quite unlike anything any of them had seen before. The mountains all around created a kind of permanent shadow, which was softened by the sun. Unless it was the other way around – light spread over the valley and the lake, but it was absorbed into the hills, which combined to create a soft but lucid glow.

Avebalderheda led them on a path down to the edge of the lake, and then on another path around it. The island was only a third of the way round, travelling anticlockwise, from the nearest shore. The path disappeared into ancient woodland, which, in the burgeoning spring, was budding with greenery. When it saw the party of dogs approach, a squirrel scampered up the trunk of an oak, and leapt through the branches, giggling loudly.

Avebalderheda kept the same silence as the night before, and all the other dogs, without thinking about it, did the same. At the most, they exchanged looks or let their attention roam the waters, the hills and the mysterious secrets of the island that fell into sharper relief as they got nearer to it.

The closer they came, the more the island took their interest. Even as they could make out more of its features, they could see nothing beyond the trees and foliage that grew on it. From the edge of the lake, it looked as if it was completely overrun by vegetation. They couldn't see how any creature could live on it.

'Here we are,' said Avebalderheda.

She nodded at a small wooden jetty, built on the rough foundation of a slate beach, which projected a short way into the water.

The pilgrims looked at the jetty, and then across to the island. The distance was not that great. It wasn't so far that they couldn't swim, but it was too far for a large animal to throw a stone. Peering across to the island, they couldn't see a jetty on the far shore, or any break in the branches, leaves, bushes and trees. The water, despite a gentle breeze, was almost entirely still.

'Where's the boat?' asked Hoo Hoo.

Avebalderheda barked.

They heard something like a startled cry from the island, followed by a rummaging in the undergrowth. The dogs looked surprised.

'I'll leave you, for now,' said Avebalderheda quietly.

She turned and walked slowly back down the path they had recently trodden. The four dogs heard something from the island splash into the water. Something which looked like the tip of a rock popped up on the water's surface, followed by another and then another. At a distance, the dogs could just make out eyes in the head of the 'rock'. Behind them came a log of wood, which emerged into the outline of a raft, with a mast rising from its centre. Ropes were fixed from its top to each corner. Finally, at its rear, they could see that rarest of things, a human – a boy in short trousers and a jumper. He had very round, chubby cheeks, and even from afar, he looked sleepy.

The 'rocks' at the front of the raft were otters, who pulled the craft. The dogs watched the waterborne creation sail over the silent waters. It was a strange and hypnotic spectacle.

When the raft reached the jetty, one of the otters leapt out of the water and tethered it to the wood.

'Climb aboard,' said the boy, without looking at the dogs.

Cloud urged everyone to do as the boy had told them. They thought twice when they looked closely at the raft. It had no floor; just a perimeter of wood. The centre of the raft was empty and led only to the waters below. When they peered into the centre of the raft, they could see rocks under the water on the bed of the lake and they just caught the darting movement of a perch.

The boy sneezed.

'Hurry up!' said the boy. 'Got a sniff.'

'Yes, hurry up!' said the otter. 'It's not as if we don't have other things to do!'

'Er… okay,' said Mouse.

He trotted lightly onto the wooden edge of the raft and grabbed onto one of the lines of rope with his teeth. Hoo Hoo followed, then Cloud. When Porker climbed aboard, the whole vessel lurched to one side. The boy's eyes widened.

'Cherub's cheek! Watch it!' he cried.

'Careful, you!' called out one of the otters.

Hoo Hoo laughed.

'Don't capsize the boat!' she said.

'I can't help it!' said Porker. 'After all, we had a large dinner.'

'*You* had a large dinner.'

When the raft was settled with all its passengers, it set sail.

Cloud looked at the boy, hoping he might be able to ask him some questions (Cloud had never seen a human before). But the boy looked into the water solemnly.

'Look!' called Mouse.

All dogs turned their attention to Mouse's cry. They saw the sausage dog peering at the water caught underneath the raft. There, they saw the reflection of Mouse, except it wasn't an exact mirror image of him. It was swimming through the water, under the raft, back towards the shore. Cloud's ears stood to full attention, and he was even more alarmed to see his own reflection, and those of the other dogs, doing the same thing. Each image of the dog was swimming through the water, trying to get back to the shore. Except, if they looked into the water outside the frame of the raft, they could see nothing.

'What's going on?' asked Porker.

'I'm swimming back to shore,' said Mouse.

'No you aren't,' said Porker. 'I can see you.'

'I can see you, too,' said Mouse, inclining his head towards the water.

'Don't tell me where I am,' objected Porker. 'I think I would know.'

'Do you?' asked the boy, a little sullenly.

'What are our images doing?' Cloud asked the boy.

'Master!' said Hoo Hoo. 'I'm surprised you have to ask. They aren't our images. Our bodies are swimming back to shore. I guess we have to leave them behind to enter this island.'

The dogs looked at each other, and then down into the stillness of the water, until, before long, they reached the island. The otters heaved the raft into a concealed entrance in the overgrown foliage, which concealed another jetty. They tied up the raft so that the dogs could disembark. The boy, brusquely and without really looking at them, motioned the way.

'That way,' he said, then mumbled. 'Be here when you get back.'

The 'way' was a narrow hemmed-in path, which the dogs were forced to follow in single file. The island was only small, so it was a short walk to its centre. The surroundings gave little sign of life, but one or two birds let their voices carry in the wind.

The path broke when it reached a clearing. It gave way to a circular area marked at the edges by trodden grass. At its centre was a pool with stepping stones leading to a small hut surrounded by a wooden walkway. Standing on the walkway, staring straight at them from the island within an island, was another dog. The dog had a perfectly white coat, and resembled a Dalmatian, but her breed was hard to make out, and she had just one spot of black above her left eye.

'Welcome,' said the dog.

By instinct, the pilgrims lowered their heads.

'Won't you join me?'

She withdrew into the hut. The travellers trotted over the stepping stones and joined their host.

The white dog settled on a cushion in the corner of her hut.

'Make yourself comfortable. I know why you have come, and we can talk about that. But since you have come so far, perhaps we could spend just a little time together. Most of all, I would like to tell you a story. Would you mind that? Would you mind if I told you a story?'

The four pilgrims settled down to listen.

'You have travelled from the East. Well, this story took place some years ago in the East. If you go back the way you have come, over the Ash Mountains, and then travel north-east, you will come to an area of moors and woodland. The highest moor in this area is called Great Thorn, which overshadows a small dwelling called Little Thorn.'

The white dog explained that, at that time, a young Border Collie called Waley lived in Little Thorn. From an early age, he had shown talent and distinction. He was lively and active, and could help with many manual tasks, but he could also study and understand things. He was good with numbers, but most of all he liked reading: he would read stories, histories, books about laws of the land, even the languages of strange animals. His teachers saw Waley's potential, and they nurtured it. They also instructed him in the ways of the Bald. He was such a bright prospect that they agreed he should be made Head Hound at a village called Beaverwick on the other side of the moors, where he would oversee all the village's affairs.

The talented young collie had also been fortunate in

another way. He had fallen in love. He had met a lovely young collie called Bee. The two were drawn to each other, like mice to cheese, and never tired of each other's company. They giggled like puppies whenever they were together. The community could see, at once, that the two were a lifelong match, so before Waley was despatched to Beaverwick, he was married to Bee. They set off together a happily married couple.

The good fortune, which had served them well in Little Thorn, however, quickly ran out, even before they reached their new home.

'Hills and mountains are the home for many lost and restless spirits, who have wandered away from the world. The more they drift away from things, and the more they roam higher into the hills, the more they lose their outward form, their body. Someone in our company understands this very well, I think,' the white dog said, looking at Mouse.

Mouse gulped.

'But the kind of spirits I have in mind have lost their form altogether. They are empty, animated forces. They might be angry. They might be clever. They might be greedy. But all they really want is to destroy. They seize creatures, or for a short time, take the form of one, so they can trick and deceive, control or manipulate. These spirits are dangerous because they see bright lights, but don't believe that these lights can shine through the lives of creatures. The world doesn't have any value at all – so they think. And we, you see, are simple, ignorant animals, too easily distracted to notice the subtle things that only mountain spirits can discern. So, they play with us. They hurt us.'

*

The white dog continued with her story. She told how one such spirit had heard about Waley's journey to Beaverwick, and his role as Head Hound. Spirits, when they are just spirits, don't have names, because they don't believe in them. Names are just a convenience to suit their ambitions when they descend on the world to shock and disturb it. This spirit, when it took a material form, took the name of Nous. And Nous was determined to make mischief with Waley's mission to Beaverwick.

On their journey, the married couple took rest at a confluence of three streams, ushered down three valleys and joining to form a waterfall which filled a large pool. A bridge ran over the waterfall and looked down on the pool. Waley and Bee were taking a rest. They peered over the edge of the bridge to admire the view. They didn't know that the spirit was loitering under the bridge.

Waley leaned out a little further to look down on the

waterfall. The spirit burst out from under the bridge. He was invisible, but made a loud bang, which erupted into the face of the ambushed Border Collie. The spirit was also carrying a noose tied to a large rock. Before Waley knew what had happened to him, the spirit had foisted the noose around Waley and let go. The rock plummeted towards the water, pulling Waley with it. Bee screamed.

Waley was dragged to the bottom of the pool. He hit his head on the way down and passed out cold.

'Waley!' cried out Bee.

She raised her front paws on the side of the bridge and looked into the pool below. She had heard her husband land in the water, but all she could see now was the surface rippling as it settled from the recent disturbance.

'Waley!' she called, louder still.

Panic made her voice quiver. She didn't want to think about what had just happened, and what it might mean.

'What is it, my love?' came a voice from behind her.

She blinked, remained on her hind legs, staring out into the valley for a few seconds. Then she turned quickly to confront the voice behind her.

When she turned, she saw her husband. He smiled back at her. She couldn't believe it. What had just happened? This dog had the same coat as her husband, the same eyes, the same markings, the same bright, wide eyes – but she was sure of one thing from that moment: this Border Collie was not her husband.

There was nothing she could do. The spirit, who had transformed into her husband, looked like Waley. He talked like him. He could quote from the same books. He knew all about the move to Beaverwick. She couldn't prove him false by any calm observation, but she knew he was false all the same.

Bee and her imposter husband travelled the remaining miles to Beaverwick, where he showed his letter of recommendation, and began his duties as Head Hound. Then he revealed his true character. Her husband would never treat anyone in the abominable way he treated the creatures of Beaverwick.

In his first decree, he told all the inhabitants of the settlement that they were wicked creatures, who led pointless, backward, corrupt lives in complete, in *total*, ignorance of truth and the light. His *only* choice – his *only* choice, he made clear – was to punish the creatures of Beaverwick brutally and severely, until they came to recognise their wicked ways. Then, and only then, once the evil inside them had been purged, might they begin to see and bear witness to the light.

Really, the spirit Nous wanted to turn the whole of

Beaverwick into a settlement of spirits that might rise up from the dirt and dust of the land into the purified air of the mountains.

He policed and punished his subjects, as he had promised. He set up a small police force, who made the creatures confess their shortcomings publicly. They enforced a curfew. They encouraged creatures to tell the public authorities about so-called 'crimes' and bad behaviour among their neighbours, and even among other members of their family.

Almost overnight the community collapsed. Some dogs tried to leave, but the police hunted them down. No one trusted each other. And all the dogs lived in a permanent state of fear and worry.

Bee couldn't stand it. She wanted to scream. She wanted to tell someone that the Head Hound was a fake, but she had nothing to prove it. She wanted to run away, but she knew the police would catch her. Most of all, she couldn't stand being near her husband. She found it almost impossible to look him in the eyes.

But she had also been pregnant by her true husband since they had first left for Beaverwick, which she found hardest of all. The thought of delivering a litter of puppies into the terrible world her imposter husband had created filled her with loathing and made her feel sick. When her time came, she raised her young pups as best she could, but each time the Head Hound cast his eyes over them, she could feel her children drifting away from her into the web of control, lies and deceit that hemmed her in.

She knew she could never rescue them all, but she was determined to save at least one of them. So early one morning, she hid her youngest son, the one with the whitest coat, in a sling, which she cast over her back. She travelled back to the confluence of three streams. Just as the sun was beginning to rise, she placed her sleeping son on a small raft in the middle of the pool, and pushed him out into the water, so that he might sail down the stream. She hoped that, in some other part of the Eastern lands, he might discover a better way of life.

The abandoned puppy drifted for miles, until he caught the eye of a large mountain dog on patrol. The mountain dog, who was resting on the side of a hill, was puzzled by what he saw. At a distance, the streak of white on the raft looked like a lonely cloud, which had somehow fallen from the sky and landed in the water. Or was it the reflection of a cloud? The mountain dog looked up but could see nothing to match the reflection.

Then, as though it were beckoning to him, the cloud ran aground on a stone beach in a kink of the river. He stood up and approached the grounded raft, where he could see clearly that the cloud was a puppy. He helped the young dog to the shore, took him home, and brought it up in his community of dogs. They never knew the name of the puppy, but true to the way he had been found, they called him Cloud.

*

Cloud's eyes were fixed on the one-spotted white dog. But when Hoo Hoo, Mouse and Porker heard the story, their eyes turned to Cloud.

There was a long pause. Cloud didn't look upset, shocked, or eager to find out more. He gave the impression that the story had scarcely affected him. But beneath the placid front, something intense was at work – a tangled knot of emotions was trying to unravel.

The white dog spoke calmly.

'Give me your pendant.'

Cloud, without hesitating, lowered his head so that the white dog could remove it from his neck. Carrying it between her teeth, she placed the locket on a red cushion, nuzzled it with her nose, sniffed it, then turned, so she was obscuring the cushion and the locket. She fiddled with it a little more, though the dogs couldn't see what she was doing (perhaps she was opening it?). Then she crouched down. She placed her front paws over it and concealed the whole thing with her head. In this position, she kept her eyes on the ground.

'So, for as far back as he can remember, Cloud has been an orphan. He was adopted by the Mountain Dog, but in some sense, he has always been a cloud adrift in the sky, bound to nothing and no one. He bears the trace of the destructive and controlling world his false father, the spirit Nous, tried to create. He has been trapped in the illusions of this arch-deceiver. Cloud is a creature purged from the world, without a real home, or a family. He is a wanderer, a pilgrim on a journey.

'Until he finds the Thumbald. And then what? What *is* the Thumbald? Knowledge? Power? Beauty? Love? How can it be these things? You can't even see it! Except on his journey, he has seen, again and again, that the way things seem when you first look at them is not always how they truly are: he saw a Wolfdog who was a tortoise; he saw three horses who thought they knew more than they really did; and he saw a bear who was really a gerbil. He also thought he was alone in the world, but now he can see that, if only he keeps looking, he isn't. So, then, perhaps the truth is not always what it seems. And perhaps knowledge, power, beauty and love are not always so obvious.

'In which case, the Thumbald might not always make much sense.'

The white dog retrieved her paws from the cushion, stood on all fours, and sniffed the locket one last time.

She nodded approvingly. She picked it up in her mouth and placed it back over Cloud's head.

'Now you can go home,' she said simply.

Cloud, slightly lost for words, looked at the floor, then back at the white dog.

'Thank you,' he said.

The white dog turned her back and curled up in a ball, apparently so she could go to sleep.

*

The four dogs were stilled by the whole encounter, by the revelations of the white dog, by the eerie calmness, even beauty, of the whole island. They wandered back silently along the path, until they caught sight of the chubby-faced boy, rummaging about for something in the undergrowth.

'All done?' he asked and made ready to launch the raft.

He gave a whistle, to summon the otters.

'Hang on! I'm not buying this old claptrap!'

Porker's voice came as a surprise in the strange and serene surroundings. A chaffinch sang out, seemingly in reply.

'Porker?' asked Cloud.

'No, no – what a lot of warmed-up leftovers!'

'What do you mean?'

'Now, let me see,' said Porker, reasoning with himself. 'How do I feel about this? Well, I'll tell you – I feel very cross. As red and raging as a bloody-minded bull!'

'Your brains are going soft and squidgy, like a mashed potato. But don't worry, I'm sure we'll find you something to eat when we get back to shore!' said Hoo Hoo.

But Porker wasn't placated.

'No, you don't understand. And, no, I won't go back to shore. Don't you get it? I've been travelling, cold, hungry and humiliated, for over a year – and what have we got to show for it?' he asked, pointing at Cloud.

'It looks the same, smells the same – if you lick it, I'd bet a favourable flea inspection that it tastes the same too! So, what have you got to show for it? Why have I come?'

'Porker...' Cloud began, trying to reason with his companion. But Porker cut him off.

'... I'm not going to listen,' he said.

He turned on his paws and stomped off back to the centre of the island.

'I'm going to have a word with that sleeping charlatan and have it out with her once and for all. I'm not starving myself of sausage for nothing!'

The others tried to halt Porker, but he was already on his way, and he was too determined to listen.

'Oi you! Patchy! Yes, the white one!' said Porker, storming over the rough stepping stones. 'What do you mean by all this, huh?! I gave up a decent life of eating and sleeping for this. All I had to put up with was a dog with a cone-shaped head. Then these busybodies came along, and it all went to pot! What do you mean by handing us back this thing?

'Don't we deserve a bit more than that? Even something to eat would be nice. A cup of tea? A slice of cake? A sandwich? I mean, I'm really hungry! But no, not so much as a flax seed! Just some peculiar story about an empty trinket – you must think we're a right bunch of jokers! Well, what have you got to say for yourself?'

Cloud scurried behind.

'Sorry about this,' he mumbled to the white dog.

The white dog raised her head slowly.

'You don't like the gift I've given you?'

'What gift?' burst out Porker. 'As far as I can tell, you haven't given us anything. You just handed back to us the thing we gave you! After you had warmed it a bit with your head. I mean, I could have done that in the comfort of my own home, while happily eating a sausage!'

'The locket was empty,' explained the white dog. 'Now it's full.'

'Of what?' asked Porker.

'The Bald,' said the white dog.

'Is it? Well I didn't see any of the Bald. Open it up,

Cloud, let's see what's inside!'

'As I have said, you can't 'see' the Bald – and anyone who tries to 'look' at it will lose 'sight' of it altogether.'

Porker looked at the white dog as if she were a bean without a pod.

'Ha, ha, ha! You expect us to believe that!'

'Yes, I do,' said the white dog. 'Let me see if I can help you. Cloud, might I have the locket once more?'

This time Cloud hesitated, but then came forward and, in the same way, lowered his head so the white dog could take the object from around his neck.

Then the white dog did something quite unusual. She placed the locket on the same red cushion. This time she opened her mouth to reveal a sparkling golden tooth. She leaned into the object and carved something on the metal holder. When she handed it back to the travellers, they could read the words she had inscribed on it.

Be Bald

'I suppose it's hard, in the end, to relate to something which can't be seen. So, for now, you must rely on a few simple words. You can rely on those words in the same way you might rely on images or stories. They won't let you see this thing, but they can point the way.'

Porker raised his head and looked into the eyes of the white dog. He smiled, lowered his head, and turned to follow the path back to the raft.

The return

'Where do we go now?' asked Mouse.

The four dogs were back on the mainland. They watched the raft sail back to the island.

'We need to visit the black dog,' said Cloud, and led the way.

When they returned to the settlement at the foot of the lake, the black dog was waiting for them in the middle of the street, flanked on either side by the two large-jawed Great Danes.

'Welcome back,' she said.

She turned and, with her guards, guided the party back into the house. She led them into a circular hall, with a ring of cushions laid out for comfort and reflection.

'Compared with the long days of travelling you have endured,' said the black dog, 'today has been easy. But you have done something momentous. You have completed your task. I think you should rest here for another night. You can begin your return journey tomorrow.'

They were all pleased to receive this invitation. The lake, the island, the settlement and valley in which they were all cradled – all were enchanting. The air was rich with mountain moisture. It cleared their minds.

'You must take the Thumbald back to Easthill,' said the black dog, 'but you can consider a large part of your quest complete. It would take the sense out of your journey, if you were to come all this way and never go back. Still, you have done well – and I know that I don't just speak for myself when I say that Hoo Hoo, Porker and Mouse, your duties have been fulfilled. When Cloud returns with his prize, you're free to make your own affairs. So long as you hold true to the changes this journey has required of you.'

Cloud's three companions looked puzzled.

'Changes?' asked Hoo Hoo. 'What changes?'

'The journey has made you all – sometimes against your instinct – direct your lives and talents to a better goal. It would be better for you all to keep that goal in sight.'

'What do you mean?' asked Porker.

'I think you know what I mean already,' said the black dog. 'Cloud found you in a remote part of the country, a prisoner to your own greed. It may have been a struggle, but on your journey, you have used your heft to help Cloud find the Thumbald. Your appetites, though you might not always have been aware at the time, have turned towards the goal of your journey rather than yourself.

'In Mouse's case, he has learned that he doesn't always have to be frightened of everything. I would say he is more prepared to show himself now than he was at the beginning, because he can see his own worth.'

'And what about me?' asked Hoo Hoo.

'You have turned from a prankster using your special powers to advance your own ego, to someone who has discovered what those powers really mean. This journey has taught you how you should understand prote-animation – it is not a tool you can use as you like to suit your own interest. Its special powers begin with an insight into the way things really are. It always follows the way to the truth, a way of humility, compassion and virtue. The way of the Bald.

'Then again,' the black dog continued brightly, 'there's one more task that will need your help.'

'What's that?' asked Mouse.

Avebalderheda gave a whistle. All the dogs perked up their ears, expecting something to happen. But it didn't. So the black dog whistled again. And again.

Then came the slow step of reptilian feet on the wooden floor.

'How many times do I have to tell you, I don't respond to whistling?! It means nothing to me. For all I know, you're doing your business on a rhododendron bush. It's not exactly an unequivocal form of communication! I don't understand why you dogs think it is.'

The tortoise wasn't in a good mood.

'I'm sorry,' said the black dog. 'I always forget you're a tortoise.'

'Forget! How can you forget? I've never been anything else. Well, except a Wolfdog, a squirrel, a paper aeroplane, an exact replica of this Border Collie, and many other creatures besides. But, in any case, I thought you were supposed to be the fount of compassion?!'

'Never mind that now,' said the black dog gently. 'Why don't you tell our guests about... you... know... what.'

'All right, all right,' said the tortoise, waddling from side to side a little. 'We meet again!' he said to the dogs.

'Hello,' said Cloud.

Hoo Hoo glared at the tortoise. She still didn't trust him.

'It was all good fun the last time we met, wouldn't you say?'

'Was it?' asked Porker.

'Yes, yes, come on – there was no real harm done. And it was a funny thing that you should have shown up at that farm to rescue the Wolfdog I had drowned. I got that idea from somewhere else. And now I think you know where. But do you know everything? When I first showed up at the farm, I appeared as a scruffy vagrant. That puffed-up Head Hound had me booted out, so I thought I would teach him a lesson. And I remembered two things: I remembered that a pilgrim was travelling that way from the East, and I remembered that if the rumours were true, I knew more about him than he knew about himself.'

'What did you know exactly?' asked Cloud.

'Many years ago, I was swimming in a lonely spot. It's a large pool fed by three streams, which come down out of the mountains. It's lovely and cool, and I was diving deep into its depths, when something fell in it. It was a dog – a dog that looked a lot like you, Cloud. He had a rope around his body, and a stone was attached to the rope. On his way into the water, he had hit his head and been knocked unconscious.

'I didn't know what was going on, but it seemed to me that something was not right. So, I decided to preserve his life until I managed to find out why he had fallen into the pool. I turned him into a large river trout and told him not to leave the pool until I came back.

'I went to investigate. And what did I find? Well, you know what I found: a wife imprisoned in a sham marriage, a malevolent spirit impersonating her husband, and a lost puppy.'

The tortoise stopped talking. The dogs waited for him to say more, but he kept quiet.

'You mean he's ...' said Cloud. 'Where is this pool?'

'That's the spirit,' said the Tortoise.

'What did you do with him? With the dog ... the trout, I mean.'

'I didn't do anything, not when I could see that a scheme was at work. It was not my role to interfere any more than I had already.'

'But that's no good – anything might have happened to him. He could have been caught and gutted by a fisherman, or some other trout-eating menace.'

'I doubt it,' said the tortoise. 'Do you really have so little faith in my abilities?'

'What do you mean?'

'You will see. If you make the journey – and I am confident you will – then you will see.'

'Of course I will make the journey. If there's any hope he's ... of course, I will.'

The black dog interrupted.

'No doubt we can help you find the way, Cloud. There are ways and means, after all.'

'What's the means of transforming a trout back into a border-collie?' asked Porker.

The tortoise shuffled with discernible pride.

'We can come to all of that,' continued the black dog. 'But suppose you find this pool, suppose you dredge up the poor creature that has been living in it – what then? What's your next move?'

'I expect my ... the trout would want to be re-united with his long-lost partner.'

'I expect you are right. But his long-lost partner is falsely wedded to the arch imposter who has caused you so much trouble. How do you feel about that? What would you want to do to him?'

'Run him out of town, I say,' said Porker.

'I could turn into a giant anaconda and squeeze the spirit right out of him,' said Hoo Hoo. 'Or become a speakerphone and broadcast German opera straight into his earhole until his head explodes in a state of Teutonic delirium!'

'I'm sure we will think of something,' replied Cloud, catching the black dog's eye.

*

The dogs travelled for many months on the road back to the East. For some of the way, they followed the same route, noticing everything in reverse, and many things they hadn't spotted on the way.

Towards the end of summer that year, they tracked north, breaking into new territory, beyond the northernmost edges of the Ash Mountains. The peaks were less forbidding and dramatic. Whether it was the summer sun or the limestone rock, everything was lighter, less heavy and enclosing. The terrain descended until it ran into gentler hills, large fields and meadows overrun with tussocks, cow parsley and dog rose. If they looked further north, they could just see the distant outline of more mountains, but none of them knew to what unknown part of the world they belonged.

None of the lands on their journey west had been crowded. But these lands were almost empty. They passed through field after field. The paths they could find were hardly trodden and difficult to follow. The tracks had fallen into disrepair and were overgrown with weeds or sedges.

'This must be the land that got left behind!' said Porker. 'It's so quiet.'

'It's pleasant, though, isn't it?' said Mouse.

'Hmm,' said Hoo Hoo, who didn't really sound interested.

'Why would no one live here?' asked Cloud.

'Because there's nothing to do,' said Hoo Hoo.

She sounded just a little bit bored.

Having flirted with the land beyond the Ash Mountains, they took a long, curved route to their south, climbing once again into foothills. Even though they could see where they were going very clearly, and the weather was fine, they still managed to get lost several times. Hoo Hoo blamed Cloud, but Porker blamed Hoo Hoo. Cloud felt guilty and Mouse stayed quiet. This meant they would walk for many hours feeling cross and uncomfortable, wondering if they would ever reach their next destination.

'Spaniels have no sense of direction,' said Porker.

'St Bernards have no sense of anything but their dinner!' said Hoo Hoo.

'I might like to be full of food, but at least I'm not full of myself!'

'It's a good job – you'd have permanent indigestion!'

A butterfly landed on Mouse's nose. Mouse crossed his eyes and looked as if the world never took him seriously. It stood still, letting its colours dazzle them and sparkle in the sunshine. It fanned its wings once, then twice.

'Over the next hill, south then east,' it whispered to Mouse.

The butterfly led Mouse's curiosity as it fluttered off towards the charm of wildflowers.

Mouse thought about what the butterfly had said.

'I think we should climb over this hill, travel south, then east,' he said.

The other dogs were shocked to hear their sausage dog declare so confidently. They were so shocked – and tired – that they agreed that this was as good as any plan.

By nightfall, they had nestled into a hollow in the side of a hill. They lit a fire and huddled up to each other, as the temperature started to drop. Owls haunted the space between the hills.

*

'Look! Look!' said Hoo Hoo excitedly.

The other dogs looked, but only after they had blinked, stretched their paws, and thought about going to the toilet.

From their vantage point on the hillside, they could just spot the weathered hump of a bridge at a low point where three valleys came together.

Morning sunlight streamed up the valley. The dogs ran down the hillside, and along the banks of one of the streams, around the corner of a hill, until they came to the bridge. The place was unmistakable: the bridge, the three streams, and the waterfall flourishing into the pool below.

'This is it! This is it! It's the pool, Master! It's the pool. You know what to do – I can help you if you like?' said Hoo Hoo, dancing about on the bridge.

Hoo Hoo, Porker, and Mouse were all visibly excited. Cloud held back.

'What is it, Master?' asked Hoo Hoo. 'Why are you just standing there? You know what to do! You know what the tortoise said.'

It was true. Cloud knew what to do. The tortoise had whispered in his ear that, when Cloud found the site of the three streams, he should drop a hair from his own body into the pool. So why was he hesitating? The answer, he also knew, was that he was afraid. He was afraid of what might come out of the water.

As a puppy, and as a young dog, Cloud had often thought about his parents, or wondered what it might be like to have parents. He had wanted them badly. Everything he had been told on this journey was true – he *was* a cloud cut off from contact with the world. He drifted, contemplated, let his mind wander. He was unmoved, unyoked, unhooked. What did it mean to have that kind of attachment? To discover love, truth, and beauty through the bonds of a family? These were things he had, at one time, wanted desperately, but he had learned to live without them. Now that they were in sight, how would he react? Would he be disappointed? Would he be hurt? Or upset?

He looked at his companions. They were all staring at him, trying to work out what he was thinking. They were all eager. They had all given so much to his journey. They were, he thought, more than companions, more than fellow pilgrims – they were friends. Their friendship was invaluable, and he would have succumbed to the rattling and ridicule of his own thoughts if he had tried to complete his journey alone.

Cloud stepped forward, plucked a hair from his chest, and dropped it into the pool.

They watched the hair sail slowly through the air, until it came to rest on the surface of the water. It should have floated down the stream with the current but it stayed there, until it sank: the water wrapped it up and pulled it down. The dogs waited. They kept their eyes fixed on the pool. They could hear nothing but the cascade of the waterfall. None of them spoke until something – they couldn't see what exactly – punctured the surface of the water below, in the same spot where the hair had fallen.

'What's that?' called Hoo Hoo.

It looked like a black brush. Rising from the bottom, it could have been a water snake, but then the long arc of its spine followed, then a head. Most of the coat was black, except one or two spots of white – almost the exact reverse of Cloud. As the nose emerged from the water, and the first pocket of air found its way into the dog's nostrils, life followed. The tail twitched. The spine arched, and beneath the surface, they could detect the kicking of legs. The mouth inhaled deeply, then started to choke.

'This way! Over here!' called out Hoo Hoo, running down to the pool. The collie dog in the water was disoriented and confused. His eyes were blurred. He felt as if he had been asleep for a thousand years (and dreaming about life as a river trout). It didn't stop him paddling towards the cries from the shore. Quicker than he could grasp, he was on the bank of the stream, shaking the water from his coat, and blinking through the bright daylight as river water dripped from his head.

'What?' he spluttered, 'Wh… what happened? Where am I? What's going on?'

Cloud walked forward to look his father in the face. He peered into his eyes. His father peered back, so he could see, just about in focus, a white Border Collie that bore a striking resemblance to himself. It was like looking into a magical mirror, which reflected the way he remembered himself when he had fallen in the pool, but with the colour of his coat reversed.

The soaking-wet Border Collie nearly asked a question, but he knew the answer before he could think to ask it.

'Hello, Father,' said Cloud.

'What's happened?' his father asked. 'Tell me.'

*

The dogs told him. Waley was a sensible dog, and the last thing he could remember was falling in the water and banging his head. He took some convincing that this was half a lifetime ago, and that he had spent the intervening years living as a fish.

'You're my son,' he said proudly, as the pieces started to settle.

'Yes,' said Cloud, unsure of himself. 'Yes, I'm your son.'

'Living as a trout is a bad enough punishment,' he said, 'but it's much worse to spend all that time without seeing your children.'

'I…' Cloud stalled. 'I didn't even know I had a father.'

Waley looked at his son, reeling from the sudden return to reality, and the shocks it had brought.

'Then we should get to know each other.'

Cloud nodded and smiled.

'That's all very well, but first you have a wife-stealing tyrant to avenge!' said Hoo Hoo.

'That's true!' said Waley. 'Let me dry my coat, have something solid to eat, and you can lead the way!'

'All right! Let's work ourselves up into a state of fighting fury and vow to squash this tyrant like a turnip!'

'I like the sound of that!' said Waley. 'You are an enterprising Spaniel, I can see!'

Hoo Hoo fluttered with pride.

'I am, it's true. I am highly esteemed in all things – and a ponderous proteanimator to boot! Master, your father has the humours of revenge in his blood, and he knows talent when he sees it. We need to show him just how much we are a winning combination – we need to cook up another plan. What's the plan, Master? What's the plan?'

'The plan?' said Cloud, sharing some of the excitement. 'Yes, we could do with a plan.'

'Yes, a plan sounds like a good plan!' said Waley.

'I know!' squealed Hoo Hoo. 'How about this? Balder's brain, I'm really good! Why don't I turn into an elephant? You can all ride on my back. Then, when we get to this place, Weaverlick or whatever, I'll jump on the head of the evil spirit until he's completely squashed and flat!'

'Is that... workable?' asked Waley, not wanting to dampen Hoo Hoo's enthusiasm.

'Oh yes!'

'I like your angle on the problem,' said Cloud. 'Jumping on his head would certainly sort out his body. But it's his mind – his *spirit* – that we need to worry about. That's where all his power lies.'

'We need to crush his spirit, you think? Mmm. Difficult. I'm pretty damn good, but even I might struggle with this one.'

'The trouble is,' said Cloud, thinking about it, 'you can't really crush a spirit. It isn't a thing like other things.'

'What should we do then, Master? What *can* we do?'

Cloud lowered his head to think.

'It's strange, I feel as if I understand this spirit. I understand him, because, in a sense, I'm his creation. He cut me off from those nearest to me. We can't squash this spirit, but we can help it to like the world, instead of purging and punishing it.'

'Yes, yes, I see,' said Hoo Hoo. 'I've got an idea, Master. Why don't I turn into a case of wine? Then he can drink me down and he will be all merry and happy. What do you think of that?'

Porker cut in.

'But then he'd have a really bad headache the next day and hate everything even more.'

'Okay, yes, I see,' said Hoo Hoo, momentarily deflated. 'Well, what about this, Master? I could turn into a giant chocolate-covered cheesecake. I bet that would make him feel a lot better about things!'

Cloud's eyes brightened suddenly.

'I have a thought. Come on, I'll tell you about it on the way.'

*

Beaverwick was much larger than any of the places they had seen on their travels. Nous had been busy. He worked the creatures who lived there like slaves. They had built many new houses, a library, a large park, and clever modern apartments. On the outskirts of Beaverwick, they had also built a large, beautiful stately home, with a sweeping parkland estate.

Late one afternoon, Nous was sitting on a balcony – completed only the previous year – surveying all the land he commanded. He smiled and thought the one recurring thought that haunted his mind. He thought about returning to the clear, thin air, high up in the mountains. Then he saw something. He looked up to find a goldfinch perched on the balcony right in front of him.

Nous examined the bird. It was a beautiful creature.

'Strange,' he said out loud, 'you birds usually keep to yourselves.'

The goldfinch fidgeted about on the balcony. It started to sing. Nous couldn't believe it. The bird seemed to be singing *for him*. Had he stamped his authority on Beaverwick so harshly that even the birds wanted to please him? He smiled at the bird and listened to it for a little while. It didn't stop. It didn't move. Before too long, it all started to feel uncanny. Nous retreated into his grand home, thinking the goldfinch would fly away. It didn't fly away.

The bird kept singing, and singing, and singing. Every day, it followed him around wherever he went, and only stopped to sleep. It scared him, and he was tempted to frighten it away or do worse. Then again, when he listened to the bird's song without these worries, he noticed how lovely it sounded. He even started to hear it in his dreams.

The more his worries about the bird went away, the more he wanted to hear it, and see it. He made a point of smiling at it, even talking to it. He studied it: its tiny straw-like legs, the pokey little beak, the streak of yellow on the wing, and black eyepatches which rested on puffed-up plumage.

'You are a beautiful thing,' he said one day to the bird.

The bird stopped singing. Nous's ears were piqued. The bird twitched its head, then flew off. Nous rushed up to the edge of the balcony to see where it had gone. He could just make it out, perched on the branch of a silver birch at the edges of the garden below. He ran down to the garden, worried that the bird might fly off again.

He was right. Just as he reached the tree, he saw the bird twitch its head again before it flew off into the parkland. Nous ran after it, becoming more and more fearful that the finch was trying to elude him.

It flew into a wood at the edge of the estate. The dog ran after it, under the canopy of trees, where he saw something else which halted his pursuit. He saw his wife standing before him. She was crying. Next to her stood the spitting image of himself.

'You!' he called. 'But it can't be. That's impossible.'

'Haven't you caused enough trouble?' said Waley.

Nous wanted to hit back.

'I haven't caused nearly enough trouble! Nothing like enough. But what happened? I thought you were lost years ago. I thought I had sent you packing for good!'

'It's… there was… a fish… never mind that now. Don't you think you have done enough harm? You drowned me in a pool. You robbed me of my wife. You cheated me of my family. You have treated Beaverwick brutally, in my name and under my charge. What do you want? Why are you doing all this?'

'A time will come,' said Nous, and nothing more.

'A time has come!' another voice replied.

It was Cloud. He walked up behind Nous.

'Had it not been for you, I would have been born here. Instead, to save me from your harsh rule, my mother smuggled me out of your sight, and I grew up in a different place, without knowing my mother and father.'

The goldfinch sang out.

Nous looked up, where he saw the bird sitting on a branch above him.

'The bird,' he said.

'You are a spirit drawn to higher things, aren't you?' said Cloud. 'And look at the damage it causes. You like the sound of that bird?'

'It's been singing to me for days,' said Nous. 'Following me everywhere. Always singing.'

'What do you think of its singing?'

Nous looked at Cloud, trying to guess his mind.

'It's beautiful,' he said simply.

Nous was about to say something else when they all heard a conspicuous rustling in the trees above. They all looked upwards (except Nous). A large and fearsome osprey had perched on a branch opposite the goldfinch. They were all shocked to see a large bird of prey at such close quarters. Cloud felt it didn't bode well.

The osprey opened its predatory beak and let out a piercing squawk, which made all the dogs recoil. The goldfinch fell from its branch, like a stone, and landed on the floor in its true state, as Hoo Hoo. Then the osprey, in a short burst of flight, swept to the floor, transforming as it landed into the shape of a greyhound.

'Francis!' cried out Cloud.

'Who?' said Porker.

'Your tricks have gone quite far enough!' said Francis.

'But they won't fool anyone here. You have no notion of what you're up against! We know what's been going on! You've stumbled about the countryside causing all sorts of chaos, bumbling here and there, surviving by potluck! You might have confused that simpleton Arouet and his idiotic friends (just as they were starting to make good progress on our schemes!), you might have appealed to that soft-hearted gerbil I tried to educate – but your run of luck stops right here!

'Then you're…' said Cloud, daring to complete what he was thinking and what he had suspected when he left Easthill.

'I am what? An osprey? A greyhound? Or something else? You simplistic creatures! I am everything this great leader taught me to be – which is everything and nothing, all at once! That, *my friend*, is the sort of power that comes from true knowledge. Something you and your motley band of adventurers would know nothing about.'

Nous cleared his throat, studying Cloud quite carefully as he spoke.

'He is no more a dog than an osprey. He is no more a dog than I am. Or, for that matter, than you are, if you really think about it. You *animals*…' Nous had to almost spit out the word it was so repulsive to him, '…you animals always behave in the same way. Pooing here. Raising a leg there. Sniffing and eating the most unedifying things!'

'Tell me about it – I've had to live with you lot for the last few years!' cried Francis.

'Then what do *you* believe?' asked Cloud, who was genuinely curious.

Nous leered at the dogs.

'I have made it my business to regulate you all – and my empire grows further and more powerful by the day. Francis here has been working on your own small hovel on the hill for some time, and he has made good progress. But he and my other servants work in many different parts of the world. I have brought everything into the orbit of my influence, so I can show you all a better way. A purer way.

'Your silly world is pointless and a waste of time. I want you to put it all aside. And I will help you put it aside by making you submit to my rules, to my world, to *my authority*! In order to be truly free, first you must be purified!'

The way Nous said this made it clear that the matter wasn't up for discussion.

Francis transformed into an osprey once more, spread his wings, and flew at Cloud, his talons out-stretched. Hoo Hoo, when she saw this, turned her-self into a lion, and started to roar. But it was no good.

Francis squawked again, which, as before, stunned Hoo Hoo and forced her to resume her shape as a spaniel.

Porker, Mouse, Waley and Bee were overcome, but they couldn't bear the thought of what was about to happen. Francis clearly had every intention of tearing Cloud limb from limb. They rushed at the bird of prey, hoping they might at least fight it off. Yet again, the bird screeched, this time louder than before. The noise was unbearable. It made them all feel dizzy and sick; they staggered about and stumbled to the floor.

The osprey gripped Cloud in its talons and lifted him off the ground. Cloud had to think quickly. No clever trick would save him now. These creatures had somehow acquired powers that he could never equal. Then a thought came to him.

His only hope was the very point of his journey. His only hope was the Thumbald, that mysterious little thing he called the *truth*. He spoke quickly, as he struggled against Francis, the bird of prey:

'D'you know, spirit, that to sing like the goldfinch, you need a body. You need to live with a family of other birds, in trees like these, so they can teach you how to sing. They also give you a reason to sing – without a family, without other creatures around you, you have no reason to sing. But what have you done, here in Beaverwick? Here, nobody sings. Nobody *wants* to sing.'

Hoo Hoo, as ever, saw the way Cloud was thinking. In an instant, everything the black dog, and the sage who had tried to educate her, had said made sense. A lion was not going to defeat the osprey. Only the truth could do that. Her ability to practise proteanimation came not from her, but from an openness to the world in its truest light. She stood up resolutely. She turned into the goldfinch. She fluttered up onto a branch. The osprey opened its mouth to squawk again, but before it could, Hoo Hoo started to sing. She had no idea where the music came from, but it flowed through her with such power and grace that it stilled everything for miles around. The osprey dropped Cloud and landed on the floor. All the creatures – Nous most of all – looked in awe, as they surrendered helplessly to the mesmerising lyric of the birdsong.

When Hoo Hoo had finished singing, they found that many other birds had congregated in the trees. Their chorus of voices echoed for the rest of the day. At the end of it, Francis flew away, high up into the mountains. Nous, meanwhile, renounced the form of a dog, which he had never really liked because it didn't come naturally to him. Instead, he became a bird.

With a little help and encouragement from the birds around him, he learned to sing.

*

Waley looked at his wife. She looked at him. Neither of them spoke. He walked up to her. He nuzzled her with his nose.

As it turned out, there was lots to be done. Waley began by making a public declaration. He told the entire small town what had happened, how they had all been tricked and deceived, and how the tyranny they had endured for so long was coming to an end.

It met with mixed reactions. Waley, after all, looked exactly like the tyrant he had replaced. Many of the dogs, who were so browbeaten and unhappy after years of servility, were doubtful. But Waley was determined to undo the work of his imposter, and to carry out his role as Head Hound in the spirit in which it had been entrusted to him by Little Thorn.

He disbanded the police. He ended the curfews, and when he discovered that no one in Beaverwick really liked the new buildings, he announced plans to rebuild. As part of his programme, he announced that he would dismantle his stately home, and use all the materials for public works. And rather than telling everyone what to do, he gave the dogs the power to appoint dogs they trusted – members from their own families and tribes – to discuss matters in a forum.

Cloud discovered that he had brothers and sisters.

They had been treated very badly by Nous, but Waley brought his family together in a small, simple cottage. Two of his sons had mates, as did one of his daughters. Cloud was overwhelmed to know that he had so many relations. He was even an uncle, many times over! Young puppies approached him to hear about his stories searching for the Thumbald. He even got to know one of his sisters (Penelope). But she disapproved of the fact that he kept the company of a Spaniel who seemed to take pleasure in turning into a miniature hot air balloon that her young pups could ride.

Cloud had spent most of his life thinking he was alone, that he had come from nowhere. It was strange adjusting to this new reality.

The pilgrims spent many months with Waley and his wife. They watched as Beaverwick transformed. It took time, but a brightness, and an optimism started to return. Things changed for the better. Beaverwick re-established contact with Little Thorn. Some of the old festivities and rituals, which Nous had banned, returned. Beaverwick had been a garden that had been cut back and killed off. Now that Nous had left, and Waley had finally arrived, everything could grow again.

For all this, Cloud felt conflicted. He knew that part of him belonged to Beaverwick, and part of him wanted to stay there, so he could get to know the family he had never known. He also knew that his mission wasn't complete. It would not be complete until he returned to Easthill with the Thumbald. He also knew that he belonged in Easthill. It was the place where he had grown up. Even if he wasn't directly related to them, the dogs there were a family of sorts, and he missed them.

'It's all right, son,' said Bee, one evening, 'we all know what you need to do.'

She could see where his mind had wandered.

'Thank you, Mother. I feel bad about going away again, when I've only just arrived. But I also feel bad about staying.'

'You have to go,' said Bee, 'but now that you are so used to travelling about all over the country, maybe it won't be so difficult for you to visit us?'

Cloud's new family all understood what he had to do. Besides, Hoo Hoo was getting restless, and Cloud knew that he was keeping Porker and Mouse in one place for too long.

'So, we need to work out how to get to Easthill from here!' said Hoo Hoo. 'This place is huge. Someone's bound to know.'

'It's easy,' said Waley.

The pilgrims turned to listen to him.

'It's obvious, isn't it – all you need to do is build a raft, take it to the place I was trapped, and sail down the river. You just need to retrace the route my son took when he was a puppy.'

Which is what they did. They built a raft, took it up to the meeting of the three streams. Wished well by the family he never thought he had, Cloud and his friends set sail down the stream.

They travelled quickly. In a day, Cloud started to recognise the contours and character of the land. It flattened out, disrupted only by occasional hills. Hedgerows marked out the edge of fields. Little lanes led off through sparse patches of woodland or jumped the stream with humped bridges. Cloud didn't recognise the territory exactly, but all the elements were right. He was almost home.

Then he saw it. He saw the bend in the river, and the little beach where his raft had run to ground.

'There!' he called out. 'That's it! We need to moor the raft there!'

This time Saddleback wasn't watching from the hillside. Only a herd of cattle came to watch the dogs disembarking from their craft.

Cloud led the way. Up a lane. Over a field. Through a wood. Into Easthill.

Porter the Irish Water Spaniel was irrigating a ditch when he saw Cloud return. He jumped up onto a wall so he could get a better view. Then he shouted:

'Look! Look who's returned!'

*

Cloud's journey to the lake in the West, the dogs and creatures he met on the way, and his return, became one of the stories Easthill told about itself. The packs all had their own versions. They picked out the bits they liked best, left out the things they liked least, and made up quite a lot of things that never really happened at all. Some even told the story in completely different ways. Leaders of the farm tried, over the years, to write official versions, but no one could ever agree on the details, and there was always someone who wanted to add more elephants.

Some of the dogs who thought the Thumbald was a silly superstition hadn't changed their minds. But one thing was clear: the journey had helped to restore its place in the community. Many also thought that the Thumbald had helped to bring the dogs together again. Before, they had started to focus more on their own affairs. Now, they found a bit more time to think about other dogs, or to see their own affairs as part of the wider community.

Did that mean the Thumbald had returned to Easthill (if it ever existed in the first place)? Even after the journey, no one had seen it – no one could explain what it was, and how its power could be felt. It was always hard to discern.

If you look for the hard edges,
Of subtle things,
You will find nothing.

So went the verse.

Cloud and a few other dogs liked to ponder and speculate about these things, but the truth was that most dogs were more attached to their daily lives, routines and rituals. And, after their long journey, it was to these lives, routines and rituals that Cloud and his companions returned.

Cloud now had a family, whom he visited regularly, and whom he invited to Easthill. He got to know his parents, his siblings, and their offspring. He also, having travelled so far, decided to explore other parts of the world, to hear the stories and experiences of other creatures.

Porker, like his fellow pilgrims, stayed in Easthill for a while, but made it clear that he wanted to return to King Cone and his daughter, First Freshness, if only to apologise for his behaviour. All through the return journey, Cloud, Hoo Hoo and Mouse had noticed how much weight Porker had lost, and that he was now no longer obsessed with food. By the time he said goodbye to Easthill, he was completely transformed. Six months later, news reached them that Porker (or Barry as they now all called him) had visited King Cone and since reunited with First Freshness – she had been dazzled by his changed appearance, the bravery of his adventures and his thoughtful and considerate attitude.

Mouse, too, stayed in Easthill for a short while, but wanted to return to Long Dale Farm. To make up for all the food he had stolen, he set up a bakery and patisserie, which made cakes in the style of the many different places he had visited on his journey to the West. The bakery was so successful that Mouse became a celebrity on the farm. He used his fame to go into politics and exert pressure on the Board for Agricultural Action. He ran a campaign. First, he said, the BAA needed to actually be active. Second, he said they should stand up more for loners, outsiders and all the many creatures who didn't have much confidence.

Hoo Hoo, after she had spent some time in Easthill, travelled back to Long Dale Farm, and then she returned to the Mountain-tarn Cave for the Deliverance of Lost Creatures. But she never stayed in any of these places for any long period. Instead, she used her powers as a proteanimator in the name of justice. She had many adventures. She transformed into a giant fire-breathing chicken to save a coop of chickens from a marauding fox. She turned into a flatulent ostrich to raise the spirits of a depressed mole whose family had abandoned him. And she punished two Pit-bull Terriers, who had been stealing from an elderly goose, by turning them into wrinkled lemons.

At the end of their journey, all the dogs had found a new focus of sorts, even if sometimes – often in fact – that also involved doing something strange, silly or confusing.

'Things are often strange, silly and confusing,' said Cherry the Red Setter. 'I wonder if that matters?'